By William Malmborg

Novels

Jimmy
Text Message
Nikki's Secret
Dark Harvest
Blind Eye
Santa Took Them
Crystal Creek

Collections

Scraping the Bone: Ten Dark Tales

WILLIAM MALMBORG

JIMMY

DARKER DREAMS
MEDIA

Darker Dreams Media
Chicago, IL

ISBN-13: 978-0-9962831-7-5
ISBN-10: 0-9962831-7-X

Jimmy/ William Malmborg. -- 1st ed.

Dedicated to Thomas Malmborg

CHAPTER ONE

Sometime during the night, the violent storms broke and were replaced by a calm, gentle rain. Later people would say the rain had been there to cleanse the town and had, in fact, washed away the terror and madness of the previous week. For many, however, this was not the case. For them the terror and madness would remain forever, and no rain, no matter how powerful, could wash it away.

It began on a clear cool Monday in May 2010. Samantha King, an eighteen-year-old senior, was walking home from school. It was a pleasant walk, one that usually didn't take more than fifteen to twenty minutes. Today it was looking like twenty because her backpack was full, the teachers having loaded her down with homework despite the fact that there were only two weeks left until graduation. It was insane.

Graduation. The word sent a chill down her spine as she walked along the wooded road. It seemed like just yesterday she had been in third grade drawing pictures of Santa and his reindeer for the class Christmas book.

Amazing how quickly time went.

Graduation in June, and then in August she would be heading to Northern Illinois University in DeKalb. Then, after four years of that, she would finally be able to live on her own, supporting herself with a career she loved and possibly raising a family with a man who cared for her deeply.

The thought of graduation wasn't the most exciting event floating around her mind though. That spot was reserved for the upcoming Saturday night, which would be spent in the school gymnasium. Prom. Not only would the dance be enjoyable, but it also was the night she planned to lose her virginity. At the moment, Steven, her boyfriend, was not in on this plan, but she doubted he would have any objections. The two had been going out for the entire year, and it was time they did more than just kiss and lightly touch each other. The question was: how would she present herself to him so he would make a move on her? Or would she make the move on him? No. The guy needed to make it or else it wouldn't be right. But what would she do?

In her mind, she always pictured the two of them in a motel room sitting on a bed. She would have loosened her dress a little and let it hang down from her breasts. He would then put his hands and lips on her. The lovemaking would progress from there.

A car sped by along the road and pulled her from the thoughts of that future night, which was probably for the best since a warm tingle had begun building between her legs.

Now, rather than thinking about that night, she looked ahead and saw the rotting mailbox for the old Hood place jutting up from the roadside weeds. A shiver went down her spine.

The Hoods had been a strange family that thought World War III was imminent. For years they had been preparing themselves while trying to recruit town and county residents into their small militia. September 11, 2001, had been the start of the war, according to them, but rather than stay and fight they had retreated to a more secure location somewhere in the Rockies. No one had seen them since. Their house had remained, and because no For Sale sign ever went up, everyone assumed they still owned it. Even if a For Sale sign ever did go up, it was doubtful anyone would buy the place. Nine years of abandonment had ruined the structure, and one would have to invest more than the property was worth just to make it livable.

Samantha slowly walked up to the driveway and turned her head. Long grass and overgrown bushes between the house and the road made it nearly impossible to see the first floor. On the second floor, she noticed a new broken window.

Something moved in the bushes to her right.

Samantha's heart jumped as she spun around, expecting to see a cat or some other small creature from the woods.

Nothing.

A kid perhaps? Someone who was throwing stones at the house and then hid when I came walking around? Perhaps he was even responsible for the broken window.

"Hello?" she called.

Nothing.

Samantha decided not to stay and find out who was lurking in the shrubbery. The house was creepy enough without the added threat of someone jumping out at her

—so creepy, in fact, that going inside and taking something on Halloween night had been a childhood rite of passage for many years, one the sheriff had finally been forced to put a stop to after a kid cut himself badly when climbing through a broken window.

She turned away from the house and started walking toward home again.

Something crashed through the brush. Samantha twisted back around and screamed as a figure lunged for her, a hand grabbing her around the throat.

"No!" she cried while pushing against him, her overfilled backpack forcing him to let go. A second later his hands were on her again, and he flung her around to the right. This time her backpack worked against her, its weight knocking her body off-balance and causing her to fall to the ground.

The attacker came at her with a long, gleaming knife.

"Ahhh," she started to scream, but then he put the knife to her throat. The blade was cold and indented her skin with its razor edge.

Warm liquid suddenly gushed between her legs.

"Get up."

Samantha recognized the voice and for the first time focused her eyes upon her attacker. It was Jimmy Hawthorn.

Okay, this is it, stay calm and focused, Jimmy Hawthorn said to himself while carefully pressing the knife into Samantha King's throat, a knife he had hidden by the back door of the Hood place this morning so he didn't have to carry it around with him all day at school. *Don't lose control, and for God's sake, don't cut her!*

Slitting her throat was his biggest fear right now,

followed closely by some unforeseen Good Samaritan coming to her rescue. *Unless it is another girl, then maybe I can get them both.* It was a pleasant fantasy, but one he quickly subdued to focus on the present situation.

"Get up."

Samantha didn't move.

For a moment, he worried that she was defying him and that he would be forced to drag her into the fallout shelter while she fought him, but then he realized her body was simply paralyzed with fear.

You'd be scared too if someone like me came at you with a knife all of a sudden.

At the same time he knew he had to get her into the fallout shelter, and with each passing second the risk that someone would come by grew, so without too much thought he moved the knife from her throat to her groin and pressed the blade up against the seam of her jeans and said, "Get up or I'll slice open your pussy!"

The bluff worked.

"Stop! Jimmy, no! Ahhh! *Please stop!*"

Jimmy ignored her cries and pulled on the rope until her toes were barely touching the concrete floor, and then he tied it off to a pipe that jutted from the wall. Once that was done, he walked into the middle of the small room and stared at her, his eyes seeming to examine every inch of her stretched figure.

Samantha stared back for a moment and then looked up at her wrists as she tried shifting them within the knots into a more comfortable position. Meanwhile her toes began to ache so she tried resting them, but this increased the strain on her wrists, and within a minute she was forced to lift her heels back up.

Jimmy continued to stare at her.

"Jimmy…" Samantha started. She wanted to say more but was forced to take a deep breath first, not having noticed how much pressure this position had been putting on her lungs. "Please let me down."

Jimmy ignored the request.

Samantha closed her eyes.

What is he going to do to me?

Rape was the first thing that came to mind but wasn't the last. Unfortunately, the possibilities were endless.

"I'm not going to hurt you," Jimmy said.

Samantha opened her eyes.

"Not unless you try and hurt me or get away," Jimmy added.

His voice caused something within her to snap, and before she even realized she was going to say it the words "What the fuck are you doing?" echoed.

Jimmy actually seemed to consider her question for a moment but didn't answer it right away. Instead, he just shrugged. It was a simple gesture, yet one that caused a chill to race down her arms. He then started to undo his belt, and the chill turned into genuine fear.

No, Samantha thought, unable to muster any actual words. *Please don't.*

Jimmy didn't take off his pants, however, and her fear of rape was suddenly replaced by a different worry as he coiled part of the belt around his right fist.

"To be honest with you," Jimmy said, "I don't really know what I'm doing. I've never kidnapped anyone before, and since you've never been kidnapped before it will be a learning experience for both of us." A second shrug followed, along with a smile that added to her fear. "Just remember that I'm in charge."

With that, Jimmy disappeared behind her.

She struggled to twist around to see what he was going to do, but before she could even move the leather belt cracked across her back and unleashed a terrible line of pain.

Tears began falling from her eyes.

She expected more but nothing happened, and then Jimmy walked back into her line of sight. The buckle end of the belt was still coiled around his fist.

"That was gentle compared to what I could do. If I wanted to, I could spend all afternoon hitting you like that, and there is nothing you could do to stop me." He sighed and started to put his belt back on. "And just think what it will be like if I cut your shirt off and hit your bare flesh."

Samantha couldn't imagine the pain being any worse than what she had just felt, but she knew it probably would be. She also knew his words were true. He could and would do anything he wanted to her. *What will those wants be?*

Though he could have stayed with Samantha for hours, his mind and body enjoying the wonderful situation he had created, Jimmy knew that word of her disappearance would spread once her family realized she wasn't coming home, and the forty-minute or so period between the end of school and her expected arrival home would be the target time used by the police to determine who had taken her. Because of this, he wanted to be home for most of that time period, looking completely relaxed and seemingly relieved to have finished another day at school. Adding to the illusion that he had been home all along would be his little brother

Alan. Normally the two walked home together, but that day Alan had needed to stay after school for detention and therefore wouldn't be home until four. Upon his arrival Alan would see Jimmy and just assume he had been there since school let out, which in turn would aid his alibi if one were ever needed. Then again, no alibi would help him if Samantha were found and told everyone that he was responsible. Thankfully, Jimmy didn't think that would ever become a reality.

The walk home from the Hood place didn't take long. Once there, however, he had trouble relaxing because he kept thinking about Samantha and all the things he could do to her, which caused an erection to press against his pants, one he didn't want to deal with because later that night he planned on going back to the fallout shelter and he didn't want to be depleted. Unfortunately, he couldn't hold back, and after looking at the clock and realizing his brother still had about fifteen minutes of detention time left, he headed up to his room and opened up one of his downloaded videos.

On screen, a girl in a leather outfit was standing with her wrists tied over her head, a large ball gag in her mouth. Having watched the video many times, Jimmy knew that it wouldn't be long before the girl was lowered to her knees and forced to suck dick, the ball gag having been removed. Later it would be put back in place once the man had deposited his load in her mouth. Jimmy didn't make it that far into the scene before he found himself burying another pair of underpants in the hamper, which already had three pairs at the bottom despite his doing laundry two days earlier, crusty patches of semen clinging to each.

An odd but familiar disgust greeted him once he was

finished, only this time it was not a result of how much money he had wasted on the kinky video downloads. Instead, it was the knowledge that he had finally given in to the desire. All his life he had dreamed of kidnapping and tying up a girl so that she had to stand with her wrists pulled over her head for days at a time, but he had always been able to keep the desire a fantasy. Now it was a reality, one which he had often feared finding himself in because it would mean he had crossed the line.

Of course, the feeling would pass. It always did with the videos and would with this situation as well. Also, deep down inside Jimmy knew it would only have been a matter of time before he did something like this anyway; once a fantasy was firmly in place in a person's brain there was no getting around it. He couldn't suppress his sexual desire anymore than a homosexual could suppress theirs, and no amount of "sexual reeducation therapy" would have helped.

Her hands began to tingle half an hour after Jimmy left, and she desperately wanted to get free. Never before had Samantha stood like this for so long, and already her legs were feeling weak and her lower back tired. Her hands were the worst, however, because whenever she relaxed her feet or legs the rope would tighten around her wrists and cut the blood flow off. Even when she was standing tall, her toes holding up her entire body, the ropes were uncomfortable.

The spot where Jimmy had hit her with the belt also hurt, though the pain from the lashing had faded considerably since his departure. *What would ten hits feel like? Or twenty? Or thirty? And what will the other things he does to me be like?* Thinking about this chilled her to the core.

Tears once again began falling from her eyes. She managed to brush some of them away with the inside of her arm, but most ran down her cheeks and fell to the floor.

She shifted her position. The pressure on her wrists grew. She tried raising her arms higher than the rope, but it was an impossible task. Even if the rope were removed, her exhausted muscles would not allow such an extension. Already they were screaming to have her arms lowered.

Curious as to what her hands looked like, Samantha forced her head back and looked up. The rope that bound her wrists had been wrapped around several times before being knotted. A second rope was tied to the first and tossed over a pipe in the ceiling before being tied to the one coming out of the wall.

Jimmy had said something about punishing her if she tried to escape, but really, given the tightness of the ropes, it was something he didn't need to worry about. There was no way she would get free without help.

Her neck began to ache, so she let it fall toward her chest again. Her eyes studied her shoes, yet her mind ignored them and instead focused on her parents.

What were they thinking?

Were they even home yet?

Samantha had no idea what time it was. It seemed as if hours upon hours had passed, yet she knew this probably was not the case.

Her eyes moved from her feet and looked around the room. There was no clock. The place was not barren though. Fear of some sort of world war outbreak had caused the Hood family to stockpile many supplies inside the small fallout shelter. Wooden shelves ran the length of the entire wall to her left, canned foods, dry goods, and bottled water piled high upon them. The other side of the room had several coils of rope stacked one on top of the other. There were only two shelves on the right side, and upon them sat light bulbs and cleaning supplies. Between the two walls was a simple doorway, the opening closed off by a huge steel structure that had no window or openings of any kind. On the other side was the stairway and the world she had once taken for granted.

"I really don't know why I even try anymore," Alan said after cracking open a bottle of Coke from the fridge. "The teachers are so focused on being right that they can't stand to see a 'kid' like me correct them."

Jimmy smiled. Alan's detention had been a result of being disrespectful to a substitute teacher in math class the Friday before. According to Alan, a girl had asked if he had an extra pencil, which he did, but then he accidentally dropped it while handing it to her. It was his vocal apology that had landed him in trouble, the substitute teacher deciding to scold him for speaking when they were supposed to be quiet. Alan had tried to explain that he was simply apologizing for dropping the pencil, and the substitute had exploded. Not long after that, Alan had been in the assistant principal's office learning his unjust sentence for being polite.

"I think you should write to Oprah about it," Jimmy said.

"Yeah, but then I'd probably get suspended or something. Remember that kid who got in trouble with Facebook?"

Jimmy remembered several stories of kids getting in

trouble for things they had written on Facebook, which the school tried to monitor either with fake profiles or with reports from kiss-up students, and not just in Ashland Creek but in places all across the country. Actually, teachers were getting in trouble too—the memory of a California teacher being fired for posting pictures of herself drinking while on summer vacation came to mind. It was ridiculous. "Which kid?"

"Oh, it doesn't really matter," Alan said with a wave of the hand. "I'm just glad summer's almost here so I don't have to deal with this bullshit anymore."

"Yeah," Jimmy said, his mind suddenly focusing in on the fact that he had no idea what he was going to do now that he was almost finished with high school. Most of the other kids in his class had plans, the majority either going to college or the military. Some had jobs lined up. Jimmy had none of that, though his grades would have been good enough to get into most colleges. The trouble was he hadn't applied anywhere because college just didn't seem right for him. He also feared going into the military, not because he was scared of going to war—he actually relished the idea of going into combat—but because he worried he would have no outlet for his bondage fantasies.

Then again, up until today, he had never had an outlet anyway, the movies online and the videos he ordered from catalogs having been his only release since hitting puberty.

"You hungry?" Alan asked.

"Um, yeah," Jimmy said. Earlier during lunch he had been too nervous to eat, the thought of grabbing Samantha after school having taken over his mind.

"Let's go to Taco Bell."

"Sounds good."

With that, the two started walking into town, a trip they often took when they were bored or hungry. The journey took them by the Hood place. Jimmy looked toward it, picturing Samantha suffering in the secret fallout shelter. Once beyond the house, however, he went back to thinking about Taco Bell and the tasty Cheesy Gordita Crunches he would soon be devouring.

CHAPTER TWO

Tina Thompson had been debating with herself for two days over whether she was going to ask Jimmy to the prom. During this time, she had been waiting for him to do it, but he hadn't, and now prom tickets were only being sold for one more day. She was going to have to do it.

Tina had first met Jimmy Hawthorn in the cafeteria way back in January when she had been forced to move from Glen Ellyn to Ashland Creek to live with her estranged mother after her father had died in a car accident coming home from a business dinner in Chicago. It had been a hard move, one she had not wanted to make, and it had only been made worse at school as she had gone from class to class on her first day at Ashland Creek High and no one wanted to talk to her. All the little groups were full and not looking for new members. Later she realized her shyness had probably played a part as well, but at the time it was an unknown factor.

Lunch, of course, was the worst because she had nowhere to sit. Seats in a classroom didn't really become group possessions, but lunch tables did, and if one sat at the wrong table there was generally trouble. There were open seats around the room, but none of the tables seemed that inviting. The students at each were happily talking among themselves and did not need her to join them.

After five minutes of standing by the wall with a tray of greasy food, Tina had noticed a boy sitting alone at the end of a half-filled table. Rather than talking with the four kids on the one end, he was writing something while eating an apple.

Tina debated for a few seconds over what to do and then finally decided to sit with him.

"Mind if I join you?" she asked.

He looked up. "Um, no, go ahead." His voice had a startled ring to it, though he did not seem at all annoyed about the interruption.

"Thank you." She put her tray of food down and took a seat. It was a relief not to be standing.

He looked back down at his apple.

An uncomfortable silence settled over them.

Eventually she said, "I'm Tina. Today's my first day."

"Oh," he said without looking up. "I'm Jimmy." His fingers began peeling away the sticker on the uneaten portion of the apple.

Tina thought for a second, desperately wanting a conversation yet at the same time not wanting to press him too much or ask the wrong question. "How come you're sitting all alone?" She regretted the question before it even left her lips, yet she was unable to stop its progress.

He shrugged while giving a weak smile and said, "I don't know. I just like to, I guess. It gives me time to think."

"Oh." *Does that mean he still wants to be alone?* "But it's okay if I sit here?"

He looked up, a partial smile forming, and said, "Yeah, of course, I don't mind."

"Good, because I don't know anyone yet and, well, it's hard." She unwrapped her hamburger while speaking and took a bite. It was awful. The bun was stale and the meat not meaty.

"Oh, well, first days are hard," Jimmy said. "Especially in a town like this where everyone has known each other since day one."

"I guess you were a new student too at some point?" Tina asked.

"No, no, I grew up here."

Yet you are sitting all alone? For some reason this intrigued her, especially since he didn't look like an outcast—outcasts usually didn't have muscles pushing against a normal, everyday hooded sweatshirt—and the two talked for the rest of the lunch period. After that they realized they had gym together during the next period and walked to class while talking. Then, at the end of the day, the two stumbled upon each other again outside the building and walked home, Jimmy and his little brother Alan showing her the way to her mother's house, which was on the way to their own.

Now, several months later, Tina continued the debate over whether to call Jimmy and ask him to the prom. She had hoped he would do it, but apparently he wasn't going to, despite the fact that the two were good friends. Unlike most teenage girls, Tina was not insulted. During their months of friendship she had learned quite a bit about Jimmy's personality and knew he rarely worked up the effort or motivation to do anything out of the ordinary—things like talking to people he did not know, staying after to speak with a teacher if he didn't understand something, walking a different route between classes, and asking a young pretty girl that he obviously liked very much to go with him to prom.

The debate ended.

She would have to make the move that brought their friendship to the next level.

"Sorry, Mom, I'm still full too," Jimmy said while pushing away his plate, which contained enough meat and potatoes to feed a starving family. "I'll eat it tomorrow for lunch. I promise."

Kelly Hawthorn gave her two sons a disappointed look, which she enhanced by crossing her arms, and said, "What on earth possessed you two to stuff yourself with Taco Bell so close to dinnertime?"

"It was Alan's idea," Jimmy said. "I didn't want to go, but he specifically said we needed to hurry over there and ruin our appetites before you got home."

"Oh, don't even start," Alan playfully warned. "I just asked if you were hungry and you said yes. I didn't force you to eat four of those cheesy crunch thingies."

"No, you were too busy stuffing your face with supreme chalupas. Mom, you should have seen him. He stuffed himself so fast that it looked like he was getting ready to shave with the sour cream."

Kelly shook her head and was about to say something when the phone rang.

"Battle?" Alan asked.

"Um—" Jimmy started.

"Don't even think about playing that game until you

two clean up the pans I slaved over," Kelly said. She then answered the phone and after a second said, "Sure, one moment. Jimmy, it's for you."

"What? Who is it?" Jimmy asked, a puzzled look dominating his face.

"I don't know, but it sounds like a girl." She covered the mouthpiece. "Have you been hiding someone from us?"

"No," Jimmy snapped. He then headed into the family room and picked up the mobile phone from the corner table near the couch. "I got it," he shouted into the kitchen.

"Say hi to Tina for me!" Alan shouted back.

Jimmy twisted away as his mother asked who Tina was. "Hello?"

"Hey, Jimmy. It's Tina. Um…was that Alan?"

"Yeah, he says hi," Jimmy said, wondering why in the world she was calling. "What's up?"

Tina put her head back on her pillow and looked up at the ceiling, her mind a spiral of colorful excitement. She was going to the prom. Jimmy had said yes. Of course, it had taken some convincing, but he had said yes, and that was all that mattered.

There was a knock on her door.

Her excitement faded. "What?"

"I'm leaving in a few minutes for my knitting group. I expect the mess from dinner to be cleaned up before I get back."

"Then it would make sense to clean it before you leave," Tina said.

The door rattled but did not open since Tina had thrown the lock before calling Jimmy. "Tina, open this door."

"Why?" Tina asked, adrenaline starting to flow.

"Because I'm your mother and I told you to." She twisted hard on the doorknob.

"Oh, you're my mother. I didn't realize that since you were gone for most of my life."

"Tina, I'm warning you. Open this door right now!"

"Why?"

"Because—"

"Because you hate it when people don't do what you say, right? Well, when Dad didn't do what you said you walked away. Seems to me like that would be a good option now as well."

"This is my house, young lady, and if you wish to live in it you will respect me."

"I don't wish to live in it," Tina snapped. "And when I turn eighteen next month I'll leave, and I'll take all Dad's money with me. So as far as I'm concerned, you can go to your little knitting group and fuck yourself with the needles."

Tina was surprised by the control her mother showed after that, and a little disappointed, but she knew it was more a result of her mother not wanting to keep her knitting friends waiting, not because she felt she had lost the battle.

Whatever the reason, Tina didn't really give a shit and just counted down the seconds until her mother left. Once she did, Tina allowed her emotions to break free, thoughts of her father unbearable right now because she knew he would have loved to see her going to the prom. She also knew he would have liked Jimmy a lot, the three of them probably having dinner quite often once the two really got to know each other.

But no, a young lady on a cell phone had made sure that would never happen, her mind too focused on the conversation to see the long line of brake lights ahead of her on Interstate 88.

Tina pressed her T-shirt to her eyes to soak up the moisture and then went downstairs to make herself some tea. While waiting for the water to boil she did the dishes, which didn't take long. The difficulty level of the task had never been the reason for her bitterness. Instead, it had been the principle of the thing, and the fact that her mother never did the dishes herself.

Finished, and with a large mug of Darjeeling tea in hand, Tina went back up to her room and started to once again think about Jimmy and the prom, concern over their status having wiggled its way into her mind while she was steeping the tea bag. Were the two still just friends or more than that? Were they a couple? Would the prom be the first date in a long line of wonderful evenings together? Or would their relationship crumble because they were only meant to be friends and wouldn't be able to handle the dating scene together?

Answers did not follow the questions, and there was no book she could look in or website she could find that would finish the thoughts. Instead, she would just have to wait and see, live life and accept whatever happened. That was the way the world worked. Nothing would ever change it.

Samantha King's hands grew itchy as the blood flowing to them slowed. Cramps had developed in the backs of both her legs, and now she was sagging forward and biting her teeth together, waiting for them to pass. The pain was intense and unrelenting.

The general ache that had developed in her back and shoulder muscles added to the misery, no doubt due to the position she was standing in. It wasn't natural for someone to have her arms raised upward and her body pulled tight for such a long time, and with each second that passed it grew more and more unbearable.

Her mind conjured the image of Moses from her old Sunday school classes and how he had stood with his arms up in the air so the Hebrews could win a battle. *How had he managed?*

Slumped forward as far as the bindings would let her, Samantha stared at the floor. Her mind could not get a grip on the situation and was a mess of random thoughts and ideas. Hours had passed with her standing in silence, and every second it seemed like she was slipping closer and closer to hysteria.

Why would Jimmy do this?

It was the only clear thought that repeated itself over and over again, and it seemed to be her only hold on reality due to the fact that she had to picture him in a real-world setting to try to grasp the reasons behind his actions toward her.

Thinking about him was also a good way to pass the time, though she wondered what exactly she was waiting for. Generally, one wanted time to pass quickly because something good was coming at a certain hour and she couldn't wait for its arrival. With her present situation, there was no guarantee of anything good happening, and each second that passed might only be bringing her toward some terrible end. Or even worse—terrible moments of utter humiliation and pain before the end.

Why did Jimmy do this?

Images of Jimmy over the years began to play across

her mind like a slide show: Jimmy in grade school, middle school, and high school came and went; memories of seeing him at the movies with his parents or at some restaurant; memories of him sitting in a classroom, at a lunch table, in an assembly; memories of him walking the hallways, or the sidewalks, or through the parking lot; memories of him everywhere. What was crazy about the images she saw was the knowledge that in each situation she hadn't really given him any thought once her mind had put a name to the figure she was seeing, nor had she felt any fear of him harming her, yet look at what he had been capable of during that time. It was mind-numbing.

Thoughts about what had happened broke through the slide show. The attack wasn't even twenty-four hours old, yet the actual events, and how they had unfolded, were already cloudy within her mind. The possible outcomes, however, were not.

Anger at herself for not fighting back followed these thoughts. Being surprised was no excuse. She should have done something to prevent the current situation. Fingernails to the face, a knee to the balls, or a backpack to the side of the head—all could have been avenues of escape, yet she hadn't set a single foot down any of those possible routes. It was incredibly frustrating.

The thought of defending herself against Jimmy brought to mind some of the incidents she had witnessed in the past. There had been times during Jimmy's school-day life when he had been the victim of bigger kids. No solid memories were present, but she did remember some fuzzy details of either seeing or hearing about fights where Jimmy had been beaten up.

Not that it mattered now. A memory of Jimmy being

beaten up didn't help her out in any way, and thinking about it was just a pleasant waste of time.

Pain suddenly raced through her arms, and all thoughts of Jimmy disappeared. She stood up fast, her toes shouting in protest, and tried lifting her arms up to a point where the ropes wouldn't have such a tight hold. The result was a fiery tingle throughout her hands that caused her fingers to squeeze into fists.

She clamped her teeth together.

It did little to stop the agony.

The terrible pins and needles that had exploded in her hands did disappear after a few minutes, but that was only a small relief when compared to the rest of the pain her body was enduring and would continue to endure until her hands were free.

"She *asked* you?" Alan said as they sat down to watch a rerun of *That '70s Show* before playing *GoldenEye*. "Why'd you let her do that?"

"What do you mean?" Jimmy asked.

"Why didn't you ask her?" Alan stared at his older brother while saying this and noted that he seemed to be both excited and upset. It was a strange mixture that produced a strange expression. *Confused* was probably the best word for it.

Jimmy shrugged. "I didn't realize she liked me, and what if she said *no* when I asked?"

Alan shook his head. "Didn't like you?" He couldn't believe it. "You two sit at lunch with each other and walk home with each other almost every freakin' day. She's had more of a crush on you than a boa constrictor could ever achieve." Alan had come up with the metaphor several days earlier yet hadn't been able to use it in any conversations. Now that he had, he wondered if it really was as clever as he had initially thought it would be.

Jimmy didn't comment on it. "What if she just liked walking home with me? What if by asking her out I ruined the friendship we already had? What if—"

Alan couldn't take it. His older brother questioned everything too much and at the same time didn't see the huge signs people were leaving him. A girl could come up to him and say, "You wanna come over tonight? My parents are out of town and I'm just dying to get your opinion on some new sexy lingerie I bought," and he wouldn't realize she wanted sex and would spend several minutes giving her real honest opinions on the lingerie and then head home. "What if she wanted to go out with you, liked you so much that you both got serious and then eventually married, and then had a wonderful family? Better yet, what if through her family she found you a great job that paid a lot and you both became millionaires?"

Jimmy looked down at his hands.

Alan had hit a sore spot without meaning to. In addition to being shy around girls, Jimmy seemed unable to find a job or get any college acceptances. The problem wasn't a lack of skills or grades but a lack of confidence, which prevented him from sending in applications or making calls or taking trips to see what was out there. Hell, Jimmy probably wouldn't even have gotten his driver's license if he hadn't done well enough in the course to take the test at school, because he never would have gotten together enough motivation to drive an hour to the DMV. It was ridiculous.

The opening music from *That '70s Show* came on and calmed the room. Alan recognized the episode. Eric's hot cousin Penny was coming to stay with them and would trick him into believing she was adopted so she could lure him into a trap in front of his parents. It was a good one.

During a commercial, Alan suddenly thought of something and asked, "You did say yes, right?" One time back when Jimmy had been in seventh grade, a girl had called to ask him out and he had told her no because he was too busy. He hadn't been, but dating wasn't something he was comfortable with, so he had rejected the girl. Alan often wondered if this refusal to date, or to really make friends, had stunted his social growth, which was one of the reasons why he had so much trouble now.

"Yeah, I told her I would go," Jimmy said.

Thank God! Alan screamed to himself and then out loud said, "Just wanted to make sure. Prom is one of those things you would care about missing ten years from now."

"No I wouldn't."

"You would."

"No, honest, I really wouldn't and couldn't care less about it."

Alan didn't feel like arguing, but he knew Jimmy was wrong. Both their parents had missed their prom and still talked about the regret they felt over not having the memory or experience of it. "Well, whatever. I'm glad you're going because I think you'll have a lot of fun."

"I hope so," Jimmy said.

The show came back on.

Alan wondered what it would be like to be inside Jimmy's head. Was it as calm in there as he tried to portray, or was his mind a mess? Actually, looking at Jimmy now, there wasn't an ounce of calmness about him. Something was on his mind and it was making him extremely antsy—no doubt the call from Tina about prom. It was about time. Jimmy needed a date. He needed a social life. So far, with the exception of a few kids through grade school, his only friend had been Alan, and though that was fine, he needed friends outside of the family.

"Hey, now you and Tina could come play pool with me and Melissa over in Haddonfield," Alan said.

Jimmy shook his head. "I don't think she'd like that."

"Why not?"

"I don't know. It just doesn't seem like something she would enjoy. Tina's not a pool hall sort of girl."

"Well, you can always ask and find out."

"Yeah, maybe."

Jimmy couldn't focus on *'That 70s Show* or the conversations Alan kept instigating because his mind was thinking about Samantha and wondering what it was like for her in the fallout shelter. Seeing women tied up with their hands over their head had been something he'd enjoyed ever since he was little, especially when it was long term, and now he couldn't wait to see what several hours of standing like that had done to her.

What is it like? What would the mind do with the time? What would it feel like?

These were questions he had been asking himself every time he came across a scene on TV or in a movie that featured a woman tied like that, ones which he usually recorded onto a VHS tape so he could watch them over and over again, often wishing he could somehow venture into the actual scene and understand it. In fact, at times he even wished he was in the scene—

in the female form, of course, since he had no desire to see men in bondage—and had recreated a few from time to time. Unfortunately, his scenes never got to last that long and often weren't accurate. Take the scene in the 1970s movie *The Four Musketeers* that had featured a moment where a young lady was chained to a wall by a set of iron wrist shackles. Jimmy had first stumbled upon it in junior high and had finally been able to add it to his VHS tape a few years later once he found it on TV again. Every time he watched the scene, he wished it were he—as the lady—who was standing there in the shackles just so he could understand what it was like. Reproducing the scene accurately by himself, however, was impossible, especially since he had no idea where to get shackles like that, nor the medieval dungeon setting, nor the dress. Worse, his inability to recreate it caused the craving to go unsatisfied. Putting himself in the mind of the person by injecting himself into a similar scene was just part of it. He also wished he could see what would happen to her as she stood there for days at a time, her body unable to relax due to the chains, her legs unable to hold her up after a while, forcing her to dangle from her wrists. He had no idea why he was fascinated by this, or why it produced such an intense sexual reaction in his body, but it did, and the more he saw the more his cravings went unfulfilled. It was bizarre.

"Still want to play *GoldenEye*?"

"What?" Jimmy asked, his mind returning to the basement. On screen, the credits for *That '70s Show* were rolling alongside an ad for *South Park*, which the two did not care for.

"Still want to play?" Alan was holding a controller.

"Oh. Sure."

"What's wrong?" Alan asked while the two set up the *GoldenEye* battle.

"Nothing," Jimmy lied while scrolling through the weapon selections for the proximity mine setting. "Um, where do I get a tux?"

"Wow, I don't really know. There's gotta be a place in town somewhere or maybe up in Haddonfield. You could always ask in the office at school. They would know. Not many kids have their own tuxes."

"Okay."

Jimmy clicked on the character selection screen and the two scrolled toward the right until they each found their favorite characters. From there Jimmy hit Start.

"We doing minutes or points?" Alan asked. He hadn't been watching when Jimmy selected.

"Ten minutes," Jimmy said. "I don't want the game to last too long since I was planning on going on a bike ride tonight."

"A bike ride?" Alan couldn't remember the last time Jimmy (or he, for that matter) had gone on a bike ride. Would their bikes even be big enough for them now?

"Which bike you using?"

"Dad's old one. I fixed the seat and pumped some air into the tires."

Alan hadn't known this. "When did you do that?"

"Last week. I've been riding every morning." He hesitated. "Didn't you know that?"

"No. When do you leave?"

Jimmy let his breath out and thought for a second. "About five. I guess no one can hear me."

"Nope. Can't hear a thing all the way down there. That's why I want the room. I could listen to music all night and no one would care."

"Well," Jimmy started. "Too bad there aren't two rooms down there." He shrugged. Nothing else followed.

The statement irritated Alan. He didn't think it was fair that his older brother had the only basement room just because of his age, but that was always the reason his parents gave.

The game loaded up.

Right away, they both went for the boxes of proximity mines and then began tossing them in all the starting locations, which they had memorized years ago. Once they had done that they went in search of each other, both of them randomly tossing mines all over the level while trying to find the other player, knowing that whoever died first was going to have a huge disadvantage since he would start several times in mined locations.

Alan was the unlucky one this time around. He saw Jimmy at the bottom of a stairway and tried to charge him. Jimmy, however, pulled out a pistol and shot him in the leg, and since they had set the battle on the "license to kill mode" it killed him right away. "Bastard!" Alan shouted as his character fell to the ground. It was no contest after that. Jimmy kept replacing the mines in the starting locations while Alan went through them and racked up suicide counts. Eventually Jimmy did get too close to one and died himself, but the cycle of starting-location death he went through wasn't enough to close the gap and he won.

"Play again?" Alan asked.

Jimmy glanced up at one of the darkening windows and said, "No, I think I'll head out on my bike ride now."

"You sure?"

"Yeah." He couldn't wait any longer. He had to see her.

"Okay," Alan said while wrapping up his controller. "Well, have fun."

"I will," Jimmy said, a nervous ring once again present in his voice. With that, he headed up the stairs and out into the garage.

Alan followed a second later but continued all the way to the second floor and then looked out a window. Sure enough, Jimmy was heading down the street on their father's old bike. He watched until his brother disappeared into the darkening landscape and then went into his bedroom where two hours of homework waited.

Samantha had actually just started drifting off to sleep when the sound of the door opening jolted her awake. All the pain came back, along with the fear.

Jimmy walked in.

Samantha stared at him as he closed the solid door and then turned to look at her. This time he was wearing gym shorts rather than jeans, and poking against them was an erection.

He's going to rape me.

Jimmy looked up at the rope and then back at her. "Is it tight?" he asked.

Samantha didn't know what to say.

"I asked you a question. Is it really tight?"

"Yes," she said dryly.

"Well, I'm going to lower you a little, but first you have to promise to do something for me."

Anything to be let down.

Samantha tried to pretend it was her boyfriend Steven who had reached up her shirt and was now fingering her nipples and squeezing her breasts, but no matter how hard she tried, even when closing her eyes, she knew it was Jimmy, and this made her feel sick.

Just tolerate anything he does to you and then spend time on the ground, Samantha said to herself. *Don't say anything.*

Her body nearly shook from the thought of being free from the ropes, and she couldn't even begin to imagine what it would feel like. She had only been tied up for half a day, but already it was all she knew. This, now, was her life.

Jimmy's hands stopped and pulled out from beneath her shirt. They were shaking.

"Let me down now?" she asked.

Jimmy nodded and then said, "But remember, there's more, and if you refuse to do it, then I'll hang you so high your toes won't touch the ground."

Samantha nodded silently, which was awkward with her arms pressing into her head, and said, "I know."

Jimmy turned and walked over to the rope and began untying it.

One moment she was stuck with her hands over her head, and the next her feet dropped to the ground as her body sagged. Relief did not come, however, because instantly her body was racked with muscle cramps. She cried out in pain.

Jimmy slowly lowered her all the way to the ground. It was basically a controlled collapse.

Samantha writhed in agony as the fierce pins and needles raced across her body. The areas of pain were so large that she couldn't distinguish where one ended and another began.

Tears fell from her eyes.

Her hands had the worst of it. For hours they had been a purplish tint, which meant blood was failing to get through to them. Now there was an onrush.

Slowly the pain began to fade and she managed to open her eyes. They drifted right to her hands, which were still bound but not suffering. Hours earlier, she had squeezed them into tight fists. Now she opened them. The pins and needles returned.

She ground her teeth together.

Jimmy came and stood over her.

She looked up at him.

He took a knee and began untying her wrists.

White impressions marked where the ropes had pressed into her skin. It would be a long time before they faded.

Jimmy suddenly took her right hand and slowly began to massage it. His fingers worked some of the tenderness away and brought a bit of life back into it.

Initially she felt warmth toward him and wondered if he would let her go, but then it faded as the situation changed quickly.

He dropped her hand and stood up.

She felt a new fright as he looked down upon her.

"Reach up into my pants," he ordered.

Samantha did not move.

"Do it or I will hang you from your wrists for an entire night."

Samantha didn't feel like she was in control as her hand went up his right leg and into the opening of his shorts.

Jimmy quivered with pleasure as Samantha's fingers got closer and closer to his penis, which was thumping with anticipation and excitement. And then her fingers wrapped around it and began stroking. Never before had a girl touched him like this, and his knees actually vibrated uncontrollably each time her fingers twisted around the head of his erection, almost as if there was a reflex point within it, one which the doctor had never explored with his little rubber hammer.

The moment was amazing, pure bliss, yet over much too quickly, the pleasure fading fast once he had spurted his load. At home, he would have stopped jerking himself off at that moment, but Samantha didn't, and when her fingers came back around over his wet penis head it actually hurt, as if the nerves were so fired up that they couldn't take the slightest contact.

His hands had been in his hair during the moment of ejaculation but then quickly went down to stop her hand, his lips going, "Okay, okay, *that's enough.*"

Never in a million years would he have thought pain would so easily follow, or that he would need several minutes to recover.

"You can wash your hands if you like at the sink back there," Jimmy said afterward. He was sitting in the corner, his breathing slowly but surely returning to normal. "The water runs. I tested it last week."

Samantha went to the sink as quickly as possible and made sure to get everything off. She didn't want even a molecule or atom of his semen to remain on her and wished the Hoods had installed a nuclear or biological decontamination shower in the small shelter that she could jump into.

"That's enough. They're clean," Jimmy said after she spent several minutes scrubbing. "I have to leave soon, but before I go you can have a bottle of water from the shelf. Drink as much as you want."

Samantha did as she was told, her mouth and body

craving the water. Cramps hit about a third of the way through the bottle, which was when she stopped, her shaky hands struggling to recap it.

"Finished?" Jimmy asked.

"Yes," Samantha said. Her voice was still weak. She then put a hand to her side, hoping the water cramp would pass.

Jimmy stood up and grabbed the rope that had bound her wrists earlier and said, "Okay, give me your hands."

"Wait," Samantha said once she realized what he was going to do. "I thought you were going to let me stay down?"

"No," Jimmy said. "You've been down half an hour. I have to go and I can't leave you like this."

"Please, don't tie me up like that again. Please don't. *Please.*" The tears returned as she slowly backed away into the corner of the room. "I won't try to get out. I promise."

"Don't make me force you. You don't want that." His voice was calm yet had a terrifying edge to it.

Samantha continued crawling backward, like a kid trying to escape a spanking, her sobs echoing through the small room.

Anger suddenly distorted Jimmy's face and he came toward her, rope in hand. Seeing this, Samantha wished she hadn't put up any resistance.

Jimmy grabbed her right wrist and pulled her toward him. Pain shot through her arm and shoulder.

"Please, I'm sorry," Samantha whimpered.

Jimmy ignored her as he twisted the rope around her right wrist several times and then grabbed the left one and did the same. He then wrapped the rope around both wrists and tied it.

"Get over here," he said while yanking her toward the rope that hung from the pipe in the ceiling. In one quick move, he had a knot tied to the rope that bound her wrists and pulled her up.

Her feet left the ground. Her wrists felt like they were on fire.

"*Oh!* Ahhh."

Jimmy held the rope. "This is what it feels like to be suspended by your wrists. Do you want that?"

Samantha couldn't say anything. Her feet kicked madly through the air trying to find the ground.

"Do you understand me?" he shouted.

"Yes," she cried, the word barely coming out.

The pressure on her wrists disappeared as her feet were once again lowered to the ground. The relief she felt was indescribable.

"You ever act like that again and I'll leave you up there all night and hit you a hundred times with my belt." Spittle flew as he spoke.

"I'm sorry," she said while crying, tears nearly choking her. "Please, I'm so sorry." A part of her was angry at the way she apologized, but the reasonable part knew this was the only way to survive.

Jimmy turned away and tied the rope back around the pipe. He then flicked the light switch off while leaving, which left the room in complete darkness. Samantha couldn't see a thing, but the relief at him being gone kept her from being upset about the darkness. He had also tied the rope in a way that allowed both her feet to be flat on the ground. In time, this position would grow unbearable as well, but at the moment, it wasn't, and that was all that mattered.

CHAPTER THREE

Megan Reed was the first to hear that Samantha King was missing and instantly thought foul play was involved. Unfortunately, her father, Sheriff Reed, did not share in his daughter's theory and had his own opinion.

"I can't put out a missing person alert, Dorothy. Not until she's been gone forty-eight hours." Sheriff Reed sighed after speaking. This was the third time he had told Dorothy King about the policy.

Megan was one room over from her father, yet despite the distance, she could hear how hysterical Samantha's mother was on the other end of the phone.

"No, it doesn't matter. She's eighteen and therefore an adult. All I can do—no, I know she's still in high school, but it doesn't matter—all I can do is put out the word to my deputies that she is wanted back home and to let her know this if they come across her." Dorothy said something frantically. "I'm sorry. She's an adult and can do what she wants as far as the law is concerned." More hysteria. "Dorothy, listen. She's probably out with friends and just lost track of time."

Megan knew this wasn't the case and found herself

growing irritated at how ignorant her father was when it came to people her age. Samantha King didn't have many friends, and the ones she did have weren't the type that would lose track of time on a school night.

What if she was kidnapped?

A shiver passed through her at the thought.

What if someone is raping her right now?

She remembered several summers back when all the kids had been disappearing around the country. Elizabeth Smart had been found alive, but most of the others were either still missing or had been found dead. Many of them had come from small towns. That was the thing people seemed to forget: small towns were just as big a target as the big cities like Chicago, or New York, or Los Angeles, maybe even a better target because no one suspected a kidnapping would happen, and the law enforcement was not really that good at handling those types of situations. She felt bad for thinking this, but it was true. The worst things her father ever had to deal with as both a deputy and sheriff were kids having sex, drinking, and doing drugs. There also was the occasional traffic violation, and once her father had been called to the scene of a domestic disturbance that almost got out of hand. That was it though. There were no murders, and up until that day, no kidnappings.

"If you don't hear from her in the next forty-eight hours, we can put out a missing person report," Sheriff Reed said. "But I guarantee she'll be back before then."

No, she won't, Megan said to herself. *No, she won't.*

Her father hung up the phone and came out of the kitchen. Megan pretended she had been reading the entire time.

He said nothing, took a seat in the chair next to her,

and turned on the TV.

"Dad, I'm reading," Megan said.

"I'll keep it low, sweetie."

Megan hated being called sweetie. She also hated it when he just turned on the TV like this. The guy had no consideration for anyone but himself.

"Doesn't matter. I can't read with it on," she snapped while closing her book. She wanted to say more but knew it would only lead to a pointless argument, one that wouldn't resolve anything, and rather than let that happen she stood up and left the room. Sadly, her father probably didn't even notice since his mind was always completely wrapped up in whatever he was watching.

Tina sat in her room thinking about Jimmy and wondered what would develop between them. She hoped they would start dating and have some sort of meaningful relationship, yet she couldn't help but think about the way Jimmy was and how he would probably never make any moves to call her or do things with her. That meant the relationship would be solely up to her and she would have to do all the hard work. If she wanted a kiss, she would have to lean into him to get one. If she wanted sex, she would have to touch him in a way that signaled this, or come out and tell him what she wanted—but then that was all for another day. Right now, all she really needed to worry about was finding the right dress for prom, one that didn't need a lot of alterations and fittings since it was such short notice.

Or I could wear my homecoming dress from last year.

The dress had never actually been worn since her date had dumped her three days before homecoming, all because she had pulled away from him while the two had been in his car out by Scooby's Hot Dog Stand in West Chicago just off North Avenue. And it hadn't even been sex that she was refusing, just sex without a condom, which they could have easily rectified. Instead, her boyfriend had been a jerk about it and told her he would pull out in time. She still said no, and when he started pawing at her she hit him in the testicles as hard as she could and then walked over to the hot dog stand to call her father, which of course sent the guy home, the words "It's over" echoing from his lips as he got back in his car.

Jimmy wouldn't do that, she said to herself and smiled. *If I said no, he would be respectful and would stop.*

Or, better yet, go out and buy the damn condoms.

I will pull out in time, she repeated to herself, the voice of the idiot boyfriend echoing in her mind. God, what a fool, and worse, she knew girls who would have believed him and then later would think life was unfair when they were knocked up.

The phone rang.

Tina hurried over and looked at the caller ID, hoping it was Jimmy. It wasn't. Instead, she saw the words *Cell Phone* followed by a local number that she recognized.

"Rebecca's House of Sinful Pleasure," Tina said. "Rebecca's not in right now, but if you'll leave your name and sexual request, she will get back to you."

"Tina," Scott Goldman said. "Your mother is here bawling her eyes out about the way you treat her, and I think you owe her an apology."

"Oh gee, I'm so touched. It is moving how much drama she can create, isn't it? I bet she even got all teary-eyed when she told you my father died, even though she walked out on him sixteen years ago."

"Just because she left him doesn't mean she didn't love

him…or you."

Tina liked how the last part was added on quickly. "Well, I appreciate you nosing yourself into a situation that doesn't really require your help, so I'm going to give you some free advice about tonight. When you fuck my mother, use a condom, because the world doesn't need any more male knitting genes in it, okay? Good. Bye, bye now!" Tina clicked off the phone, completely disgusted with the fact that her mother was sleeping with a twenty-four-year-old guy who loved knitting.

Jimmy sat in his room for a long time after coming home, his hands holding a pair of handcuffs that he'd had since he was five. He had asked for them for his birthday, after the plastic pair that had come with a police costume had broken, and his parents had gotten them for him. Today most would probably think such a gift was crazy, but back then things had been a little different. The handcuffs had actually been geared toward kids, a tiny little switch making it so one could escape easily if needed. Young female friends had become familiar with the switch. His teenage babysitter had worn the handcuffs quite a bit as well, and Jimmy had been startled to see a home video of himself sitting in the family room waiting for her to arrive one night, handcuffs in hand. It was weird, and he wondered if his parents had ever thought something was odd about how much he enjoyed handcuffing the girls in his life. With his being so young, they probably hadn't thought much about it. Looking back, especially if word about what he had done to Samantha ever came out, they would probably be horrified and even blame themselves for what he had done, thinking they had triggered his desire at an early age just like some parents of homosexuals thought their parenting actions had caused the "abnormal" desires. Jimmy knew this wasn't the case though. He knew that the desires had already been in place. After all, why would he have asked for the handcuffs if they hadn't been?

CHAPTER FOUR

Alan woke up early the next morning and discovered that Jimmy was gone. At first this startled him, but then, remembering the bike-riding thing the night before, he went out to the garage to see if the bike was still there. It wasn't. Jimmy had gone on another bike ride.

It was about six o'clock.

Probably still nervous about prom, Alan said to himself, thinking the bike rides helped Jimmy relax. *What will he be like on Saturday?*

Hopefully his brother would be able to relax by then and enjoy himself. At the same time he knew just how nerve-racking such a situation would be for him. After all, it wasn't just his first dance, but his first date and girlfriend. Experiencing all of that during one night— Alan couldn't even imagine what that would be like. It did, however, bring to mind his own first date two years ago and how much of a disaster it had been.

Samantha woke weary and tired, her body having been unable to relax enough for her mind to drift away for long periods of time due to the ropes. Every time she did manage to doze off, something would happen that would pull her back. The tug of the ropes was the worst. People were not designed to sleep while standing, so whenever her mind entered the dream world the ropes would yank her back. Of course, just relaxing enough to fall asleep was nearly impossible. All her mind could think about was her situation, which kept the fear of having to live the rest of her days tied up like this constant. To make matters worse, every time she did fall asleep and then woke up, she thought Jimmy was in the room with her, concealed somewhere in the darkness.

It was also very cold and her body had no way of keeping the heat in, which was why she was shaking when Jimmy did actually appear the next morning.

"Here," Jimmy said while handing her a wool blanket. He had gotten it from the stack of wool blankets that had been folded and left in the rear corner of the shelter. Before doing that, he had untied the ropes from her wrists and told her to sit against the wall.

Samantha nodded a thank-you and wrapped herself with the warm blanket. It felt wonderful, despite the itchiness, yet it didn't get rid of the shakes right away. The comfort of finally being free from the ropes, however, made it difficult for her eyes to stay open.

Jimmy uncapped the bottle of water she had drunk from the day before and helped her take a few sips. For the first time in her life, Samantha was glad the water was warm.

"Do you need to use the bathroom?" Jimmy asked.

"Y-yesss."

"Okay, stay here a second." Jimmy stood up and walked over to the wall with shelves and picked up a metal bucket. He then brought it back. "Use this."

Samantha had assumed he would take her into the house and let her use one of those toilets since this little shelter didn't have one. Now she just stared at the bucket with disgust and humiliation. "I ca-can't go in th-that."

"If you need to go, you can."

Samantha looked at Jimmy and then back at the bucket, disgusted. *How can he be doing this to me? Why is he doing this to me?*

"If you don't use it now, I'll just tie you up so your legs are straddling it. But then you'll be stuck with the smell until I get back from school."

"S-school?" she asked. "What time is it?"

"It's just after six o'clock in the morning."

As soon as he said it, the hunger that had been showing up on and off throughout the night hit full force. She was starving.

"Can I e-eat something?" she asked, hesitation gripping her as her eyes studied the shelf with canned goods.

"Oh, yeah." Jimmy got up and walked to the shelf. "What do you want?"

Samantha didn't know what was over there, so she didn't respond. Anything would satisfy her as long as it put an end to her hunger.

Jimmy turned. "Crackers?"

Samantha nodded.

Jimmy moved a few cans around, took out a box of crackers, and then returned to Samantha. "I bet this started out as the Hoods' Y2K shelter but then wasn't enough for the coming nuclear war with Islam they thought was going to occur."

Samantha wasn't sure if she heard him correctly, but it seemed like Jimmy was trying to start up a simple conversation. Why would he do that? Rather than answering him, she just waited for him to bring the crackers.

A day earlier, crackers for breakfast would have been a joke unless she was dieting. Now her stomach opened up with just the thought of a single small square.

"Let me see your wrists," Jimmy said once the box was open.

Her arms felt like they had gone through a heavy workout, and she had trouble holding them out to him.

Jimmy looked at the red marks the rope had left and slowly began rubbing them. He then asked, "What was it like standing there all night?"

Samantha didn't respond. Last night had been the worst night of her life, and now he was asking the question like it was nothing. It could have been a bed he was asking about, and how comfortable the new mattress had been.

"If you want some crackers, you better answer me," Jimmy said, his voice growing stern.

"It hurt," she said. Her voice wasn't as shaky as before, and now her body actually felt warm.

"I've always wanted to know what it would be like," Jimmy said. "Standing there like that, arms over your head, the bite of the ropes, knowing you couldn't get free." He shook his head. "I envy the experience you had."

Samantha couldn't believe what she was hearing. Was he serious? Could he actually be envious of what he had forced her to do all night and would force her to do again? He was crazy.

"That and the stocks, or pillory as they are really called. I've always wondered what it would be like to stand locked in the pillory all day, the way the girls in medieval and Puritan times were forced to do. I don't know when that desire started, but I love looking at videos on YouTube of girls at Renaissance events being locked in the pillory."

Samantha didn't reply. She had no idea how to.

Jimmy didn't seem to care and continued. "One of these nights I might lock myself up with you. I'd tell my parents I was sleeping over somewhere and come here, put handcuffs on, tie them up like yours, and just wait until morning before unlocking them. What do you think of that?"

Samantha struggled with a response. She didn't know what to say but knew he was expecting an answer. "I guess it would be nice to have some company."

"Was it lonely last night?" Jimmy asked.

"Yes." Tears began to well inside her eyes again. She wasn't sure why his comment about being lonely had gotten to her. Perhaps it was everything coming together. The tears did not fall. She wouldn't let them. She didn't want him to see her cry.

"Here," Jimmy said while handing her some crackers. He waited with the water.

They were the most delicious things Samantha had ever eaten. She had another handful before washing it all down with a sip of water.

Jimmy then handed her the box of crackers and set the water next to her. For a moment she thought he was going to leave and let her stay sitting there all day, but he was only getting up to stretch his legs and look at some of the things the Hood family had brought down.

"I wonder when they made this place," Jimmy said while examining the concrete walls.

Samantha's mouth was full of crackers.

"I don't remember ever hearing about it being built, and no one ever mentioned it, so maybe they didn't really build it. Maybe it was an old atomic shelter from the fifties that they converted into a Y2K shelter."

Samantha took a big swallow of water and then said, "My dad talks about it all the time." It was a lie but one she thought might work.

Jimmy whirled around. "What?"

It had worked.

"He remembers them asking him about concrete and cement and how much would be needed. He owns that construction company, you know, and so they asked him all about it." She tried to sound genuine, but then her voice started to waver. "He talked about it with us at dinner a lot."

Relief suddenly swept over his face.

"You're lying," he said.

"No."

"Yes. I can tell, but just to make sure"—he started to take off his belt—"I'll whip you until you admit it."

Her eyes went wide. Why had she said that? "No, wait, please." She then thought of something else. "If you hurt me, I'm just going to say it's a lie so you stop." She could still feel the belt hitting her the day before and did not want that again.

"Tell me, right now. Were you lying?"

Fear coiled itself throughout her body. If she said yes, he was going to punish her. If she said no, he was going to punish her until she admitted it. It was a lose-lose situation.

"*Were you lying?*"

"*Yes*," she cried. "I'm sorry."

He came over and grabbed her right wrist. She tried to hold back but couldn't. He forced her to her feet.

"Tell me, why'd you lie?"

"I-I—"

He swung the belt low and connected with her leg. Samantha cried out and tried to fall to her knees. Never in her life had anyone treated her this way.

"ANSWER ME!"

Somehow she spoke through her sobs and said, "*I wanted you to think people knew about this place so you'd take me somewhere else.*"

Jimmy calmed down.

Several seconds passed.

Her tears continued.

"That's what I thought," he said. "Come here."

He pulled her to the rope. "What are you doing?" she asked.

"You've just earned yourself ten minutes of being hung from the wrists."

"No, please, don't."

"If you fight me, I'll make it twenty minutes." He was no longer angry. Actually, he seemed excited.

Samantha realized she was making things worse for herself and stopped fighting. She wiped away some tears and then held out her wrists. *Ten minutes. It's nothing. Don't worry.* However, she remembered the day before when he had pulled her off the ground and how there had been instant pain throughout her arms and wrists. That had been a few seconds. What would ten minutes be like?

Jimmy wrapped the rope around her wrists several times and then attached it to the one hanging from the ceiling.

"Please," she tried again. "I'm sorry."

"Too late for that."

He gave the rope a pull. Samantha felt her arms rise up, but this time rather than stopping when she was on her toes he kept pulling until her feet left the ground and then tied off the rope. The pain was instantaneous, almost as if someone were putting a ring of fire around her already burned wrists.

Jimmy looked down at his watch. "Ten minutes," he said.

"Please. *I'm sorry*." She gasped for air, her chest feeling as if a giant weight were compressing it. "Let me down!"

Her toes stretched toward the ground, trying to find the surface, but they fell short by nearly ten inches. This desperate attempt to reach the floor caused her body to twist to the left. It stopped once she was completely sideways and then twisted back.

"Nine minutes to go," Jimmy said.

The ropes felt like razor teeth chewing on her torn flesh, and her hands, squeezed into tight fists, felt lifeless.

Jimmy's hand suddenly reached up between her legs from behind. Samantha jerked, but her body wasn't going anywhere. His fingers began rubbing up and down against her groin. Samantha wanted to protest but kept silent.

Embarrassing warmth began to develop.

The fingers continued to caress her pubic region for several seconds and then stopped.

Samantha felt both relief and disappointment. For a few seconds his fingers had taken her mind off the rope. Now it was back full force. At the same time, she was disgusted at how her body had reacted.

"Seven minutes to go."

* * *

Despite having ejaculated twice the day before, Jimmy had once again grown excited that night when thinking about all the scenes he had watched where women were hanging from their wrists, and he had developed a craving to see Samantha actually hanging for a good chunk of time, her feet unable to touch the ground. The craving had gotten so intense that he nearly rode his bike back to the fallout shelter again to see her and produce the scene, but then he realized how dangerous that would be in the middle of the night, especially if someone saw him and then reported it to the police. Being out at night wasn't against the law, especially since he was eighteen, but once word of Samantha's disappearance spread, people would remember the little oddities in everyone around them and might grow suspicious of him. Once that happened, he had a feeling people would learn about his interests, which in turn could eventually lead them to Samantha. Or lead to her death from dehydration if he wasn't able to get to her for a long period of time due to the scrutiny put upon him.

So, rather than going out to see Samantha, Jimmy had opened up his computer and watched a short scene he had downloaded from a bondage site in 2008, one which he legally shouldn't have been on at the time given his age, yet had no trouble seeing thanks to the simple click of the *Yes, I'm Over Eighteen* button. The scene had been from a site called Into the Attic, which featured amateur girls on the West Coast who wanted to try out bondage. Most of the videos didn't interest him, yet he checked the site regularly just in case something would appear that he craved (same thing with Kink.com and, more recently, the Clips4Sale sites). In August 2008, just such a scene appeared with a girl who called herself Syn that he couldn't resist. In the video Syn stood on a chair while the owner of the site tied her wrists to a bolt in the ceiling and then removed the chair. She then hung there until she used a safe word to get down, which took quite a while, her toughness and determination making her last longer than most would be able to. BDSM fans probably thought the scene was boring due to a lack of nudity, sexual penetration, or painful implements being put upon her, but Jimmy had loved it and never regretted the thirty-dollar membership fee he had paid just to be able to see that one scene. In fact, Jimmy would have paid hundreds of dollars for hundreds of scenes like it, not caring if there wasn't any nudity in them because he loved seeing the girls tied up in everyday clothes anyway. It seemed more real that way.

Watching the muted scene and then masturbating to it had stifled the craving that night, and then, after a long hot shower, he had been able to sleep. The craving had returned that morning, however, and now, seeing Samantha hanging from her wrists, her feet trying to touch the ground, her breathing shallow due to the pressure the position put on her lungs, was amazing. It was so hot he wanted to masturbate while she hung there, but he didn't for fear that he would spend so much time in the shelter with her that he wouldn't have time to shower before school and people would smell the semen once he got to class.

Instead, he just watched her, savoring the intense position as her body slowly swayed back and forth, the single strand of rope making it impossible for her weight to find the proper balance to stay still. It was incredible.

Samantha felt the ground beneath her feet and almost

cried out with thankfulness. But then Jimmy's hand was upon her right breast and she once again felt anger and disgust. Adding to this was the terrible pain that raced into her wrists now that the blood flow was no longer cut off. Her hands screamed in agony.

At the same time, there was a strange numbness to certain parts of her left hand, which had seemed to take most of her weight while hanging. Pins and needles covered most of her flesh, with the exception of a small area near her thumb and another right below her pinky. Due to the painful tingle, however, her mind wasn't too concerned with the lifelessness that distorted her left hand. She gritted her teeth, waiting for it all to pass.

It wasn't just her hands that were suffering. Her elbows felt as if she had gone through a strenuous workout and wanted to stay straight. She bent them a little and felt her muscles throughout her arms gasp.

Jimmy's hand continued to work her right breast, his fingers sending shivers of humiliation through her.

Pretend it isn't him.

Her mind was unable to accomplish this.

The pins and needles in her hands grew worse, almost as if someone were heating up the imaginary torment, which caused her to grind her teeth back and forth.

Jimmy stopped touching her and went over to tie off the rope. Rather than pulling her up to the tips of her toes, he gave her a considerable amount of slack. It was almost enough for her to be able to reach down and touch her face, just a few inches short.

Samantha took several deep breaths while he did this.

Jimmy returned to her side.

Samantha stared at him.

The pins and needles were fading and her breathing

was returning to normal. Her fear, however, wasn't dissipating. What was he planning to do now?

Without warning, he reached out and began to unbutton her jeans.

"No," she gasped. *"Please don't!"*

Jimmy ignored her plea and struggled with the button. His fingers were not experienced at undressing another person and it took him several seconds to break the connection. He then pulled down her zipper, exposing her panties.

She hopelessly struggled, her mind unable to come to terms with the moment she had been dreading since the abduction. She did not want him to rape her. She did not want him to be the one who took her virginity.

"Stop," he said.

She didn't.

"Stop." He grabbed her legs while saying this and forced her to stay still. Her struggles were no match for his strength, but this didn't mean she was going to give up. She continued to fight against his hands until he said, "I'll hang you again and then whip you hard."

Her struggles ceased.

In the end, he would have won anyway. Nothing she could do would stop him from raping her.

"Lift your legs," he ordered while pushing her pants down to her ankles. Her panties were now completely exposed.

The ropes tightened on her wrists as she lifted one leg. He pulled her jeans from that one and then from the other.

Samantha felt completely vulnerable, even with her underwear still in place. It was humiliating.

Jimmy carefully folded the jeans and set them next to

the stack of blankets. He then returned and reached for her panties.

A chill raced through her as his fingers went beneath the fabric and brushed up against her pubic region. No guy had ever touched her there before. There was no pleasure. His hand felt dirty.

Her panties came off quicker than her pants had.

The vulnerability she had felt before multiplied itself several times.

Why me? she pleaded. *Why did he take me?*

Tears began to well in her eyes again. She didn't want him to have her. Not like this. Not ever. Panic erupted.

Jimmy didn't rape her.

Instead, after looking at her nakedness for a few seconds, he went over and grabbed the bucket, which he then set next to her bare legs.

"If you had listened to me earlier, I wouldn't have to leave you like this." He shook his head. "You'll have to go eventually, and I don't want to clean your clothes."

Samantha looked down at the bucket. Disgust at having to use it should have filled her, but it didn't. Instead, she was relieved that he wasn't planning to rape her. Unfortunately, the thought that he probably would eventually didn't go away. There would come a point when he would want her and then there would be nothing she could do about it.

"I'll be back tonight," Jimmy said.

Alan was eating a bowl of cereal when Jimmy came back from his bike ride. A second later the shower downstairs was on and Jimmy in it.

Fifteen minutes went by before Jimmy was finished and came upstairs to eat something before school.

"How was your ride?" Alan asked.

"Pretty good. You know, I never realized how nice it is in the morning when it's still dark out. Everything is so peaceful and the air smells nice."

"Oh," Alan said. Jimmy was speaking quickly, which made Alan wonder if everything was okay. Something didn't seem right, but he couldn't put his finger on what it was. He had never before seen his older brother like this. Could it all really be because of the prom, or was something else worrying him?

After a quick search of the kitchen, Jimmy settled on a bowl of cereal just as Alan had. He ate fast. It was almost seven twenty, which meant the two had to leave soon.

"I wish I could just go out and ride all morning, from like three to seven, without anyone else out there," Jimmy said while finishing his cereal. "It's just so peaceful. I love it."

"You just ride around, nothing else?" Alan couldn't understand why this was something so *great*. It seemed boring. Though, he would admit, a nice stroll through the woods was cool every now and then, but *every morning*? Nah, that would get old quick.

"Yep. I go down the trails through the woods and out onto the edge of the soybean fields. Watching the sun come up over those fields is one of the most beautiful things you could ever imagine. I wish I could go back in time to when the country was all woods and prairie and just walk for miles. Ever wonder what that would be like?"

"I guess," Alan said. In his mind he thought, *Jimmy, you're getting weird.*

Actually, Jimmy thought to himself while talking with

Alan, *I wish I could go back in time and build a house way out in the woods far away from any civilization with a secret dungeon in the basement that no one could find and bring dozens of girls that I kidnapped from farms there.*

It was a fantasy he had had for a long time, one which would never become a reality even if he were able to find such a place in this day and age, because in his fantasy he left girls tied up in the woods hanging from their wrists, their bodies subject to whatever nature forced upon them. In his fantasy, no one would ever be able to find them, but in real life, there was a chance someone would stumble upon them, even if he were hundreds of miles from civilization. It was just too risky.

CHAPTER FIVE

Megan went to school with the need to find out what people knew about Samantha's disappearance and almost immediately began asking classmates if Samantha had said anything to anyone about running away or going out of town for a while. Every answer was no, and by noon several students were speculating about the Samantha King disappearance. Unfortunately, due to the small-town mentality that nothing terrible could happen, only a few people were actually worried. Megan was one of them.

"But she wouldn't just leave," Megan said to Alison Ellis.

"You don't know that," Alison replied. "Maybe she got in a fight with her parents."

"No. I could hear it on the phone. Nothing happened. Samantha just disappeared."

"Megan, come on, she wasn't kidnapped. This is Ashland Creek. Okay? That just wouldn't happen here."

"Why?"

"I don't know. I gotta go." The bell signaling the start of class was about to ring, and Alison wanted to get to the bathroom before going to biology.

Grrrr, Megan moaned to herself. It was so frustrating. No one was taking this seriously. They were acting as if people just left all the time.

Her next class was world literature, a class she had regretted signing up for the moment she stepped foot into the room last winter when second semester began. It wasn't that she disliked reading, but the teacher was an old bitch and for some strange reason didn't like guys or any girl who participated in sports—especially cheerleading. She was also vocal in her support of the Republican Party and hated Obama because she felt he was a socialist Muslim who wanted to ruin the nation, one who was even responsible for the terrible oil spill in the gulf, even though there was nothing he could really do about it.

Megan knew her teacher was not alone in her opinions, and she wouldn't have cared about them if she kept them to herself. The teacher didn't, though, and seemed to find ways of comparing every negative aspect of Obama and the Democratic Party—both real and fabricated—to the literature they were reading and then would go on a rant. Making the situation worse was that most people in town felt the same way, including her father and the school board, so no one cared when Megan complained. Plus, the teacher had been working there since Megan's parents were students, and no one had the guts to get rid of her. Still, it made Megan sick every time she went on a rant, especially when it was fueled by something like a passage within the novel *One Day in the Life of Ivan Denisovich* by Aleksandr Solzhenitsyn, which she would use to show what life would be like once Obama turned the nation into a socialist country.

Most students brushed that away and wouldn't have despised the teacher if that were her only flaw. The one that pissed off Megan's fellow students was the teacher's thought that kids their age couldn't help but get in trouble and be destructive during their free time and needed to be shackled down by the burden of homework and reading assignments in order to prevent such unacceptable behavior. It was really bad.

Even Jimmy Hawthorn, the guy who sat behind her and never really said a word to anyone unless spoken to, had voiced his opinion of the teacher on several different occasions. She was awful, yet there was nothing Megan or any other student in class could do about it.

"Hey, Jimmy," Megan said a minute before the bell was going to ring. She twisted in her seat so she could see him.

"Yeah?" Jimmy asked, his eyes drifting away from hers.

"Did you hear about Samantha King?"

"What about her?" he asked quickly, his eyes back and staring into hers.

"She disappeared yesterday after school." It surprised her that he hadn't heard about it, even if he rarely ever talked to anyone. By now, it was common news.

"Oh yeah, I think I did hear something about that. She ran away or something, didn't she?"

"No," Megan snapped. "Samantha wouldn't run away. Something happened to her."

"Like what?"

"Like she was kidnapped by someone. My dad doesn't think so, but—"

"Whoa," Jimmy interrupted. "Your dad doesn't think

she was kidnapped?"

"No, but I know she was. Samantha had no reason to run away. Something happened to her."

Ms. Gliek walked in just as the bell rang. Anyone who wasn't in their seats, even if they were just standing next to them, was marked tardy. It made Megan so angry. Teachers, even ones she liked, focused too much on stupid disciplinary rules, tardiness being one of them. If a student walked in twenty minutes late, that was one thing. Marking them tardy because they weren't sitting in their seat properly when the bell rang, that was something else.

Jimmy had expected there to be a huge uproar over the fact that Samantha King had never returned home the night before, but aside from a few speculative comments, no one was really saying that much, and apparently the police weren't even involved yet, which was amazing. He had thought for sure every single police officer would have been at the school asking questions, similar to the scene in the movie *Scream* after the two kids were murdered in the beginning, and that the FBI and news media would have all descended upon the town. Instead, the only one who even seemed remotely concerned was Megan Reed, the daughter of the town sheriff and a good friend of Samantha's. It was amazing and a huge relief.

At the same time, he knew that things still had the potential to turn hectic and that his visions of the town being swamped with reporters and FBI agents and other law enforcement agencies could still happen, especially if Samantha wasn't heard from. Once she'd been missing for a week or so, people would start to panic. Until then he felt like he could relax a bit, though of course he still had to stay alert.

Brett Murphy saw Jimmy Hawthorn and that new girl Tina talking in the hallway before school ended and knew he had to interfere somehow. He had to inform this Tina girl that she was much too pretty to be hanging out with the likes of Jimmy.

A look of fear spread across Jimmy's face as Brett approached (at least this was what Brett saw).

"Hey, Jimmy, how's it going?" Brett asked.

Jimmy and Tina swiveled around to look at him. "What do you want, shitface?" Jimmy asked.

Without warning, Brett had Jimmy in a headlock. Tina gasped.

"Who's the shitface now, you stupid cocksucking bastard? Who is it?" Brett looked over at Tina while holding Jimmy and said, "Why do you hang out with this loser? Don't you know he's the punching bag of the entire—" All the air rushed out of him as Jimmy's elbow connected with his stomach just below the rib cage.

His arm loosened.

"Let's go," Jimmy said to Tina after pulling free.

Brett, gasping for air, straightened himself and looked around. The bitch who had once reported him for using a hall pass to go get a Coke from the vending machine during class hours was looking at him. God, he hated all hall monitors, especially that one.

Before she could get close, he walked away, his mind thinking about one thing: *Jimmy*. The bastard was going to pay for this.

"I don't know why, but he's picked on me ever since the

first grade," Jimmy said. "It all began with the game four square, if you can believe that," he added with a smile.

"Four square?" Tina asked. "Really?"

"Seriously. When I was little, that game was all the rage during recess. The school had like five four-square patterns laid out, yet huge lines still developed all the time at each one. I wasn't very good at the game but liked it and always got knocked out, but then one day I started to do really good and got to the king square and was allowed to make the rules. It was really cool, but everyone ganged up on me to knock me out, which obviously is how the game works, but being that young and being ganged up on and then being knocked out right away really got to me, and I started crying and ran behind a tree. After that, Brett never left me alone."

"What a jerk," Tina said.

"Yeah, but now it doesn't really bother me. He thinks it does, which is why he keeps at it, probably because it used to make me cry in junior high school, and he once pinned me on the ground and pushed my face in goose shit. I started working out my freshman year though since they had a weight room, and now every time he tries to hurt me I just push back. He doesn't seem to realize that I could kick his ass if I wanted to."

"Plus you sit alone every day, so people probably think it still gets to you."

"Well, it doesn't. I just prefer to sit by people whose company I enjoy."

Tina smiled, which caused Jimmy to blush.

After that neither one knew what to say, but thankfully their silence didn't last long since Alan came and joined them for the walk home, the words "So I hear you two are going to prom together" leaving his lips.

"Yeah," Tina said, again smiling.

"Aw, that is so cute," Alan taunted them.

"Watch it," Jimmy said, though it didn't really bother him all that much because the more he thought about it, the more he enjoyed the idea of going to the prom with Tina. In fact, he couldn't believe he had previously gone so long without even thinking about asking her, his mind fine with the idea of missing what would be such a wonderful moment for the two of them. It was going to be great.

He really likes her, Alan said to himself as he watched the two hug before parting at Tina's place, their conversation having carried them there without interruption, which seemed unreal since their talks on the way home usually consisted of several moments of silence and then a hesitant "See you tomorrow" before separating.

Jimmy watched as Tina walked up to her house and then gave a quick wave when she turned to look back before stepping inside, a huge smile on her face.

Jimmy had a smile too, one that didn't fade away as he rejoined Alan on the sidewalk.

"What?" Jimmy asked.

Alan smiled. "You're glowing."

"Shut up."

"And now you're blushing too. My God, man, you've completely fallen for her."

"I…" Jimmy stopped. "Okay, maybe I like her a little, so what? I'm allowed."

"Yes, you are allowed," Alan said as the two started walking. "But only just a little, and you can only like her, not love her. Those are the rules for Mr. I Never Will Be Infatuated by a Girl Like All Those Losers at School."

"Oh, you are so asking for a beatdown," Jimmy said.

"You couldn't hurt a fly," Alan said.

"Wanna bet? I elbowed Brett in the stomach right before leaving and was going to punch him too if a hall monitor hadn't been coming around the corner."

"Epic! No wonder you're glowing. You kicked ass and have a hot girl going to prom with you. Jesus."

Jimmy didn't reply, and Alan wondered if he was pushing it too far. The trouble was that Jimmy's relationship was exciting for him and he couldn't help it. His older brother had been alone for so long due to his self-imposed prison, and now it looked like Tina might help him break free.

"So, what happened?" Alan asked.

"Nothing really. He just put me in a headlock and I elbowed him right under the rib cage." Jimmy shrugged. "I may have knocked the wind out of him, but I don't know for sure."

"Sweet."

"It was nothing."

"Yeah, but you know how everyone is. By tomorrow people will be saying you beat him up."

"True."

Physical contact always turned into more than it really was in school. Simply being pushed against a locker could turn into a person having the shit kicked out of him by the end of the day. Jimmy had experienced this quite a bit. Someone would trip him in the hall or knock him off-balance so he hit the divider between two doors, and he wouldn't retaliate, even though he could have beaten the crap out of him. Within a day word about the "fight" would have spread, especially on Facebook. Jimmy never seemed to care though, probably because he knew if the kids really wanted to fight with him they would be in for a world of hurt, not to mention the threat of being expelled once the school board got involved.

"It's too bad Brett wasn't in the weight room that day when you showed everyone up," Alan said.

"He had to have heard about it."

"Yeah, but if he had seen it, he probably wouldn't be such a jerk."

"The guy's a dumbass and is always going to be a jerk. Being able to out-bench someone with free weights isn't going to change that."

"Most seemed to shut up after that though."

"They did, didn't they?" Jimmy said, his sagging smile getting a booster shot of ego enhancers.

"Of course your strength is no match against my mad kung fu skills." Alan did a pretend hand chop with his statement. Laughter followed.

Samantha heard the latch of the door click open and looked toward it. Despite being forced to do it, she was embarrassed by what was sitting in the bucket. She had no idea why this embarrassment filled her—it wasn't like she was trying to impress Jimmy with her ladylike qualities, yet her actions and the resulting smell caused her face to go red.

Jimmy's face and the small gasp that escaped his lips as he walked in only added to her embarrassment. Several hours had drifted by since her use of the bucket, but during that time the smell had not weakened. Actually, it had probably gotten worse.

Samantha wanted to say something, but no words came.

Jimmy didn't say anything either. Instead, he just took the bucket from between her legs and went back outside for a few minutes. When he came in again, the bucket had been emptied and washed out. He set it aside.

Samantha's body ached from standing and she wanted down. Boredom had gotten to her as well. During the peak of it, she had actually wished for Jimmy's return just so she'd have some company. Now, however, she wanted to be alone again, her mind cursing her earlier wishes.

"Please let me down," she begged.

Jimmy nodded and walked over to the tied-off rope end and undid it. Samantha collapsed to her knees and then down to her butt. Pain erupted everywhere. The sudden freedom to move around had its costs.

Jimmy stepped over and undid the ropes from around her wrists. This added to the pain as the blood raced back. The pins and needles attacked.

Once again, Samantha found herself grinding her teeth together as a way of distorting the pain. It wasn't really a conscious action.

Jimmy walked over to the shelf, took a new bottle of water down, and handed it to her. He then grabbed a bag of pretzels, opened it, and tasted one. Satisfaction ran over his face as the pretzel went down. He brought the bag over.

Hunger twisted her insides at the sight, and she stuffed several in her mouth. A large gulp of water helped down the mouthful.

Jimmy just stared at her.

Samantha realized something as she took another handful of pretzels. She was naked from the waist down. Jimmy could see everything, and he was looking.

Where were her pants?

Her eyes caught sight of them over by the blankets on the opposite side of the wall. In order to get to them, she would have to crawl, which would expose her even more. It was not an action she wanted to take part in.

"Can you bring me my pants?" she asked, hesitation straining her words.

"If you do something for me first," Jimmy said. He then stood up and unbelted his pants.

No, she thought while backing away.

"Don't make me force you," Jimmy said. "All I want is another hand job."

A hand job? she questioned. Why was that all he ever wanted? Here he could have her body at any time, yet he never took it. What was wrong with him?

Are you complaining? a voice asked.

No.

Knowing everything would get worse if she denied him, Samantha crawled over and sat before him. She then reached up a hand and took hold of his erection.

Jimmy shivered beneath her.

"Don't close your eyes this time," he said. "And look up at me."

Samantha obeyed him, her hand slowly moving back and forth against him.

Jimmy groaned and his body started to hunch forward. His hands were restless and couldn't figure out what to do. His knees shook.

It took about thirty seconds and then he came, his seed splattering her hand and shirt. It was warm, sticky, and sickening.

"Keep going," Jimmy gasped.

Fighting the urge to be sick, Samantha continued to

move her hand back and forth, the thick liquid oozing between her fingers.

More dripped out and eased itself to the floor.

Jimmy pulled away with a gasp, his hand grabbing himself and squeezing the last of his seed out.

Samantha held her hand out before her, semen clinging to it. The hand felt contaminated. She wanted to clean it off.

Jimmy saw this and suddenly said, "Lick it all off."

"What?" she asked.

"Lick it off your hand. I want to see you put it in your mouth and swallow it."

"No, I can't." Her stomach turned over just thinking about it, nausea building.

"If you don't, I'll hang you for twenty minutes."

Her hands still had numb spots from the last time, and she knew she didn't want to do that again. But she also didn't want to put that disgusting stuff in her mouth. No. She couldn't do it. Just the thought was going to make her sick.

"One, two, three—" he began, his own hand wiping the residue from himself onto his bare leg.

Samantha took a deep breath and brought the hand to her face. Hesitation gripped her. Her eyes looked up at Jimmy. He was staring down at her, his face hard, his eyes mean.

She stuck out her tongue and touched it to one of the globs on her finger. The taste was unlike anything she had ever had inside her mouth, and it disgusted her. It seemed salty and—she didn't know what flavor it was.

"Do it," Jimmy ordered, his impatience growing.

Samantha ran her tongue against her finger and scooped up a gooey strand. This time the taste was ten times worse than the small sample she had taken and caused her to gag. The urge to vomit almost got the better of her, yet somehow she forced it back down. She then took another lick from her hand, this glob nearly falling off her tongue as its weight shifted, and quickly swallowed it. No gag followed, and she took another quick lick and then another and another until her hand was cleaned off.

Once she finished, the sickness hit again. Like before, she managed to fight it off. She wondered if it was a fight worth winning. Did she really want that stuff swimming inside her?

"I'm going to reward you tonight," Jimmy said while handing her panties back. Satisfaction and excitement filled his words. "You're not going to stand all night."

"Really?" she asked while pulling the panties on. Relief at having that area covered nearly overwhelmed her.

"Yes," he said. "Stand up and put your hands behind your back."

She obeyed.

Jimmy began wrapping the rope around them and then pulled the knot tight. "Walk over to the pipe."

She did.

"Sit with your back to it."

She sat and he tied the rope around the pipe. This gave her about a foot or two of movement in her arms and also made it so she could move to the side and lean against the wall. Her mind was so warped by this that she actually said, "Thank you," and hoped the night would never end. She just wanted to sit there forever. It felt so good.

* * *

"Do you know a girl in your class named Samantha King?" Rebecca asked Tina that night at dinner, which had started out pretty quiet thanks to the bitterness from the night before.

"Maybe," Tina said. The name sounded familiar, but she couldn't put a face to it.

"Well, I was talking to Martha today, and she said a girl named Samantha King was kidnapped while walking home from school yesterday." Her mother spoke slowly, the way people did when something terrible had happened and they wanted to show concern yet didn't really feel it.

Now Tina knew exactly who her mother was talking about. Her disappearance had been an impromptu topic in a few of her classes today. Some had even gone so far as to speculate about her being kidnapped, but most thought it unlikely.

"Everyone I talked to says she ran away," Tina said.

Rebecca shook her head. "Martha says the girl was an honors student and was planning on going to college in the fall. Girls like that don't just run away."

"Maybe you're right. After all, you're the expert when it comes to running away."

Her mother slammed her palm against the table, causing the dishes to jump, and said, "You know, I've just about had enough of your attitude and guilt-trip attacks. You think you know everything that happened between your father and me, but you don't."

"Maybe if you had picked up the phone once in a while, you could have filled me in," Tina said.

"Maybe if you had picked up the phone yourself, I would have known you were interested," Rebecca said back.

"Yeah, blame the kid," Tina said. "That always looks really good. While you're at it, why don't you just go ahead and tell me that you left because of me too? Tell me everything was fine until I showed up."

"You were the reason I left, but not in the way you think," Rebecca said.

"So it was my fault," Tina said, unwanted tears starting to fall. "Good, I'm glad we cleared that up, though now I guess I have to accept the fact that my father was a liar, because he always said it had nothing to do with me." With that, Tina left the table and headed for the backyard.

"Tina, stop," Rebecca called from the table.

Tina ignored her and stepped out into the backyard.

A few seconds later, her mother was at the back door and called out to her. "Tina, I'm sorry, that didn't come out right."

Tina tried to ignore her but could only walk so far before she hit the fence of the neighbor's yard.

"Tina, at least come back and finish your dinner!"

Tina didn't respond, wishing she had grabbed her purse on the way out so she could drive into town. She didn't want to walk back into the house to get it, not with her mother trying to be all sentimental. No. Instead, she would rather have her mother stop pretending like she cared and leave her alone, almost as if the two were roommates that hated each other rather than mother and daughter.

Now how are you going to get the dress?

Earlier that afternoon before Rebecca had come home from work, Tina had gone into town and looked at some of the prom dresses that were on sale, several of which she liked. Her favorite had been a beautiful burgundy gown that fit her nicely when she tried it on, her body "displayed like a delicate flower," according to the salesman. Unfortunately, the price had been too high for her savings account, which had dwindled considerably since her move to Ashland Creek that winter, the local businesses barely able to provide part-time work for adults, let alone teenagers. Had Tina been a year older this wouldn't have been a problem, because once she turned eighteen she could access the money left to her by her father, which had been an eye-bulging sum— apparently her father had made some really smart investments during the stock market bottom in early 2009. Now, though, it seemed her only option was to ask Rebecca for some money, which she had been planning on doing at dinner.

Guess again, her mind taunted. And then, *Just face it, you're not getting that dress.*

Her fingers gripped the fence rail while thinking this, her knuckles turning white.

Jimmy had never planned on letting Samantha sit on the ground all night, but after seeing the embarrassment on her face about the bathroom bucket, and then actually feeling bad for forcing her to eat his semen even though it was a huge turn-on, a soft spot had gotten the better of him and he couldn't help himself.

Ideally, he would have used handcuffs or some form of locking shackles to attach her to the pipe, but he didn't have either. Thankfully, he was confident that his rope work was solid. He also was pretty sure that her exhaustion from standing up for an entire day, coupled with the mental exhaustion of being in a state of constant fear, would make it so she pretty much fell asleep right away. The blanket he had wrapped around her added strength to his theory, though he was sure it would fall off once she started moving around.

Either way, he knew she would be grateful for being allowed to sit all night long, which made him feel good as he started up the stairs to the trapdoor, which he slowly eased open.

Voices echoed.

Startled, Jimmy lowered the trapdoor back down, his mind having been prepared for someone to be around at some point but not expecting it.

"Dude, if he came through here half an hour ago, then he's probably long gone by now," a recognizable voice said.

"Yeah, man," someone else said. "Besides, where the hell would he be going? He probably just pulled in here to take a piss or something."

"No." This voice belonged to Brett. "I pulled up and waited so I could clip him with my door or something, but he never came back out, so wherever he was going, he went through this way."

"But there is nothing through there but forest and soy fields, man," the first voice said, one which Jimmy now knew belonged to Matt.

"And the school," the other voice said, this one belonging to Ron. "You can get there through there."

Matt and Ron were Brett's little sidekicks and had pretty much been by his side since the fourth grade when all three shared a class, one that Jimmy had unfortunately shared with them as well. As single identities, the two couldn't inspire fear in anyone, especially Matt, who was about five three when walking with good posture. Alongside Brett, though, who would have been a formidable obstacle on the football field if he had the grades to play, the two had been able to instill fear in plenty of classmates and underclassmates in earlier years. Now most didn't give a shit and just saw them as idiots, ones who the system was going to leave behind eventually, but the three didn't realize this and still felt like they were in control over everyone. They thought the lack of confrontation from other classmates was out of respect or fear, but really, it was due to indifference. No one cared anymore.

"I don't give a fuck where he's going," Brett said. "I just want to be here when he gets back. The little shit has been disrespecting me and needs to be taught a lesson."

"Man, I don't want to sit around here waiting for him," Ron moaned. "What if he's already gone?"

"If you want to be a pussy, go on home. I don't give a flying fuck."

"Do we still have beer inside?" Matt asked.

"We should, unless some cocksucker stole it all," Brett said.

"So there," Matt continued. "We can chill here for a while with a beer and see if he comes back."

No, no, no! Jimmy silently screamed. He didn't want to wait around for them to get bored and leave, especially with his bike tucked away in the bushes, because they would find it if they decided to look for it. Even worse, he didn't want any sort of confrontation near the fallout shelter even though it was well hidden, because if he could find it by accident one day when not even looking, they could do the same, especially if they were interested in why he was hanging out here.

Jimmy lifted the trapdoor a little more so he could see out into the yard of the Hood place. Brett and Ron were sitting on the back porch lighting cigarettes—or what appeared to be cigarettes. A second later Matt came out through the broken window with some beers, the plywood covering the window, which they had probably pried open a bit at one point, slamming back into place.

"Seven?" Brett snapped while looking down into the bucket. "How much did we drink last time?"

"Don't know," Matt said, "but this is all that's left."

"Fuck me. I'm gonna have to get my brother to buy us more."

"Man, can't you find someone else to buy us beer?" Ron whined. "He charges too much."

"Maybe you can find someone to buy it, shithead."

Ron didn't reply.

Jimmy considered his options. The three were about thirty feet away, which meant he could get on his bike and ride away from them without a problem, so long as he didn't get tripped up somewhere. The only trouble was he didn't want them seeing him anywhere near the fallout shelter.

What a mess.

He lowered the lid and looked back down at the main door at the bottom of the stairs and thought about heading back inside with Samantha, but he really didn't feel like it at the moment. He also had to pee really bad thanks to the hand job, something that always happened after he ejaculated, and he didn't feel like using the bucket.

Thank God they weren't back there when I went to clean out the bucket, Jimmy said to himself. He had taken the bucket all the way around to the hose on the other side of the house and sprayed it clean. While doing that, he would have been completely vulnerable, and while the metal pail would make a great weapon, especially if he hit one of them in the face, he would still have to contend with the questions about why he was hanging out at the Hood place, both from them and from the police who would undoubtedly investigate the fight, especially if he used the bucket as a weapon. Without it, however, he wouldn't stand a chance. One on one he could take any of them down without too much trouble. Three on one, well, that was a different story.

He lifted the trapdoor again and looked out. The sun was setting, but not fast enough for his liking.

He lowered the lid and waited.

Once it was dark, he would be able to sneak away, though hopefully the group would get tired of waiting and leave before that. Until then, he was stuck.

CHAPTER SIX

Alan looked out the window to see if Jimmy was coming back on his bike yet, but his brother was nowhere to be seen, which surprised and frustrated him because the two had planned on playing some more *GoldenEye* the moment he came back home from his bike ride. That agreement had been several hours ago, however, and he still wasn't home.

Where the hell does he ride too? Alan wondered.

The town of Ashland Creek wasn't heavily populated, but it did encompass quite a bit of space, which was something most people from up in the suburbs didn't realize. They thought "small town" meant "small area," but when compared with the suburbs Ashland Creek actually had more landmass. Most of it was farmland, though, like the suburbs, they also had neighborhoods and a downtown area, both of which were pretty close. Unlike the suburbs, one couldn't simply hop a fence and be in another town. Instead, one would have to hop a fence, cut through some woods, and then cut through a farm field or two, then cut through more woods. Once in those woods, he would hit a town line of some sorts, but one that he wouldn't know for sure he had crossed until he entered the scrubland beyond the woods, scrubland that butted up against more farm fields. A walk like that would take hours and could be pretty dangerous. Alan had done it once with friends one summer day many years earlier, all of whom had started vomiting that night thanks to insecticide poisoning from the fields that had just been sprayed. Ever since then Alan had stuck to the roads when near a farm field, and even then he didn't like to be exposed to the fields for a long time and always urged whoever was driving to keep the windows closed.

Is Jimmy riding that far?

Alan couldn't see why his brother would do that, but then at the same time he couldn't understand why Jimmy would be riding every day to begin with. It just seemed really boring.

But maybe he isn't really riding at all. Maybe he's seeing Tina.

Jimmy was the type who would hide something like this just because he wouldn't want his parents knowing, though not because they would disapprove, but because they would make fun of him. It wasn't mean-spirited teasing, and in fact, Alan was pretty sure they didn't even know they were doing it, but it was still annoying and something Jimmy wouldn't want to experience. The question was, *Why wouldn't Jimmy tell me about it?* Getting together with Tina like this would be exciting for him and most likely wouldn't be something he could hide for very long. From his parents, yes, from Alan, no. The two were best friends and shared everything with each other.

Wait and see. If he really is seeing Tina when he goes riding, he'll tell you soon.

With that, Alan headed into the living room to watch TV with his parents. The two were flipping back and forth between *NCIS* and *The Office*. Actually, his father was flipping back and forth, and his mother was telling him to stop because she wanted to see the new episode of *NCIS*, which was one of her favorite shows. Listening to the bickering, one would think the family only had the one television set, but like most households, they actually had more televisions than members of the family. This one was just in the best spot in the house.

Not liking the channel flipping—watching one show during the commercials of another always drove him crazy—Alan sided with his mother in the debate. His father had the remote, however, which evened out the odds considerably.

Brett Murphy grew weary of waiting for the fuckhead to return and eventually called off the ambush, one that probably wouldn't have gone all that well anyway, considering they were being so loud that Jimmy would have been warned of their presence. Before leaving, he needed to take a piss, so he started toward the old shed, which stood in the left rear corner of the yard. Actually, the area was so overgrown with weeds and tiny trees that it probably no longer belonged in the yard category and instead was now just part of the woods.

"Me too," Ron said after Brett announced his intention.

"Same here," Matt said.

The two started following him.

Brett went to the corner and started peeing, his spray helping to remove some of the flaking paint from the shed wall. Ron joined him. Matt went into the trees.

"What's the matter?" Brett called. "Can't piss with us?"

"Yeah, got something we don't know about going on down there?" Ron added.

"I call it a penis," Matt shouted back.

Brett laughed for a moment but then realized Matt was making fun of him. Unfortunately, he couldn't think of a comeback. Even if he had though, Matt would have cut him off.

"Hey, guys, look at this," Matt said.

"No thanks," Ron said. "Seeing mine is enough."

"It's a bike," Matt said.

Brett zipped up and came over. Sure enough, a bike was lying in the brush right next to a tree.

"Is it his bike?" Matt asked.

"How the fuck should I know?" Brett asked.

"You're the one that saw him riding it."

"Yeah, but I didn't like examine his bike. I just saw him and called you guys." He shook his head. "Fucking moron."

"Dude, if it's his bike that means he's still here, so where the fuck is he?"

"Probably hiding in the trees somewhere," Matt said.

"Yeah, he probably saw us and got scared and was waiting for us to leave."

"Well, if he wants his bike back, he'll have to come and get it," Brett said while grabbing hold of the handle and wheeling it back into the yard.

"Wait, what if it isn't really his?" Matt asked. "What if some kid left it here or something and is going to come back for it?"

"Why the fuck would I care? Kids should know better than to leave shit like this lying around. Finders keepers. Come on, let's go." Brett started wheeling the bike to his car.

* * *

Rebecca was sitting in her room, hands folded in her lap, when Tina came back.

"What are you doing in here?" Tina demanded.

"Waiting for you," Rebecca said.

"Wait somewhere else. This is my room."

"Well, this is my house."

Tina felt heat rising in her face, yet at the same time knew there really was nothing she could do. If her mother wanted to sit in her room, she could. Still, it pissed her off, especially since her father had never disrespected her space and had once even yelled at his girlfriend for going into her room. The girlfriend had liked the idea of being a "mother figure" to Tina and kept trying to act like one. Tina, of course, would have nothing to do with it, and one day she came home to her room having been searched, the girlfriend thinking she probably was using drugs like most teenagers her age. Thankfully, the two had broken up shortly after that.

"Fine," Tina said. "If you want to sit in this room all night, go ahead. I'll go somewhere else." She grabbed her backpack and purse while saying this and started heading toward the door.

"So, the prom is this Saturday," Rebecca said.

Tina stopped.

"I have to admit, I was growing curious about whether or not you were going, you know, since you are my daughter and every mother wants their daughter to go and have a good time."

Tina looked down at her purse. Normally she kept it zipped shut, but when she grabbed it from the desk it had been open, a fact that hadn't registered until that moment.

She turned around.

Rebecca was holding her prom ticket, a nasty little smile on her face.

"Give that back," Tina said, her voice barely able to stay calm.

"Why should I?" Rebecca asked.

"Because it isn't yours," Tina said.

"This house isn't yours, yet you feel like you can do whatever you want within it, so maybe I should act the same way." She held the ticket up and prepared to rip it in half.

Tina was about to lash out but somehow managed to hold it back. At the same time, she wondered if the school kept an electronic record of who had bought the tickets just in case something like this happened.

"What, no comments? No cuss words? No angry outbursts?"

"The school knows I bought a ticket," Tina said. "If you rip it, they'll just print me a new one."

"Even if I call them and tell them I don't want you to go?" Rebecca asked.

"Why would you do that?"

"Oh, I can think of plenty of reasons, but let's see, what would I tell the school?" She looked as if she was pondering several different possibilities. "Oh, I know. I'm worried because a girl was kidnapped while walking home, and I don't want the same thing happening to my daughter."

Tina didn't reply.

"Do you think they would buy that?"

Tina knew they would. Schools bent over backward to accommodate parents, even if what the parents wanted went against the school's basic principles. Just last year a teacher in her old school up in Glen Ellyn had told the class about a group of seniors who had cheated on a test somewhere out west and were caught. The teacher gave them all zeros due to the cheating policy, which in turn made it so they couldn't graduate. Once the parents found out they complained, and the teacher had to allow them to take the test again.

"I think they would," Rebecca continued. "But even though I am entitled to be that cruel given how poorly you've treated me these last several months, all after I welcomed you into my home, I won't do that."

She *didn't welcome me into her home. The courts told her she had to take me.* Tina kept the remark to herself.

"This is conditional. If you keep treating me poorly, I'll tell the school you can't go. If you respect me and do as I say this week, then on Saturday you can have this back. Understand?"

Tina didn't reply.

"Understand?"

"Yes." It was everything she could do to not fly across the room and beat the woman to a bloody pulp.

"Yes what?" Rebecca asked.

Tina stared at her, unsure what she wanted.

"How about a 'Yes, ma'am'?" Rebecca said.

Tina couldn't believe this.

"Of course, if you don't want to respect me as your mother, I can always call the school right now," Rebecca said.

"Yes, ma'am, I understand," Tina said.

"That's better." Rebecca stood. "Now I don't want you coming out of this room tonight unless I give you permission, understand?"

Again, Tina did not reply.

"Understand?"

"Yes, ma'am," Tina growled.

Rebecca smiled. "Don't act like you have it bad. You just have to respect me for a few days. I had to respect my mother her entire life, and if I didn't—well, society was more accepting of physical punishments back then, and to this day I can still taste the bars of soap she made me suck on while taking me over her knee."

The words were right there. She wanted so hard to lash out at the woman, but she knew doing so would be disastrous.

"By the way, what are you wearing to the prom?" Rebecca asked. "I didn't see a dress in the closet."

"I have a dress being made...*ma'am.*"

"Really? I hope it is ready in time. We should go pick it up together. It will be a nice mother-daughter bonding experience." With that, Rebecca left the room, pulling the door shut behind her.

Tina wanted to scream.

"Where's your bike?" Alan asked after meeting Jimmy in the street. He had been getting a Coke from the kitchen during a commercial and had just happened to look out the window and saw Jimmy walking home. Knowing something had happened, just not what, Alan hurried outside.

"Brett took it," Jimmy said.

"What?"

"I set the bike against a tree to pee, and I guess he was following me in his car, because all of a sudden he grabbed it." Jimmy was obviously pissed off, his anger showing in both his words and his face.

"Why didn't you stop him?"

"Because I was in the middle of peeing and because his friends were there." Jimmy shook his head and slammed a fist into his palm. "I can beat the shit out of any one of them by themselves, but together…"

"Good point." Alan could see the three of them overwhelming his brother and then viciously pounding the shit out of him once they had him down. It would not be an honorable fight, but they wouldn't care. Bullies like that never did. "But now there are two of us, so let's go get it back."

"I don't—"

"We are doing this, so don't even think about putting it off," Alan said, shooting down what he knew Jimmy would say. "They won't be expecting both of us to be there so quickly, and we won't stick around. Just grab the bike and go. If they want to come after us, so be it."

"But he's on the other side of town and it's getting dark," Jimmy said.

"So we take Mom's car. She won't care. Come on."

Jimmy finally agreed.

Samantha couldn't believe it, but the rope was actually slipping off her wrist. A shiver went through her.

Jimmy usually tied each wrist separately and then attached the second rope to the rope between her wrists. This time he had just wrapped it around both her wrists, and now her right hand was actually coming through.

Oh my God! she thought. *I'm going to get out!*

The burned areas of her wrist screamed as she pulled against the rope, but the pain was masked by her determination to get free. Hell, she could probably slice off her own thumb to free herself and not feel a thing.

On cue, the rope snagged against her thumb joint,

which stopped her hand from sliding out. All hope fled.

She tried squeezing her fingers into the smallest fist possible, but still the rope would not move.

No! No! No! she silently screamed while pulling with all her might.

It came out.

Samantha was so stunned that she failed to realize her right hand was sitting in her lap, and that the rope around her left had fallen to the floor.

She was free.

Panic hit.

She turned her head toward the door while her right hand rubbed the rawness of her left, and then the left rubbed her right. *If it's unlocked, I could—*she failed to finish her thought, the idea of freedom after the longest day of her life almost too much to bear.

Oh God, what if I'm home tonight? Please, God, let me get home.

She crawled over to the door and used the handle to stand. Her legs shook with exhaustion while her hands shook with excitement. Her mind was racing.

Please...

She twisted the handle.

It was unlocked.

She pressed her body against the cool metal door and then eased herself back and pulled. It opened less than a centimeter before catching on something.

No, her mind said weakly.

She pulled again.

The door didn't get past the obstacle.

NO!

Somehow, the door was locked on the outside, only not through the knob. Something was attaching it to the wall.

Samantha fell to her knees crying, her fists clenched, her mind screaming with frustration and sadness. Jimmy had planned for this. The little bastard had put some kind of lock on the outside just in case she got free, and now, once he found out she had tried to escape, he would punish her.

He would do—

Knowing how awful it would be, Samantha couldn't finish the thought and collapsed into herself on the floor, her body rolled into a crude ball, her hands hanging against her knees. Sobs echoed through the room while tears dampened her face and then the floor.

If only she had fought him off in the beginning. If only she had been more alert while walking home. If only this, if only that—the list could go on and on.

The word "fought" stuck in her mind.

She brought her head up from her legs as an idea made itself known. Her wet eyes looked across the room and stared at the shelves of food and water.

I could fight him off.

This hung in the air as if spoken out loud, waiting for criticism. None came. Using an object from the shelf as a weapon, or the shelf itself, would give her an advantage Jimmy was not expecting, which meant he would not be prepared for it, which meant she could easily get the upper hand. All it would take was one good solid blow to the head and Samantha could be free. One hit as he walked through the door and Samantha would be on her way home.

In her mind, she saw Jimmy toppling over as the blow knocked all sense from him. She would then run through the door and out into the yard. From there she would get to the road and head home.

HOME.

The word sounded fantastic, unlike anything else she had ever wanted. Never before had it seemed like such a wonderful place. All she had to do was hit him hard enough. Once down, Jimmy would have no chance at catching her, and she would get home.

What if it doesn't work?

The question went unanswered. If she thought about failing, she would fail, and if she failed, the consequences would be far worse than anything her mind could conjure up, of this she was sure.

When one thought of bullies, one often pictured them living in nasty run-down houses or trailers whose outside walls were just a preview for the horrors inflicted upon them within while growing up, something that they were always trying to make up for by picking on the weaker kids at school. This wasn't the case with Brett Murphy. Instead, his house was like all the others in the neighborhood areas of Ashland Creek, alas, a bit worn from the harsh winter, but nowhere near as run-down as Hollywood would have pictured it. To everyone that knew the family too, his parents didn't seem that bad, and in fact, they weren't. Like most middle-class families, they had provided Brett and his older brother Brian with a wonderful childhood, one free from the dramas that many unlucky kids faced all across the country. They also had stayed together despite a marital affair that had occurred when Brett was ten. None of it mattered, though, because Brett still had grown up bad and, judging by the path he was taking, would continue to be bad well into adulthood.

Of course, Brett never thought about any of this, nor would he have cared if someone had pointed it out to him. In fact, all he cared about at the moment was making Jimmy pay for elbowing him in the gut earlier, and now that he had his bike, he was pretty sure that outcome would arrive soon. What he wasn't counting on was it happening so quickly, or that his older brother Brian would side with the two fuckheads.

It all started the moment Brett pulled into the driveway, parked, and started to get the bike out from the backseat—the piece of shit had actually scratched his car while the three had been getting it in, which pissed him off even more.

Brian was sitting on the front porch when Brett pulled up, drinking a soda, relaxing after a day spent getting in shape for the military, a career he would be starting in June after having talked to a recruiter in Haddonfield a month earlier—all because the construction company he had been working for ever since he graduated in 2004 had gone bankrupt.

"Where'd you get the bike?" Brian asked once he saw Brett struggling to get it out of the backseat.

"I found it," Brett said.

"Really?" Brian's voice was skeptical. "Who did you 'find it' from?"

"What do you care?" Brett asked. The bike popped free, the tires bouncing on the ground.

"I really don't, unless it was 'found' from someone who didn't know they had lost it and might want it back."

Brett shook his head and started walking the bike toward the house. A second later, a car pulled up to the house. Shouts followed.

Brett turned and saw Jimmy and his little brother coming up the driveway, the brother shouting at him to give the bike back.

"Make me!" Brett shouted back at the stupid sophomore.

"Oh, we'll make you, you motherfucker," the brother said, his pace quickening, fists clenched.

Brett wasn't sure if he could actually take the two of them by himself and quickly started running with the bike toward the backyard. Once back there, he would grab the shovel he knew was lying by the rear of the garage. Brian stopped him before he even made it to the gate.

Jimmy and his brother were soon there as well.

"This is your bike?" Brian asked while looking at Jimmy's brother.

"No, it's his." He nodded toward Jimmy.

"The fuck it is. I found the bike in the woods," Brett said and tried to jerk the bike away from Brian.

Brian's grip was too strong and the bike stayed within it.

"After you saw me lean it against the tree to take a piss," Jimmy said.

"Bullshit. You were nowhere near it, unless you were hiding in the woods because you know you can't take me in a real fight."

"I'll take you right now," Jimmy said.

"Whoa," Brian snapped. "No one is taking anyone." He turned to Brett. "If the bike is his, give it back to him."

"But—" Brett started.

"I said *give it back to him.*"

"What's going on out there?" Brett's mother echoed

from the porch.

"Nothing, Mom," Brian said. "Just a little high school misunderstanding that is being worked out." He turned back to Brett. "Right?"

"Fine!" Brett snapped. "I'll give it back."

Brian let go of the bike. The moment he did that Brett rammed it into Jimmy's shins and then tried to jump on him but tripped over the bike.

"Fucker!" someone shouted, and the next thing he knew someone—probably the little brother—was on top of him pressing his face into the grass with both hands.

"Hey, get off him," Brian snapped.

Brett felt the weight removed from his back. A second later, he felt himself being pulled to his feet and yanked away from Jimmy and his little brother. "Stupid idiot, let me go!" Brett snapped.

Brian didn't and said, "Take your bike and get out of here." He then pushed Brett to the ground and said, "Don't you realize you could be arrested for taking his bike like that? What were you thinking?"

Brett didn't answer him, but not out of defiance. Instead, all he could think about was Jimmy and how badly the shithead was going to suffer for this. He was going to get him for embarrassing him in front of his brother. He would make him pay.

Megan got in an argument with her father during dinner about the Samantha King situation and eventually stormed out of the room. *How can he not realize it?* Samantha King had been kidnapped. Anyone could see it.

Unfortunately, most in town had not seen it. Megan had realized this at school and that had been part of the reason why she was so pissed off. Everyone just agreed that a kidnapping couldn't happen in Ashland Creek and that Samantha King had run away. But it simply wasn't true. She would not have run away.

In the backyard, Megan sat on the porch swing and looked out at the surrounding forest, wondering if Samantha was out there somewhere. Hadn't she once heard that most kidnap victims were kept within a few miles of their homes?

Most kidnap victims are killed in forty-eight hours.

This thought didn't settle well in her head. Samantha was her best friend, and the thought of her being killed by someone was too much to bear. Not to mention the fact that other terrible things were probably happening to her as well.

If only her father would do something about it. Then, if Samantha were close by, they would find her. What if she was out in the woods at that very moment, tied to a tree or something? Why couldn't her father just get together a search party and explore a little?

Why couldn't her father act like a real police officer? Why couldn't he just investigate a little?

"Megan?" her father called.

"What?" she asked without turning toward him.

Her voice changed his mind and he went back inside. That was fine by Megan. There was no way for her to convince him of what she knew, so what was the point in even talking?

Slowly the sun began to set. Megan watched it for twenty minutes before getting up and going inside. Her butt and back hurt where the wooden slats had been pressing into her. She rubbed the indentations away and went up to her room, where she grabbed her car keys and then headed out to the driveway. It wasn't unusual for her to just go for a drive through town without telling anyone, so her parents weren't too concerned when, for the next hour, they didn't know where she was. No one thought anything terrible had happened. Terrible things didn't happen in Ashland Creek. Small towns were perfect.

Jimmy's right shin had a nasty gash in it, yet it didn't hurt all that much once the pain of the blow to the bone went away, that was, until he poured peroxide all over it in the bathroom at home. That hurt like a son of a bitch but then was over as abruptly as it started. Finished with that, he and Alan played some *GoldenEye* battles, all of which Alan dominated.

"Wow, I kicked your ass, just like I started to kick Brett's ass once he was down on the ground," Alan said after winning the second game. They had played in a neutral level—neutral meaning neither one had a clear advantage, this one being Facility—and Alan had started out in the bathroom area, which he mined really well and then ventured out into the main areas. Jimmy, whose mind wasn't really on the game, started on the opposite side of the level and began mining those starting locations but then ran into one of his own mines, killing himself, and was thrown into the cycle Alan had created. After that it was one-sided for the rest of the game, and Jimmy never even came close to beating Alan. "Did you see that dumbass trip over the bike? Man that was priceless."

Jimmy smiled.

"And that guy that was there. Who was that, like his brother? Man, that guy is cool. He like totally realizes

Brett is a loser. Good thing too, because he lifted me off him without any trouble and probably could have kicked both our asses if he'd wanted to."

Jimmy knew that lifting Alan was no easy feat because even though he was only a sophomore he was no lightweight. The two of them worked out together all the time, and while he was no bodybuilder by any stretch of the imagination, he was stronger than most in the school and could handle himself pretty well.

"The only problem now is that I really have to watch my back because he is going to be royally pissed," Jimmy said.

"Oh, I know," Alan said.

In the movies, bullies would back off once they realized their victims had outgrown them and could stand on their own two feet. Brett wasn't like that though, and Jimmy doubted most real-life bullies were. No. Rather than seeing this as a fight he couldn't win, Brett was going to escalate things and would keep escalating them until they got out of control. It was just the way he was. And given how stupid he was, he would act without thinking, which could cause a serious problem. Jimmy wouldn't put it past the guy to ram him with his car when he was on his bike, just because he would think it was funny and would not consider the resulting consequences.

"The only way to stop him for good is to beat the living shit out of him to the point where he is hospitalized for a while," Alan continued. "That would probably teach him a lesson, especially if he had to pay the bill."

"Maybe, but more likely it would just make him more determined to do something worse, or I would end up in jail for assault," Jimmy said. "I'm telling you, he's like one of those dogs that's too far gone to be redeemed and needs to be put down because he won't stop biting people to death."

"Ah, man, you just insulted some poor dogs."

Jimmy smiled.

"Another game?" Alan asked.

"Nah," Jimmy said with a shake of his head. "I think I'm gonna call it a night."

"Oh, okay. I'd probably just beat you easily again anyway, so for the sake of your ego it's probably better not to do another round."

Jimmy laughed and said, "I'll get you tomorrow."

"We'll see," Alan said while putting the controllers back on the shelf. "We'll see."

"Good night."

"Night."

Only Jimmy didn't go to bed. He tried, but thoughts about that night's situation kept him up, as well as thoughts on the entire Samantha King thing, ones that made sleep impossible, especially once the sexual fantasies started. Once that happened, he had no choice but to get up and take care of the situation.

Alan was still awake when Jimmy left around eleven thirty and wondered what he was doing. It was one thing to go riding once or twice a day on the bike, but after eleven at night, and after already riding a few times that day, it started to get weird and was making him think something else was going on. Something that Alan couldn't even begin to comprehend because Jimmy was so different from everyone else, different to the point where normal teenage activities just didn't fit with

Jimmy.

Samantha had taken the shelf off the wall and then sat down with it, the long board cradled in her arms, ready to be used as a weapon.

The waiting was difficult.

With her back to the wall, she listened to every second tick away in her head, knowing that at any moment Jimmy could walk through the door. At that point, she would spring up, connect the board with his face, and then run like hell.

She slowly drank a bottle of water while waiting and ate several different bags of stale chips and pretzels. The cans of food she left alone because of the risk they had spoiled. What she didn't know was that the Hood family had been concerned about this as well and had gone about getting foods that wouldn't spoil, along with military rations of all kinds. Samantha didn't realize that the small square packages on one of the shelves were the same type of rations soldiers over in Iraq and Afghanistan were consuming, and really, she didn't care. The chips and pretzels were fine, and she ate them rapidly to fill her aching stomach.

The worst part of the wait came when she suddenly needed to use the bathroom, and it wasn't urine that wanted out. The urge hit and there was no denying it, yet she still tried to wait.

Any second Jimmy could walk in, and if she wanted to surprise him, she could not be squatting over a bucket. But then ten minutes and then fifteen minutes went by, and the urge became more and more powerful.

If you had gone earlier, you would have been finished, she scolded herself. Now if she went, there was the likelihood that Jimmy would walk in.

Samantha could not wait, however, and retrieved the bucket. She put it up against the wall where she had been sitting so she could press her back against the concrete as leverage. Leaning against the wall to her right was the board. If Jimmy came in while she was going, she would grab it and nail him with it. The fact that she would be naked with stuff coming out of her would have to be ignored. Escaping this situation was too important, and people who saw her running from the Hood place would eventually understand. Actually, being half-naked would be better because people would notice her.

Using the bucket as a toilet when she had to pee was disgusting but mild compared to what she did now. Taking a shit into a bucket with your back braced against the wall was pure humiliation—even when alone.

Jimmy did not enter while she was doing this, and she even managed to clean herself off with a rag. Samantha was then back against the wall, waiting, board in hand, bucket as far away as possible.

And then she dozed off.

There was a ten-minute battle in which her eyes fought to stay open, but in the end they fell shut and her body drifted off into a deep sleep.

She dreamed of Jimmy chasing her. The air was thick and made it difficult to run for her but not Jimmy, and he quickly caught up. And then she was back in the room hanging from her wrists, naked, while Jimmy forced himself into her. His penis then became a knife and suddenly started slicing her body open upward. The sound of skin tearing filled the air.

The sound changed as her eyes opened, but it did not

disappear with the dream. She jerked her head around, trying to see where she was, but could not focus on anything, her mind confused as to why she wasn't asleep in her own bed.

The sound grew louder.

Samantha looked to the left.

The door was opening.

Oh, shit.

Both hands scrambled to find the shelf board. It was in her lap, yet her fingers could not grasp it.

Using the wall, Samantha stood up, let the board flip over into her waiting palms, and then took hold of one end. Jimmy entered the room at the same time.

A terrible charley horse lumped up in her left calf and she nearly fell over. At the same time, she swung the board in a wide arc toward the door.

Jimmy turned at the sound, his face full of surprise.

In the microsecond before the board struck him in the face, Jimmy fell back and pulled the door halfway shut. The board hit the end of the door and vibrated terribly.

Samantha could no longer hold it as it wobbled, and the board went crashing to the floor. As it did, all hope was lost.

NO! her mind cried.

She watched the board falling the way a person would watch a winning lottery ticket go up in flames.

Then Jimmy came in and grabbed her by the throat. Her body was forced back against the wall, her left leg screaming and her lungs crying out for air.

Jimmy held her like that for several seconds, his face full of fury, his eyes almost turning red, and then threw her across the room.

The strength he had in that one arm was amazing,

though Samantha did not appreciate it as her body went tumbling to the ground several feet from him. In fact, she could not think at all because of the terror that held her.

Jimmy was behind her, and both arms came down around her chest. The charley horse in her leg was forgotten as he lifted her from the ground and forced her up against the opposite wall.

His breathing was rapid and warm against the side of her neck. She didn't even try to break free, only wondered to herself what had gone wrong. At this moment, she was supposed to be running home, Jimmy lying unconscious—maybe even dead—upon the floor. How had he known?

Tears welled up in her eyes and began to fall.

Anger overwhelmed Jimmy to the point where he did something he never thought he would do, something that he had seen countless times on TV and in bondage videos but never thought was sexually stimulating, that being to slap a woman across the face. Yet he did it now, and not just once. He slapped Samantha several times while holding her against the wall, both fronthand and backhand until his skin hurt, and then dragged her to the overhead pipe, his anger having failed to dissipate and mixing in with the adrenaline that had erupted.

Samantha cried out as her feet left the ground and all her body weight was supported by her thin wrists, which the knotted rope was painfully pushing together. Both her hands became fists, and her legs kicked about trying to find something—anything—to rest upon. Nothing was there.

Jimmy tied off the rope to the pipe and then walked

over to her. Before tying her, he had stripped her down to her underwear and now stared at her half-naked body.

She felt his eyes and then his hands on her uplifted breasts. At first, they gently caressed them, but then became rough and squeezed.

Samantha tried to squirm out of his grip but it was no use, so without thinking she kicked a leg up and connected it with his side. Moments later, she would regret it.

Jimmy shouted as the blow landed and let go of her breasts. She still felt his hands upon them, however, and knew there would most likely be bruises in the shape of his fingers in a few hours.

"God," he said as his hands rubbed where her ankle had connected. They then dropped down to the buckle of his belt and undid it.

"No, *I'm sorry*," Samantha gasped, her lips sore from his repeated blows. Even without the pain from her lips, talking was difficult when hanging like this, yet her words managed to be loud and audible.

Jimmy didn't say anything.

Samantha closed her eyes as his hand went back, and prepared herself for the pain.

Nothing happened.

She opened her eyes again.

Jimmy swung the belt toward her. It snapped across the side of her body and danced across her breast.

Glass would have shattered from her scream.

The strike was so powerful that her body started swinging from it.

A line of white-hot sting sprang up across the skin of her midsection.

And then there was another from the other side as he

brought his hand back, and then a third right into her stomach. Both hurt as much as the first, and she started sobbing while screaming, tears and mucus sliding down her face.

"Only twenty-seven left," Jimmy said.

Samantha passed out after only eleven.

A few moments later, a splash of cold water jolted her back into her terrible situation. Now she was wet, and the next nineteen hits stung even more, though, thankfully, they were across her back this time, which wasn't as bad, though the difference was hardly noticeable while actually being whipped, each blow causing a sharp painful line upon her skin, one which would slowly expand with a strange and unpleasant warm feeling. It was horrible.

When he was finished, Samantha could not speak or move. Her body was broken for the moment and she just hung there, tears plastered to her face, sweat to her body. Had he lowered her to her feet, she still would have hung there because her legs would not have supported her body, but that did not happen.

Instead, he came up from behind and pulled back her hair, bending her head at an awkward angle.

"Ahh," she moaned softly and then gagged as something ran down her throat.

"You made a big mistake," he said, his voice sending shivers through her. "By this time tomorrow, your hands will have no life left in them, that is, if you don't pass out and suffocate first."

Samantha could feel the pressure on her lungs and thought that suffocating would be a blessing. It wouldn't happen though, not unless weight was added to her feet. It took a lot of pressure to actually suffocate a person like this. So much pressure that the chest would be sucked inward and crush the lungs.

"Please," she started but could not finish.

Jimmy reached around and took hold of her breasts again and squeezed while her head sagged forward. Samantha hardly noticed.

It had been about ten minutes since she had first been pulled off her feet, and already her hands felt useless. There still was a tingle in them though. It was a painful tingle.

The fists she had made upon being pulled off her feet had loosened a little but not much, her fingers only able to open slightly and with great strain.

Jimmy let go of her breasts and started to walk away. Before leaving, he turned and looked at her. His hand then flicked the light switch into the off position.

Samantha was left alone in the dark, in a state of constant pain. Each passing second felt like thousands, and she could not wait for his return so he would let her down. She would do anything just to feel her feet against the ground. *Anything.* In the meantime, she would spend an eternity hanging from her wrists by a rope that had already torn most of her skin away, each strand feeling as if it were willfully digging deeper and deeper into her flesh.

Her body felt stretched as it hung there, and she could not imagine anything worse than what she was going through. Every moment was noticeable, the ropes and what they did to her body unrelenting.

Jimmy put his face in his hands for several seconds while sitting atop the fallout shelter trapdoor, his mind unable to even comprehend how close he had come to losing

Samantha, and thus his freedom, all because he had tried to be nice. He just couldn't believe it. How could he do something like that? How could he be so stupid?

Samantha was his prisoner and he her captor, and nothing he could do would ever make her view the situation differently. Furthermore, he couldn't allow himself to view it differently, because if he did, he would slip up, and if he slipped up too badly, well, the outcome would not be pleasant.

Self-preservation was now the name of the game.

For her as well.

If she tries to be nice to you, it isn't because she is being generous; it is because she is trying something.

Maybe in time, once she was completely broken to the point of being unable to think of anything but pleasing him, things would be different, but right now he had to be careful. One day of standing with her wrists tied over her head wasn't enough to make her devoted to him. Hell, one week probably wouldn't be enough.

But by this time tomorrow she will be sorry, which will be a step in the right direction.

Earlier he had developed a soft spot and felt bad for being cruel to her. Now that wouldn't be the case, and any time he felt a soft spot starting to develop he would smother it. The risk of her getting the better of him was just too great. He couldn't allow it to happen. He couldn't allow himself to see Samantha as anything more than an object he used for his own pleasure. Two days ago, such an idea would have been unthinkable; now it was absolutely necessary. He wasn't a mean person and hated making people feel bad in normal everyday life, but now he didn't have a choice, not unless he wanted to spend the rest of his life in jail.

No mercy, ever. If she misbehaves, you punish her.

At the moment, he had accomplished that and had her in a position that she wouldn't forget for a long time and that would make her regret what she had done.

Jimmy knew this because he had hanged himself from the wrists many times when no one was home, and in the fallout shelter from time to time just to see what it was like, always imagining he was some poor medieval peasant girl locked in a dungeon, hanging from her wrists until she confessed to some trumped-up charge.

It was an incredibly painful position, especially when rope was used, and the longest he had ever been able to endure it was ten minutes, and only then on rare occasions, because once he ejaculated, which happened every time even without genital contact, he usually grew weary of the fantasy and let himself down. Sometimes, however, his determination to experience it got the upper hand and he stayed like that for the set time limit, which was always ten minutes because of his fear of getting stuck, which had nearly happened once, his fingers and hands too numb to undo the knots. It had been frightening, especially since his parents would have found him if he hadn't been able to get free.

Samantha's been hanging there much longer than ten minutes already, he said to himself, thinking it had to be nearing midnight. *And will continue to hang there until tomorrow afternoon.*

God, what would that be like? A part of him wanted to feel the experience without the damaging consequences just so he could understand it. Another part couldn't wait for the time to pass because he wanted to see what she looked like after all of it—her hands especially—and how she felt once she was lowered back to the ground.

These thoughts, mixed in with everything that had happened during the last half hour, caused an erection to build, one that he knew wouldn't go away.

In his mind, he saw himself going home and looking at some computer porn to get rid of it and then taking a shower, but then he dismissed the idea because it just didn't seem all that exciting. Plus he would have to wait for the computer to boot up and then connect to the Internet, and then he would be sucked in to a dozen different sites, all of which would cause him to spend hours online that meant he would never get to sleep.

You could fuck Samantha.

The idea stuck, and even though he wouldn't be tall enough to reach her pussy with his dick, he knew he could move some of the giant containers down there and stand on them. That would get him high enough for sure.

What if she has an STD?

The thought chilled him to the core, especially since he didn't have any condoms.

What are the chances a high school senior has something?

Jimmy didn't know the statistics on this, but he knew the rate was growing and that there was a chance she had something.

At the same time, he really wanted to know how it felt to have his penis up inside someone, though not as much as he desired the feel of having a mouth around it.

At least you won't have to worry about taking care of a baby if you get her pregnant.

Jimmy smiled at the thought as he considered his options, marveling at the fact that he had just eliminated one of the greatest of all the high school fears. However, it also made him admit the fact that he was never going to let Samantha go and that, in all honesty, she would die at some point, his own hands being responsible.

To his surprise, the thought didn't upset him all that much, even though he didn't like to think of himself as a killer. In fact, it brought to mind something he had seen in the past that he was curious about, something that also sexually stimulated him at times, though it wasn't something he had ever dreamt he would truly get to see.

His hand started rubbing his penis through his pants. A few seconds later he went back into the fallout shelter, the words, "Let me down, please," greeting him and causing his erection to thump even more.

CHAPTER SEVEN

Jimmy woke up the next morning completely exhausted and sore and wished he could simply lie in bed for a few more hours, his mind focused on nothing but the TV and whatever programs they liked to spit out between six and ten. Of course, knowing the consequences of such actions, Jimmy didn't allow himself to be sucked in and forced himself to his feet, his body moaning with protests as his joints popped and his muscles flexed.

Oh God, he said to himself while putting his hands on his lower back and stretching his chest upward.

A smile followed.

Upstairs a pot of coffee was waiting along with Alan, who was just finishing a bowl of Honey Nut Cheerios.

"You're up later than usual," Alan noted.

"Yeah, couldn't sleep," Jimmy said while pouring himself some coffee, which he added plenty of cream and sugar to.

"I know, me either. I was too worked up about the fight with Brett."

"What fight?" Kelly Hawthorn asked while stepping into the kitchen.

"Ah, it wasn't really a fight," Jimmy said.

"Yeah, Brett Murphy snagged Jimmy's bike while he was taking a break from riding, and we went and got it back from him," Alan said.

"Was anyone hurt?" she asked.

"No, well, maybe just Brett's ego," Jimmy said and then took a sip of coffee. "Ugh, God."

"Your brother made it," Kelly said.

"Hey, I've never made coffee before," Alan protested. "It's always ready when I get up."

"Tell him how many scoops of coffee you added."

"Ten."

"What?" Jimmy looked down at his cup. "It's only supposed to be five, and that's when you make a full pot."

"Yeah, well, I made us ten cups and thought that meant ten scoops." Alan shrugged. "And I didn't really think it tasted all that bad."

"Not that bad? It's terrible. And how in the world did you fit ten scoops in that thing?" While asking this Jimmy noticed coffee grounds floating in his cup, which meant it probably hadn't all fit.

"I just kept pressing it down with my fingers."

Frustrated because coffee was the cornerstone of a good day, Jimmy set his cup down and said, "You could have just woken me up. I would have made it."

"I figured you wanted to sleep in after your bike ride last night."

"Another bike ride?" Kelly said. "Wow, you're becoming quite the little athlete."

"*Mom!*"

"Actually I think he's riding a lot because he's nervous about the prom," Alan said.

Jimmy watched as his mother's eyes actually seemed to grow while also slightly popping forward. "Jimmy Hawthorn," she said while crossing her arms, "you *have* been hiding a girl from us."

Jimmy could feel himself blushing, which turned into a glare when he looked at Alan.

"You should see them together, Mom. They make the perfect couple. They even sit together at lunch and walk home together, and sometimes they bump into each other on the way to school too and get all shy."

"How sweet," Kelly said. "What's her name?"

"Tina," Alan said.

"Well, Jimmy, I think you should invite Tina over for dinner one of these nights so we can meet her."

"No!"

"Mom, remember how he used to always say he would never fall in love with anyone, or marry anyone or ever date anyone?"

"I do, and now I really have to meet this girl."

Thanks a lot, Alan, Jimmy said to himself while dumping his coffee in the sink. "Mom, can I borrow the car for a moment so I can get some good coffee?"

"Oh, honey, I have to leave for work soon."

"I'll be really quick."

"How about you guys get ready for school, and I'll swing you by McDonald's and then drop you off."

"Oh man," Alan said while looking down at his nearly empty bowl. "I just ate."

"Oh, look at the tears rolling down my cheeks," Jimmy said to his brother while pointing at his own face, and then said to his mother, "That would be great."

Ten minutes later the three were heading toward McDonald's. Eventually Jimmy would realize he hadn't thought about Samantha once while in the car, nor what had happened the night before. In fact, it wasn't until he was at school, quickly finishing his bacon, egg, and cheese bagel and drinking his large, five-cream five-sugar coffee, that he started to think about it, wondering how many of the guys around him had to still fantasize about being with girls, whereas he now knew what it was like. Even better, he didn't have to wine and dine them in hopes of luring them into bed. Instead, he just had to be in the mood.

Megan's day did not start out well. First, her alarm clock didn't go off for some reason, or maybe in her sleep she had switched it off without knowing. Because of this, she didn't get to spend much time in the bathroom and would look like shit for school. Worse, there had been nothing in the kitchen to eat for breakfast.

"I could make you some eggs," her mother said as Megan frantically looked through the cabinets.

"*Mom,* I don't have time for eggs." She whipped open the cupboard again and looked at the cereal selection. Nothing. She slammed it shut. "There's nothing to eat."

"How about some grapes?"

"Grapes? That's not enough food." God, her mother's help was only making things worse.

"Toast?"

"Not enough. I want Frosted Mini-Wheats. Why does Tim always eat it all?" When her brother ate cereal, he would fill the bowl to the brim and then top it off completely with milk. Five minutes later, he would grow full and dump most of the cereal down the garbage disposal, wasting it. This pissed her off, especially since she would now have to go to school hungry and her stomach would be growling all day.

It began at ten.

She was sitting in calculus, listening to the teacher drone on, when suddenly her stomach noisily cried out for food. Petrified, Megan slammed her fist down into her gut to stop the noise. The damage had been done, however, and everyone knew it was her.

A few moments later, it happened again.

She looked around to see if anyone had noticed. No one was looking at her, but she knew they had all heard. God, it was so embarrassing.

How far can the sound travel?

She wanted to shrivel up and disappear.

There were a few more roars from within before calculus was finally over. Unfortunately, she still had world literature, and knowing the bitch Ms. Gliek, she would get a detention for her stomach noises because they would be disrupting the class.

That didn't happen, though her stomach was continuing to growl angrily. Thankfully, this was the last class before lunch, so she thought the worst of the day was almost over.

This wasn't the case, but she wouldn't realize that until later.

"Hey, Megan," a voice said.

Megan turned and saw Steven Charlton coming toward her in the hallway, his class—American Politics— having just gotten out as well. "Hey, Steven, how you holding up?"

"Okay, I guess. I was just wondering if you've heard from Samantha at all, or if your dad has learned anything."

"No, nothing really. My dad says he can't do anything

until she's been missing for a few days, and even then he thinks she left and went to Hollywood or something."

Steven's face twisted while he shook his head. "Samantha didn't want to go to Hollywood. Why does everyone keep saying that?"

"Because of Misty all those years ago," Megan said. In 2005, a girl named Misty had dropped out of high school on her eighteenth birthday and left for California to become an actress. Instead of being in blockbuster movies, however, she could be found moaning and groaning all across the Internet in a series of low-budget porn videos. It had been quite a scandal, one that caused her parents to leave town, their shame too great. "Everyone thinks all girls want to be actresses and will throw their lives away to try and become one."

"But that wasn't—"

"I know she wouldn't do something like that," Megan said.

"You know, if something happened to her and she was kidnapped or attacked, your dad is losing time. I watch these crime shows on TV when I can't sleep, and they say the first twenty-four hours is the most important, and your dad hasn't even started to look for clues."

Megan thought about something for a second and asked, "You two would almost always talk to each other after school, right?"

"Yeah," Steven said. "It usually took her like twenty minutes to get home, so I'd always give her a chance to get settled. Sometimes we would go out too. I would swing by and pick her up and we'd get ice cream or something, but this week she didn't want to do that at all because she worried about not fitting in her prom dress."

Megan saw emotion in his face when he said this and

grew even angrier with her father for not doing any investigating, especially knowing Samantha would not want to miss the prom. "Did she answer when you called?"

"No. At first I thought maybe it was taking her longer to walk home, but then when she didn't answer the second time I just figured she didn't want to talk." He shook his head. "I should have known something was wrong and headed over there, but—"

"It's not your fault," Megan said. "And whatever happened, I don't think it happened to her at her house. I think something happened while she was walking home from school. You know, like someone grabbed her from the side of the road or something. There is that stretch by the old Hood place that is pretty much deserted. If someone saw her there walking alone, they could have just—" She saw Jimmy Hawthorn standing there listening to them and turned to him. "You walk by the old Hood place on your way home from school, don't you?"

"Um, no," Jimmy said. "I'm a few streets over, and that road curves the wrong way."

"Oh, for some reason I can picture you by that house."

Jimmy shrugged. "I ride my bike sometimes, so maybe you saw me over there."

"Hmm, maybe that's it," Megan said. She then asked, "That area is pretty wooded, right? So do you think someone could have grabbed her from there without anyone seeing?"

Jimmy shrugged again. "Maybe, though why would someone do that?"

"Because there are some sick motherfuckers out there

who can't get a girl on their own who—"

The bell rang, cutting Steven off. Right before it rang, Megan thought she saw Jimmy glare at Steven, though maybe it wasn't so much a glare as a moment of surprise at how quickly he had lashed out at his suggestion. Whatever the reason, she didn't think too much of it right then or there. Later she would, but by then everything would make perfect sense.

"I saved you a seat," Tina said with a smile as Jimmy came toward their side of the table, which, as usual, they had to themselves. When he didn't reply to the joke she asked, "What's wrong?"

Jimmy shook his head. "Oh nothing, I just got caught up back there. It's nothing though. How are you doing today?"

"I'm okay," she said, desperately wanting to tell him about what Rebecca was doing, but knowing he probably didn't want to hear all about her problems. "I looked at dresses yesterday."

"Oh," Jimmy said. "That's cool. I'm probably going to go get a tux later today. What does the dress look like, or is it supposed to be a surprise?"

"Hmm, it doesn't have to be a surprise, but maybe I should keep it one."

"Very well, then I won't tell you what my tux is going to look like."

Tina laughed.

"I should ask though, what are your favorite tie-dye colors?"

"What?"

"For my tux," Jimmy said. "I was thinking about tie-dyeing it, but I need to know what colors you like."

"Have you ever seen a rainbow?" Tina asked.

"Um, I believe so," Jimmy said. "One of those colorful things after a thunderstorm, right? Pot of gold at the end if you can find it?"

"Exactly. Well, I don't like any of those colors. In fact, the only colors I like are white and black."

"Ah, I see. Black was actually my first plan, but if that didn't work I would go with the tie-dye. Unless you mean a black-and-white tie-dye? That would look pretty cool, though people might get dizzy if you spin me on the dance floor."

Tina smiled. "It's usually the other way around."

"What is?"

"The guy spins the girl."

"Oh." He shrugged. "I've never danced before."

"Me either."

The two talked for the rest of lunch and then during gym class as well, the random spread of topics helping keep Tina's mind off her mother and the frustrating situation she found herself in.

"Hey, sorry about this morning," Alan said to Jimmy once Tina had disappeared into her house. "I couldn't resist."

"Oh, don't worry about it. Mom was bound to find out about her soon anyway." Jimmy sighed. "I just wish they wouldn't make such a big joke about it, you know? It's like they think me dating someone is cute."

"Like an 'Ah, Jimmy has a girlfriend' kind of thing," Alan said.

"Yeah. It drives me crazy."

"I know, but what can you do about it?"

"Nothing." He took a sip of Coke while saying this.

"Hey, let me have some of that," Alan said.

Jimmy handed over the Coke and watched as his brother chugged a third of it before handing it back. "Thanks, man. I was dying of thirst and couldn't watch you drink that thing all the way home. I'll spot you one tomorrow after school."

Jimmy shrugged and then took another gulp.

"Sounds like you two are getting excited about prom?"

"Yeah, we are," Jimmy said. "I'm a little nervous though."

"How come?"

"Well, I've never been on a date before, and I'm not really sure what is expected of me, especially with it happening at prom," Jimmy said. He then took a sip of Coke.

"It's no big deal really. All you do is dance, eat some cookies, and drink punch. You two could probably go to dinner too if you wanted before the dance. A lot of guys take their dates out beforehand." Alan almost said he could also get laid afterward but decided not to mention that. He doubted Jimmy would make a move on Tina, and even if he did, Alan didn't really want to think about it.

"Still, this is like the biggest night of a girl's life up until her wedding, you know, and what if I screw up?"

"There's nothing to screw up," Alan said.

"How do you know? You've never been to a dance before."

"I know, but…" Alan didn't really know what to say. "It's not going to be as intense as you think."

The two went quiet after that.

"Do you think a lot of people will make a big deal out of me being there?" Jimmy asked after nearly a minute.

"I know no one really makes fun of me anymore, but I can't help thinking they will think it's strange that I'm there, especially since I've never gone to any of the dances or games before."

Alan shook his head. "No one will care. Everyone will be so focused on their date and hoping they don't make a fool out of themselves that they won't even notice you, unless…"

"Unless what?" Jimmy demanded.

"Unless Tina is wearing something really hot, like so hot that other guys have to hide their boners. Then you'll be in trouble because all the girls will get jealous and come after you two."

"Shut up."

"Really, it's happened before. Girls go crazy when other girls outshine them, and it gets messy. I've read about it in *Newsweek.*"

Jimmy shook his head and said, "What if I disappoint Tina and she doesn't have any fun?"

"Jimmy, she likes you," Alan said, his voice once again serious. "You can see it in her eyes when she is looking up at you. Just act like yourself when around her and everything will be okay. Trust me. She'll have the time of her life."

The two stopped at an intersection and waited for a few cars to pass. While standing there, Jimmy looked to his right and thought about the Hood place and how two days earlier he had been rushing that way through the woods to get a good spot ahead of Samantha, who would have been crossing the same street down there at Lambert. Less than a mile from there was the Hood place.

Less than a mile from here Samantha is still hanging from her wrists.

Jimmy knew he had to let her down soon.

Without warning, he watched as Megan Reed appeared on the side of the road over there and waited to cross.

Alan noticed him looking and said, "What is it?"

"Oh, I'm just wondering what she's doing over there since the sheriff lives on the other side of town."

"Probably retracing that girl's steps, you know, the one that disappeared," Alan said. "She lived down over there somewhere, and that girl—that's the sheriff's daughter, right?"

"Yeah," Jimmy said.

"Well, she's been talking like crazy at school and says she is certain something happened to her while walking home, and she was going to start looking around herself to see if there were any clues."

"Okay, that just seems weird."

"I know, but she may have a point."

"What do you mean?" Jimmy asked.

The two started crossing the street.

"Well, I think something had to happen to that girl, but I don't think she was kidnapped. I think she and her boyfriend probably had a fight or something—maybe he even tried to screw her and she fought back or something and he accidentally hurt her—and now her body is lying out there in the woods. You read about things like that all the time."

"In *Newsweek*?" Jimmy asked.

"Shit, I'm serious. You read about stuff like that all the time in the papers or hear about it on the news. It's crazy. People don't think when their sex drive starts up. In fact, I was watching something on the Discovery

Channel a few weeks ago that said a man's mind loses the ability for rational thought once their body gets really turned on, which is probably why so many guys say screw it when they don't have a condom but still dive into a girl's pussy and then get her pregnant."

Jimmy thought about that and about all the times he had purchased subscriptions to bondage sites when getting turned on, something that he almost always regretted afterward once he was finished and thought about the money he had wasted. It made sense.

"You know, if something did happen to that girl, no one will really care right now because of the oil spill," Alan said. "No one outside of town, that is, because the news won't care. A few years ago they would have, because kidnappings were like a news fad, but now, not so much."

Jimmy hadn't really thought about this, but now he realized his brother was probably right.

"Do you think she will find anything?" he asked.

"Who, the sheriff's daughter? What's her name again?"

"Megan."

"Maybe, but only if there is something over there, and only if it isn't like buried ten feet beneath the surface of the forest. I mean, there still is the chance she just split town. I know some don't think so because of the prom, but it's still a possibility."

"Yeah," Jimmy said, not really hearing what Alan said and instead just focusing on Megan Reed and the chance that she might find the fallout shelter.

He couldn't let that happen.

Megan wasn't really sure if she was going to accomplish

anything, but she thought it was better to go out and take a look around than just sit at home angry, which is what she would have done. Now at least she could feel somewhat productive.

She had made the decision to look around while talking with Steven, whom she felt sorry for because she knew he loved Samantha yet wasn't being recognized for it due to the fact that it was just a high school relationship. What most didn't realize was that their relationship was special, one of the ones that seemed almost like a fairy tale, especially ten years later once they had kids and were enjoying a perfect life.

She started her little investigation by walking the route to Samantha's house. Once there, she started walking back toward the school, slowly this time, trying to see if anything jumped out at her.

Something did, but it wasn't what she was expecting.

"Jimmy, what are you doing out here?" Megan asked as he rode up to her on his bike.

"I saw you walking this way on my way home and remembered what you said in the hallway today, and it made me remember something I found a few years ago that might help."

"Oh, what is it?"

"Come on, I'll show you."

Megan followed Jimmy down the wooded road. He was now walking his bike so she wouldn't have any trouble keeping up. The two did not talk.

Five minutes later they came upon the Hood place, Jimmy still in the lead, Megan behind him wondering why he wouldn't just tell her what he thought was so important. She also wondered why, if it was important, he hadn't mentioned it to anyone else, but she didn't really think too hard about that because she knew from the books she read that people sometimes didn't realize how important something was until something else clicked. Like the odd bulge she saw beneath Jimmy's sweatshirt, which he hadn't been wearing at school given the warm day they were having. Though familiar, she never realized it was identical to the bulge she saw beneath her father's sweatshirts when they would go out as a family and he was required to carry a gun. Of course, he could have carried the gun on the outside of his clothes and no one would have said anything, knowing who he was, but he always preferred to tuck it away. Had she made this realization sooner, the coming events might have been different.

Jimmy couldn't believe she was still on the street walking around when he came by. He had figured he would have to call everything off if he couldn't find her, knowing he could only grab her if she was near the house, because anywhere else and it would be too difficult to get her to the fallout shelter, especially without a car.

He also couldn't believe how uncomfortable carrying a gun could be, especially while riding a bike, and wondered why so many people across the country were pushing for open firearm carry laws. After all, who would want to carry something so heavy all over the place? Sure, it would be cool at first, but after a while, it would become an annoying burden.

"It never even occurred to me that she could be down here," Jimmy said. "I mean, I've known about this place for a long time." He reached toward the ground while saying this, his fingers grabbing hold of something

Megan couldn't make out. "But I kind of forgot about it until you mentioned this place and the possibility that she was attacked." It was a ring he was holding, one that completely blended in with the dirt, and without warning a giant square of dirt lifted up.

"What the hell?" Megan said.

"It's an old fallout shelter," Jimmy said, "one the Hoods built for something back in the eighties or nineties, maybe Y2K or just out of fear from watching *Red Dawn* too many times."

"Is there anything down there?" Megan asked while peeking down the stairs.

"I don't know, but you know what? You see that padlock right there, the one that someone forgot to close when leaving?" Jimmy pointed down with his free hand.

"Yeah?"

"That was never there the last time I looked down there, and why would someone lock up that door from the outside?"

"Oh my God, did you look inside?"

"Not yet."

"We have to look inside," Megan said. "What if she's in there and she's hurt?" With that Megan started toward the door but then froze, suddenly realizing that Jimmy would have looked himself earlier if what he said was true, and she quickly turned around, fear suddenly gripping her.

Jimmy was pointing a gun at her.

Jimmy's heart was racing as he held the gun, which had actually snagged on his jeans while being pulled out and nearly fell to the floor while he fumbled with it. Thankfully, her back had been turned to him during that, and now that she was facing him he had a nice firm grip.

"Go on, open the door," he said. "Your friend is waiting."

"You fucking bastard!" Megan shouted, spittle flying from her lips. "I should have known you were a sick twisted freak."

"Inside!" Jimmy snapped, motioning with the gun.

Megan reluctantly did as he ordered, her face red with anger yet also hinting at fear.

"The light is on the right," Jimmy said. "Turn it on and walk into the middle of the room."

Megan did, her hand fumbling for a moment before it found the light. Once it was on, she gasped. A second later, she ran into the room.

"Don't touch her!" Jimmy shouted as he followed her inside, his left hand pushing shut the door behind him.

Megan ignored his command and tried to console Samantha, her hands caressing her bruised face and then reaching up to try to untie the knots from around her wrists, which, of course, was a hopeless endeavor.

Jimmy rushed forward and tried to pull her away.

Megan spun around, and before he even realized what had happened the gun was knocked from his hand.

A second blow came toward his face, this one from the same forearm that had knocked the gun away.

Jimmy deflected it with his elbow, hurting both of them, and looked toward where the gun had landed.

Megan followed his gaze and dove for it.

Jimmy was a second behind her, panic starting to overwhelm his senses.

Megan grabbed the gun.

At the same time, Jimmy stepped on her hand, hard,

and heard what had to be a bone crunching, though he couldn't be sure. A second later, he kicked her in the chest, his foot actually recognizing the feel of her boob compressing despite the fact that Samantha's breasts had been the first ones he ever touched.

Megan grunted and tried to grab the gun again.

Jimmy kicked her hand away, took hold of it himself, and pointed it down at her.

Megan still didn't stop and grabbed his leg and tried digging her nails into it, but she couldn't get much of a grip thanks to the jean fabric.

Jimmy kicked her again and screamed at her to stop, wondering how the hell he would get her hands tied with her fighting so much.

Megan didn't listen.

Heart racing, Jimmy kicked her again, hard, and then grabbed hold of a chunk of her hair, which he used to lift half her body into the air, her hands digging her nails into his own hands.

"Let go!" he demanded while pressing the gun into her temple. He didn't want to pull the trigger, not when he knew he could have so much fun with her down here, but he would if forced to. After all, it was better to shoot her in the head and kill her than to risk her escaping and bringing her dad here.

Megan dug deeper.

He hit her with the butt of the gun, not hard, but with enough force to hurt her.

Megan's fingers relaxed but still didn't release, and then started to tighten again once she regained her senses.

He hit her again, harder, and then pointed the gun at Samantha. "Let go or I'll shoot your friend!"

This time he received the compliance he was looking for, but it only lasted a second, because the moment he lowered the gun and looked at the damage done to his hand, which still held her hair, she grabbed his testicles and twisted, a cry of fury echoing from her lips as one of pain echoed from his.

Jimmy tried pulling away but couldn't and had no choice but to hit her with some serious force.

The hand released him as her eyes rolled backward.

Hurt, but knowing he only had moments, Jimmy set the gun on the shelf and began tying her wrists together, making sure the rope was as tight as possible when he knotted it.

CHAPTER EIGHT

Samantha was broken and didn't even realize Jimmy had returned to the room with another girl until the hand touched her face. Even then, she couldn't really register what was going on, the pain being the only thing her mind understood, though even that was fading and turning into nothing more than a noticeable ache.

Sounds echoed from her left.

Samantha eased her eyes toward the source of the struggle but didn't really see what was going on, nor did she care because it didn't seem to have an immediate effect upon her. The idea that one of them could free the rope didn't enter her mind because the very idea of being free no longer seemed real. Instead, she just watched what was happening without any emotion or opinion, the way a dog might watch a Little League game outside the window.

Megan drifted in and out of consciousness the way a person on a twilight drug during a medical operation would come and go, her mind seeing and registering things but not really processing them, at least not at that point in time. Even the tug of the rope above that secured her hands wasn't fully understood, yet the discomfort was. She also made several attempts to stand up, even though her body couldn't balance itself, her feet always trying to find a firm spot on what seemed to be a wobbly floor. All of these attempts failed and caused the tug of the ropes to be more intense, though the association between the two wasn't understood.

"What happened to you?" Alan asked as Jimmy walked into the kitchen to get a glass of water.

"I fell off my bike into a thorny weedy mess on the side of the road," Jimmy said.

"My God, are you okay?"

Jimmy looked at his left hand and wrist, which had suffered the worst of Megan's nails, huge gouges marking where the flesh had been peeled away, and said, "Yeah, I think so, though these hurt like hell."

"Was it Brett?"

"No, though it might as well have been him, because I was looking back to make sure it wasn't him coming up behind me when I hit a broken patch of road and went right into the brush." He winced as he ran his arm under the water. "But I guess I should be thankful nothing is broken and that I didn't hit the bump and fall right in front of the car."

"Yeah, really."

He added soap to his arm, not even wanting to consider trying the peroxide on this, and squeezed his lips together for a second before saying, "Fuck!"

"You know, on *MythBusters* they found out that swearing helps you manage pain."

"You're shitting me!"

"Honest."

"*Fuck! Fuck! Fuck!*" he shouted while rubbing the soap in. "It still hurts!"

"But maybe it doesn't hurt as much. Cut up the other arm and try it without the swears so we have a baseline to compare it to."

"Fuck you!"

"Did it hurt less during that microsecond?"

Jimmy rinsed off the soap and then toweled off his arm with a disposable sheet.

"Better?"

"I hope so. The last thing I need is an infection from her." He tossed the paper towel away.

"Who?"

"What are you talking about?"

"You said get an infection from her."

Jimmy froze but then quickly said, "The bush. *Her.* Get it?"

Alan stared at him.

"Bush as in pussy. STD. It was a joke."

"Okay, yeah, a real Jimmy original—all the greatness of a professional joke, minus the annoying need to laugh afterward."

"Fuck you," Jimmy said, though with a smile.

"Okay, on a scale between one and ten, how was your pain while swearing?"

Jimmy shook his head.

"Did you at least get measured for your tux?" Alan asked.

"No, I didn't make it to the place before falling and then came right home. You want to go with me later on once Mom is home with the car?"

"Sure, or we could just walk there."

"Let's drive. I'm sure they will still be open after five."

"Probably. Battle?"

"Battle!" Jimmy confirmed, one arm raised up in the air as if wielding a sword and commanding a charge.

Megan's understanding of the situation returned slowly and wasn't pleasant, especially when she vomited all over herself. With the vomit came a kind of clarity, one that allowed her to focus on the situation, though some parts of it still took a few moments to register.

Her hands being tied was one of them.

A part of her knew they were tied, and that the constant pull from above against her wrists was a result of it. Her understanding of the ropes, however, wasn't fully realized until she tried to touch the back of her head, her fingers wanting to assess the pain. The ropes would not allow this.

She looked up at the bindings, her head moving slowly due to the dizzy spells that threatened.

The knots seemed tight and very far away.

A nasty tickle hit the back of her throat, one that she recognized as a precursor to throwing up. Thankfully, nothing ventured toward her mouth, and everything settled once she lowered her head back through her arms.

I want to show you something.

The words echoed in her mind, but without reason, the memory fuzzy.

She pushed it away and carefully tried to take in her surroundings. Earlier, while only semiconscious, she had thought she was inside a small boat, one that was rocking in the waves. The idea now seemed ridiculous due to the concrete floor and walls. Plus the events from that afternoon were starting to fade in again.

I want to show you something.

She could see Jimmy Hawthorn talking to her, but it didn't make sense. Wariness about his presence, or supposed presence, did appear, however.

She saw herself trying to grab the gun and then felt the pain of his foot coming down on her fingers.

Megan looked up again, slowly.

Though slightly shadowed due to the light being behind her, she could tell her right hand was busted up.

Pain followed, though because of the ropes, it wasn't as bad as it should have been, the numbness working to her advantage.

She thought about her failure to fire the gun. Just a simple pull of the trigger would have been enough, even when the gun had been on the floor and his foot on her hand, her mind thinking he would jump away from the blast, but her finger hadn't been able to make the necessary movement.

Frustration swelled.

She looked down at the floor.

Small bits of vomit decorated her shoes.

A moan echoed.

Megan slowly twisted to her right.

Someone was sitting on the floor next to her. No, not sitting, hanging, only low enough that she could have been kneeling on the ground, her hands raised over her head. Instead, her body just lifelessly dangled there, her legs making no move to support her weight.

Samantha!

Everything flooded back to her.

"Samantha," she said, voice barely audible.

Nothing.

Megan moistened her lips, the taste of vomit being activated again.

Once a good glob of spit was ready, she hawked it onto the floor. Some of the vomit taste went with it; most stayed behind.

"Samantha," she said again. This time her voice was able to fill the room. "Can you hear me?"

Her friend didn't respond.

Silence settled.

Megan screamed while pulling at the ropes, but this didn't help the situation, and after a few seconds, she gave up.

Samantha shifted, moaned, and then peed herself.

Megan watched with dismay as the urine pooled on the floor beneath her, its journey hindered only by the thin pair of panties her friend wore.

Fear followed, not of the waste, but of the fact that her friend was so badly hurt that she couldn't even control herself—so badly hurt that she didn't even seem to realize what was going on, nor care.

How could this happen?

She examined her friend, her eyes taking in the colorless hands that jutted out above the knotted ropes, and then looked at her own hands, which were starting to turn purple as the blood pooled in them. What would they look like tomorrow or the next day?

Two days.

Samantha has only been here for two days.

This frightened her even worse than the fact that Samantha had peed herself, because she wondered what Jimmy could have done during those two days to make her like this. Worse, would he do the same thing to her?

Yes!

Megan pulled at the ropes again, thinking that with enough force she might be able to snap the pipe or the rope, or both. All she managed to do was hurt her hands.

At the same time, the smell of the room hit her. Of course, it had been there the entire time but just hadn't fully registered. Now it did, and made her gag. Nothing came up, her stomach already empty.

Will there be anything to come up ever again?

Her eyes settled on the shelves of food and wondered if she would be fed, a thought that caused her stomach to shrivel. Later she knew this wouldn't be the case. Once the hunger really began to set in, she wouldn't care about the smell or even the condition of the food and would eat it all.

I won't be here that long.

Not if I focus and find a way to get free.

She looked around again, her mind envisioning her seeing something long and sharp and slowly but surely working it toward her feet, which then would carefully lift it into the air and cut the rope.

On TV, things like this happened all the time when someone was caught in a situation like this.

Unfortunately, nothing but her purse was within reach, and even if something sharp had been, she doubted she would have actually been able to use it the way a TV or movie character would. Still, it would have given her some hope.

Samantha stirred and cried out, the sound startling Megan.

Nothing followed.

"Samantha?"

Her friend twisted a bit and looked at her with lifeless eyes.

"Samantha, it's me, Megan."

Samantha just stared at her, eyes completely vacant.

Tina hesitated for a while once she was home, a debate over whether or not Rebecca would leave the prom ticket at home or keep it on her while at work raging within her mind.

And even if you find it, she could still call the school.

The question was, would the school really listen to her, especially if Tina went to the office and explained the situation? Furthermore, would the people at the door checking tickets actually inspect the name to see if she was on some sort of "Her mother doesn't want her attending" list?

Tina didn't really have an answer for this but did know one thing, having her prom ticket would be better than not having it, because without it she couldn't get in —especially if Rebecca called them too.

Tina got a glass of juice while thinking about this and decided she had to look. If the prom ticket wasn't there, then it wasn't there, but if it was and she found it, things would be much better.

Unless Rebecca really flips out.

Tina thought about this while heading up to Rebecca's bedroom, which apparently had been Rebecca's mother's bedroom before the old woman had died from colon cancer a few years earlier. *That's gotta be a pain in the ass,* Tina had said when Rebecca had explained this the day Tina had moved in, which wasn't received very well —and she pictured Rebecca trying to punish her. Last night Rebecca had said her mother used to take her over her knee while also putting a bar of soap in her mouth, her gasps from the spanking causing the soap to hit the back of her throat. It sounded absolutely horrible, and Tina felt sorry for Rebecca's younger self for suffering at the hands of such a bitch. At the same time, she knew if Rebecca tried something like that with her, she would just find herself suffering even more, because Tina would kick her ass. It was one thing to raise a kid to fear you, something that often seemed to follow the kid up through adulthood. It was another to expect a grown woman of seventeen, who was the same size, who you'd never spent any real time with, to fear such things. Nope. The minute Rebecca touched her Tina would split her lip and break her nose, no questions asked, no apologies given.

The image of this brought a smile to Tina's face. It quickly faded once she actually stepped into Rebecca's room and began her search. It was the faces that did it. Rebecca had lined the walls of the room with pictures of her late mother, ones that seemed to glare at Tina as she examined the contents of each dresser drawer.

It was the actual location of the prom ticket that stopped her dead in her tracks. It was sitting on the surface of a drawer full of unframed photographs, the small blue and white slip of paper clipped to one of the pictures.

At first, Tina didn't think much of this and just slipped the ticket free of the connection. A second later a chill slipped down her spine as she realized what the picture displayed, her father's face easily recognizable despite the time that had passed. Rebecca's face was harder to make out, the years between then and now having taken a serious toll upon what was once an incredibly pretty and youthful appearance. The two were formally dressed, her father wearing a tuxedo with a flower, Rebecca wearing a royal blue gown, which seemed to enhance her beauty the way a nice frame will enhance a painting. Her father's tuxedo didn't have the same effect and instead made it look like he was trying to outsmart everybody.

Enchantment Under the Stars—Prom of 1992.

Tina stared at the picture for several seconds and then peeked into the drawer to see what else was in there. A wedding photo greeted her. It sat atop a wedding album.

She pulled it out. *Together Forever—Memories of Stanley Thompson and Rebecca Collins Wedding—August 26, 1992* was embedded in gold on the thick cover, an image of the two kissing in front of the altar pressed into it beneath the words.

Tina opened the book and started looking at the pictures, her eyes growing wet as she saw the happy, yet nervous face of her father captured repeatedly throughout the wedding ceremony and celebration. Rebecca looked happy as well, though her thick white gown did not have the same effect that her prom dress had in the other picture. Truth be told, the wedding dress almost looked as if it was holding her hostage, the thick layers of fabric acting like restraints.

Your mother probably picked out the dress and made you wear it, whereas you were the one deciding on the prom dress.

Tina shook her head and closed the book, wondering what the hell her father had been thinking. Why marry the bitch, especially right after school like that? Why not go out and enjoy life for a while? It just didn't make any sense. Her father should have been smarter than that. Shit, her father *was* smarter than that.

But he was in love.

She looked at the prom picture again and saw it in his eyes. Rebecca had it too.

Puppy love.

She peeked into the drawer after that. Other photo albums were there, as were dozens upon dozens of loose pictures that had just been dumped in. Each one was a picture of Rebecca and Tina's father, or just her father.

Tina pulled out a pink album that had the words *It's a Girl* printed across the front.

A chill crept down her spine.

She opened the book.

A picture of Rebecca lying in a hospital bed, face plastered with sweat, looked back at her. Her father was in the picture as well, leaning over the bed and looking at the camera, smiling. Tina lay between them, eyes closed, her tiny body wrapped in a small blanket, pink socks covering her feet.

Several more hospital pictures followed, and then one of the two standing outside an apartment building, Rebecca holding Tina. Snow covered the ground, and each of them was wrapped up tightly, Tina included, a warm baby outfit hiding just about every part of her body. Written beneath the picture on the caption spot was *Home for the First Time—January 1993.*

Tina smiled.

She remembered the apartment, but not her mother being there. Instead, she had memories of her grandparents coming over and staying with her during the day while her father went to work and then night school, something that he finished when she was in first grade. Her grandparents and she had sat in the hot sun while her father had gotten his diploma, her grandmother taking pictures like crazy, her father looking funny in the black square hat. Tina remembered the event. She had no idea what was going on at the time, just that it was important and that soon after they were able to move into a house rather than an apartment, the same house they had lived in until his death last year, a house that wasn't displayed in any of the pictures she found in the drawer.

Daddy, where is Mommy? Tina remembered asking once.

She lives with her mommy, her father had said.

Why?

The answers had stayed pretty simple until she had been old enough to understand the reality of the situation.

She put the baby album away and looked at some of the stand-alone pictures. In some her father and Rebecca looked happy; in others they just looked like any other married couple who had grown used to the constant companionship.

Tina dumped the pictures back into the drawer and then replaced the two albums, her mind still startled by the wedding one because she had never seen any of those pictures before.

She wondered why Rebecca had been the one to get the album, especially since she had been the one to walk away, but then figured her father probably hadn't wanted the constant "in your face" memories the album would carry. Plus he probably figured it would act like a thorn in Rebecca's side, its purpose being to constantly remind her that she had abandoned her family.

He wouldn't think that way, Tina said a few seconds later.

She looked at the prom picture.

God, if only you knew what she would do.

She wondered what her father would have thought at that moment if he had known that within a year he would be married and have a daughter.

Hell, not even a year, more like—she quickly counted the months in her head—*nine months.*

She shook her head, put the picture away, and started for her room, the prom ticket safe and sound in her pocket where it would stay until prom night.

Megan was staring down toward her purse but not really seeing it, her mind projecting a pleasant fantasy as she took one of the boards in the corner and beat in Jimmy's head until his skull split like an oversize eggshell, when suddenly the purse sprang to life with a series of barks and growls.

Shouting, Megan tried backing herself away from the small leather bag, but the ropes wouldn't let her get very far, and for one brief moment she had a vision of something horrible exiting the purse and coming for her, her body unable to get away and moving in small circles as she danced around the angry creature.

But then things clicked and she realized it was not the leather coming back to life, or some other horrible monstrosity, just her phone, which had different ring settings for different people, her mother's being a dog barking and growling because sometimes the lady could be a real bitch. Her other family members had personalized rings as well, her little brother's being "If I Only Had a Brain" from *The Wizard of Oz*, and her father's being a series of Barney Fife statements from *The Andy Griffith_Show*, though she had been planning on changing the latter one because none of her friends understood what they were.

The phone stopped growling after six series of rings.

Please, no voice mail, Megan said to herself, but then the happy little half ring echoed once the message from her mother was complete.

Oh God!

Her phone was programmed to beep every ten minutes when she had a message. Normally such a feature didn't bother her because she didn't get that many messages, and when she did she usually listened to them right away. Now, however, the stupid phone would beep every ten minutes, driving her crazy, and she would have no way of turning it off. Even worse, the thing was fully charged and had a really long battery life, one that lasted even longer when no one was talking or texting.

At least they are wondering where you are, her inner voice said.

The question was, would they be able to find her in time—in time meaning before Jimmy spread her legs and fucked her? Or would she be a withered mess of flesh, simply dangling from the ropes when they finally discovered the secret location?

Or a rotting mess of flesh tossed in the woods—one that the coyotes and birds have been picking at for days?

The thought chilled her to the core and once again brought up the question of why Jimmy had done this. *Why would he kidnap Samantha? Why would he kidnap me?*

Not to kill me, obviously—unless of course killing is just the dessert after a very satisfying meal.

Her eyes once again took in Samantha.

What has he done to you?

More important, what is he going to do to me?

Dozens of different possibilities ran through her head, none of them pleasant, all of them frightening. After a few moments of this, she tried to block everything out, but her mind wouldn't stop.

The phone beeped.

Ten minutes since the call.

Time was moving slowly.

Megan shifted her arms and stretched herself so that she was on her toes for a moment, all in an attempt to ease an ache that had started to develop in her back. At first, the stretch worked, but then the ache returned the moment she allowed her body to sag against the ropes again.

Samantha moaned.

Megan twisted around to look at her, but her friend still had an empty look behind her eyes.

She didn't bother trying to communicate with her, not yet, maybe not ever. It all depended on how badly Jimmy had hurt her.

Don't let him touch you! her inner voice ordered. *Even if he threatens to hurt you, make him pay dearly.*

Megan could see herself hitting him in the balls every time he tried to fuck her, to the point where he lost all his desire to do anything. Of course, if she did that he might kill her, and then her family would never find her.

They might not find you anyway!

She thought about the entrance to the fallout shelter and how she had never known about it, or heard anyone ever talk about it. That said, someone had to know about it, and Jimmy had been able to find it, so there was a chance she would be found.

Still, would she want to give in to Jimmy just to stay alive? If rescued, could she live with herself after being raped repeatedly?

She thought about that girl in California who had been kidnapped as a young teenager, or maybe even before she was a teenager, and held in that pervert's backyard in a tent for something like twenty years. The girl had given birth to his children and raised them in the tent, finally being found only when the family went to the police station or something. Megan hadn't paid too much attention when the story had been on the news, but now she was curious about what that girl's mind was like.

Will Jimmy make us bear his children?

The thought sickened her, especially when she imagined it all taking place in the small little concrete room, which didn't even seem to have a toilet or shower.

Worse, she saw herself giving birth while standing tied, Jimmy trying to pull the child out, his actions those of someone who had no clue what he was doing and screwed everything up.

And then, even worse than that, she saw the baby as a girl, one who grew up thinking this was all the world was, her body there solely for Jimmy, who would spend years molesting her.

No! No! No! Megan's mind screamed. The horrible timeline would not stop, however, and got more and more disturbing until she finally tried to rip her hands free, the ropes tearing the damaged skin to the point where blood actually hit her face.

The cell phone beeped.

"Shut up!" she screamed and kicked at the purse.

Her foot caught one of the straps and jerked the purse in the air, but at a sideways angle, which caused several items to fall out, the lipstick getting a good bounce and rolling all the way to the wall.

The phone, however, stayed within.

She let the purse fall back to the floor and removed her foot from the strap.

On cue, the phone started to ring, the growls of an

angry dog once again echoing through the fallout shelter.

This time her mother didn't leave a message, not that it mattered since the phone still beeped every ten minutes to remind her of the first message.

"Will you guys be home for dinner?" Kelly Hawthorn asked once Jimmy and Alan told her they needed the car. "I was going to make spaghetti."

"Um, yeah," Jimmy said. "I think?" He turned to Alan while saying this last part. "How long will this take?"

Alan shrugged. "I don't know. They just have to measure us."

"Us?" Jimmy said.

"Oh yeah, I forgot to tell you," Alan said with a shrug. "I'm going to prom too. Let's go."

"Wait," Kelly said. "Who're you going with?"

"Some senior chick. I guess her boyfriend bailed on her."

"And how did you come into the picture?" Kelly asked.

"Art class. We sit together."

"What's her name?" Jimmy asked.

"Good question," Alan said while scratching his head. "I should probably figure that out."

"Seriously, who is it?"

"Rachel something or other. Long brown hair, cute face"—he checked to see if their mother was looking, and when he saw that she wasn't he cupped some imaginary breasts—"and huge…"

"Huge what?" Kelly asked while turning toward them.

"Huge stores of art talent and opinions on history, science, and philosophical theory," Alan said.

Kelly nodded. "Go on, get those tuxes. Oh, and Jimmy?"

"Yeah?" he asked.

"See if you can teach your little brother how to be respectful toward women and understand how to treat them as a person, not some eye-pleasing object."

"Hey!" Alan snapped. "I look for more than just beauty in women. I know they need to understand how to cook, clean, and fold clothes."

"Oh, you better run," Jimmy said.

Alan did, though his mother was still able to nail him with some spray from the sink.

A few seconds later, the two were in their mother's car heading into town, both of them laughing.

"You know," Jimmy said as they neared the shop where they could rent tuxedos. "We should probably stop by Taco Bell on the way home."

"Why?"

"Because Mom is so going to poison your food."

"Well, what do you know," Brett said as Jimmy and his little brother walked into the clothing store on the corner, which had been pretty busy lately thanks to the upcoming prom and their tuxedo rental program. The place even had a large banner telling those planning to attend prom to hurry up and get their tuxedos before it was too late. "You don't actually think he's going to prom?" He stood up while asking this and then added, "Let's go make sure he gets something nice."

"Ah, man, just leave him alone," Matt said.

"What?"

"Leave them alone."

"Like hell I will. I told you what he did to me

yesterday."

"Yeah, after we took his bike."

The two were sitting on the bench in front of the old run-down video store, where Matt had worked for two years before it finally closed its doors and sold off its inventory. They had been there for twenty minutes watching the grocery store a few doors down, hoping someone would help them buy beer.

"Since when did you become such a pussy?" Brett demanded.

Matt shrugged. "I'm just not in the mood." Truthfully, he hadn't been in the mood since a year earlier when Jimmy had shoved him up against a gym locker between classes back in the corner of the men's locker room where the gym teacher couldn't see from the office, pissed that Matt had told everyone what he had rented from the video store. Matt couldn't remember what the movie title was, just that it had been a kinky soft-core porn flick, nor did he really care. Instead, all he remembered was the look in Jimmy's eyes, a look that said, *If you ever fuck with me again, I will kill you.*

Since then, he had slowly started to lose heart in the torment of Jimmy, yet for some reason he couldn't bring himself to separate himself from Brett and Ron, not after spending so much of his childhood by their sides.

He was also a little scared of Jimmy, though he would never allow such a thing to become known. Something was seriously wrong with the guy, something that he couldn't put his finger on but knew to be true nonetheless.

"Oh, *not in the mood,*" Brett said, voice rising. "I'm so sorry; I didn't know you had such a delicate schedule."

"Can we just get the beer and go?"

"Yeah, as soon as someone takes the stick out of their ass and helps us buy some," Brett snapped.

"Why don't we just call your brother?"

"I'm not fucking calling my brother. I told you what happened."

Yeah, Brett had told him. He had told him a dozen times, his mind completely obsessed. Matt, however, hadn't really cared and like so many other moments when he had been around Brett, started to realize just how immature the guy was and wondered why he still put up with it. It was stupid. Even worse, he knew that ten years from now Brett would still be like this, and it brought to mind something one of his teachers had said a few years earlier about her high school reunion and how the "cool kids" had become the "lame adults" yet didn't realize it and still expected everyone to think they were all that. It was a position he didn't want to find himself in ten years from now.

"Come on, let's—" Brett started but stopped as a sheriff's cruiser pulled up, the deputy inside giving them the look that told them to move it.

Matt stood up to head to Brett's car, but Brett stood his ground.

The passenger window slid down.

"You can't arrest us for just sitting here, Paulie," Brett said before the deputy even got a word out.

"You want to test that theory out, Mr. Murphy?" Deputy Paul Widgeon asked. "Now move along and do something productive for a change."

"Come on, Brett, let's go," Matt said. He reached an arm out to tug Brett away, but Brett shrugged it off.

"You should listen to your little friend, Brett."

"Why's that, Paulie?" Brett asked.

"Because even if he was missing half his brain, he'd still be smarter than you," Deputy Widgeon said. "And that's on the conservative side of things."

"You know, you think you're tough shit now that you've got a gun and a badge, but I know how you used to run home crying because my brother and his friends shoved rocks and leaves down your pants on the way home from school and made you eat dog shit."

Matt had heard about the first part, but never the dog shit part, and had a feeling Brett was embellishing the story.

"Yeah, well a lot has happened since then, Brett. Now move along before I run you in for failure to comply with a sheriff's deputy."

"More like failure to comply with a wannabe police officer who sadly lost his package in Iraq," Brett said, though he did start heading toward the car.

Matt hesitated before following, watching Deputy Widgeon for a moment to see if he was going to do something. Thankfully, the deputy kept his cool, and a moment later Matt followed Brett to the car.

It wasn't a conscious decision to start counting the message beeps from her phone. Instead, it just started to happen because there was nothing else to do. Sometimes Megan would even try to count down the time until the beep occurred, her mind saying something like, *It will be in ten, nine, eight, seven*…until she reached *zero*, her mind never able to actually match the countdown with the beep. Sometimes the beep would just happen, her mind not really focusing on anything when suddenly the beep would echo. Other times she waited for it, her mind wanting and needing the beep. No matter the situation, however, her mind always registered the number, even if she was simply staring at the wall, drifting. The phone would beep and her mind would say *five* or *six*. It didn't make a big deal out of this, nor did it attach any significance to it, until the twelfth beep.

Twelve, her mind noted. This happened at one of her staring-at-the-wall moments, her mind wondering how thick the concrete was and whether or not it had been built to withstand some sort of blast, or just to provide a place to hide for a little while.

After the beep, she thought to herself, *Twelve beeps means it's been two hours since she called*, and then went back to thinking about the wall thickness.

Another beep echoed.

Two hours and ten minutes, her mind said.

It was then that she realized she was able to keep track of the time, something that momentarily seemed monumental despite its simplicity. Of course, being able to pinpoint that time passage on a clock would be even better, but she would take what she could get. Other discoveries would follow, ones that seemed even more significant, but at the moment, she relished this one.

Waiting for Rebecca to come home from work was nerve-racking, and for the hour or so after finding the prom ticket Tina did nothing but pace the house, her body unable to relax, her mind envisioning the horrible confrontation that would take place. Rebecca would be pissed, there was no doubt about it, and once things got started, there would be no stopping the verbal abuse that would follow. Tina also had the feeling things would turn physical, especially if Rebecca tried to forcefully take the ticket away from her. Tina would not tolerate it, and if

Rebecca laid one finger on her, Tina was going to hit back and she wouldn't hold herself back.

She'll call the school.

This thought was a constant companion to the vision of the fight, one that chilled Tina yet also made her question how effective the call would actually be. Parents and guardians always had the ultimate say when it came to things like prom, but her situation was so different, and Rebecca was so weird, that the school might let things slide.

It was a risky bet, one that Tina hoped to God would pay out in the end. If not, well, there wasn't much she could do about it. All her cards would be on the table.

Occasionally during this hour of pacing, another thought would enter her mind, one that had nothing to do with her own prom and instead focused on her father and Rebecca's prom.

Was I conceived that night?

It was a question she had never really given any thought too, mostly because the possibility had never occurred to her. She always knew her father and Rebecca had married young and that her father had been forced to cut back on the amount of classes he was taking due to the financial responsibilities, but the true reason for this never really clicked. It was the year changes that did it. Her father had graduated high school in 1991, prom and their marriage had been in 1992, and her birth had been in 1993. Because of this, she had always assumed things had been planned out—not well, yet still planned out—and that she had been conceived after the marriage, the two feeling that they could bear the responsibility despite the burden it would place upon them. In reality, Rebecca must have gotten pregnant around the time of prom, and her father did the honorable thing and married her, which of course explained why everything was so ill-fated and eventually broke apart.

Stupid teenagers, she said to herself. *Probably didn't have any condoms.*

At the same time, she knew she wouldn't have been born if they had been wiser, which meant she couldn't condemn them too much. It was crazy.

Did Rebecca plant the ticket there so I would find it?

This was another question that was bothering her, one that she couldn't seem to figure out a reason for. When first starting the search, Tina had had a strong feeling that it was a fruitless endeavor because Rebecca would never leave the ticket where she could find it. A part of her had even tried to convince herself not to search altogether because it would be a waste of time. The other part had needed to try it, though, just in case it wasn't. Now it seemed incredibly doubtful that Rebecca would have left the prom ticket lying around, because she would have known Tina would search for it. Sure, the two still didn't know each other all that well, but the experiences learned from living together gave them enough insight to predict the other's actions with a high degree of accuracy.

Why leave it?

Whatever the reason, Tina knew it wasn't going to be so she could simply stumble upon the photographs and come to the realization that she had been conceived out of wedlock. No. As horrible as such a situation might have been for Rebecca and her family, she was sure Rebecca understood that it wouldn't faze Tina. Another reason was behind it, and whatever it was, it wasn't going to be pleasant. To the outside world, Rebecca could portray herself as a poor tragic woman who was being abused by her newfound daughter, who she just wanted to be loved by, but with Tina, she knew she couldn't pull this off and for the most part didn't even try. Tina knew the truth and knew that anything that seemed calculated was supposed to hurt her.

It won't work.

Nothing Rebecca could say or do would get to her. Tina just didn't care.

Downstairs the garage door suddenly opened.

Tina put the prom ticket in her pocket, which would be its permanent place until the actual dance, and went to her room to wait. The calm before the storm would be broken soon, and Tina was ready for it.

Megan was waiting for the eighteenth beep to echo, marking the third hour since her mom had first called, when she heard a sudden gasp from Samantha and turned.

Her friend was moving around, only this time her actions seemed calculated rather than the simple shifts her body had been making earlier.

"Samantha?" she asked.

Samantha twisted her head and looked up at Megan, her eyes growing wide as she recognized her friend.

"Megan?" she asked, her lips unable to muster much sound.

"Yes," Megan said. "It's me."

Samantha closed her eyes for a moment and shook her head. A second later, she started gagging and twisted her body away from Megan. The vomit came in small harsh-sounding clumps and instantly filled the room with its stink.

Tears began falling from Samantha's eyes as she spit out some leftover residue. Small bits clung to her lips and chin. Snot dangled from her nose.

Megan felt terrible for her friend but didn't know what she could do. Above her head, she could feel her hands automatically straining against the ropes without much success. There was no way to get free.

A few more gags followed, but nothing else came up. Hearing it, however, and smelling the fresh stench as it flooded the room, made Megan feel nauseous once again. Fortunately, there was nothing within her stomach to come up.

Samantha moaned on the floor and straightened herself into a sitting position, one that would allow some slack in the rope if she were able to lift her hands. At the moment, such action did not seem possible, however.

Watching Samantha move about like this intensified Megan's discomfort, and for a moment, she yearned to be on the ground as well.

But at what cost? her mind warned.

Jimmy hadn't allowed Samantha to lie on the ground like that because he was kind; he had done it because she was broken. The question was, what had the bastard done to her to make her this way?

Rape. That was obvious. But what else?

The phone beeped.

"Eighteen," Megan said without much thought.

Samantha looked up at her and then toward the purse.

"My phone," Megan said. "My mother tried calling me three hours ago and left a message. Ever since then it's been beeping every ten minutes."

Samantha did not reply to this.

Megan didn't like how quiet her friend was being and wished she would talk with her, but she also knew not to push it. Samantha would talk when she was ready, and then the two would be able to start planning their escape.

Samantha herself couldn't remember much of what had happened, the pain being the only exception. Every second she had been hanging from her wrists had seemed an eternity. It had gotten so bad that she had actually scolded herself for trying to escape and had wanted nothing more than to have Jimmy come into the room so she could apologize and be let down.

Freedom no longer seemed possible. No one was going to find her, and Jimmy wasn't going to make the mistake of tying the ropes too loose in the future. Hell, even if he did, she wouldn't be able to use her hands afterward, so it didn't matter. Despite the time she had been sitting on the ground, her hands still felt as if they had been cut off at the wrists.

"Samantha," Megan said. "What did he do to you?"

Samantha looked over and up at her friend, still unsure if it really was Megan or just her imagination. She didn't answer the question for several minutes.

"What did he do to you?" Megan repeated, her words a bit forceful.

"Hung me," Samantha said while looking down at the floor.

Hanging from her wrists had been so terrible and exhausting that she had actually forgotten about the whipping Jimmy had given her, though the bruises and welts that covered her body still throbbed.

She shuddered at the experience, hoping he would just

kill her next time.

There won't be a next time, unless…

She looked up at Megan while thinking this and pictured her friend fighting with Jimmy. Some of the images were real images from earlier, though she didn't realize this. Instead, she just saw everything as a future event, something Megan would do if given the chance, which then would result in them both being punished.

Emotions hit.

Jimmy would be punishing her again, and this time it wouldn't be her fault. It wasn't fair.

Tears started falling again and carved new paths through the drying dampness of her earlier tears.

"It's okay," Megan said.

Samantha didn't reply. It wasn't okay.

The phone beeped again.

"Three hours and ten minutes," Megan said.

Samantha looked over at her friend and then back at her own wrists, her mind realizing that she might be able to take the pressure off them by bending her legs a bit and resting her elbows on her knees.

Would Jimmy be okay with that? she wondered.

He wouldn't have lowered you to the ground if he wasn't, another part of her mind countered.

Samantha agreed with that part of her mind and quickly shifted herself so that her knees were scrunched up toward her chest. The movement hurt her back a bit, but only in an "it will only hurt until something pops" kind of way.

A few twists and the pop echoed up her spine, relief following close behind.

Slowly Samantha lifted her arms, the muscles barely able to function, her mind having to focus everything on the simple task of getting her elbows on her knees.

It took several seconds, but eventually, despite the numbness and exhaustion, she got her elbows positioned correctly and balanced them on her knees.

Pain followed as the blood flow increased, her fingers once again filling with the much-needed fluid. At first, it wasn't much more than a discomfort, but within moments it got to the point where she couldn't stop herself from screaming, her dry crusty lips opening just enough to allow her anguish to bounce back and forth across the concrete room.

Megan couldn't stand the screams as Samantha tried to keep her wrists elevated above the ropes and quickly tried to distract herself by looking at the shelves of food. She also pressed her biceps into her ears, but that did little to drown out the sounds. Thankfully, they didn't last too long, though the gasps Samantha continued to make once the screams faded indicated that the pain hadn't eased up any. Megan didn't care, just as long as the screams had stopped.

Tina could somehow tell that Rebecca had made the discovery, and she prepared herself for the coming confrontation, but it never happened. Instead, her mother stayed in her room for a long time and then headed downstairs for a while, never once speaking to Tina or even venturing down the hallway toward her room. The situation was unnerving, especially given how uncharacteristic it was. Just the fact that Rebecca hadn't said anything about Tina not making dinner since it was her night to cook was bizarre, but stirring it in with the prom ticket situation, that made it unreal.

It's all part of a scheme, Tina said to herself while waiting on her bed.

Unfortunately, she had no idea what that scheme was, which in turn meant she couldn't prepare herself for it, thus causing her anxiety to skyrocket.

What is she waiting for?

The silence almost made Tina want to go confront her, but she knew that would be a mistake. Instead, she would just mirror Rebecca. If she wanted to play the silent game, Tina would play as well.

"Did you two stop by Taco Bell again?"

Jimmy looked up at his mother and then down at his plate, which he had barely touched.

"Jimmy did," Alan said. "I told him not to and tried to stop him, but he wouldn't listen and forced me to go with him and then threatened to tie me up and shove tacos down my throat all day if I said anything."

"Shut up!" Jimmy snapped. He shook his head and said, "We didn't stop at Taco Bell. I just got lost in thought there for a moment."

"Were you able to get yourself all measured for your tux?" Kelly Hawthorn asked.

"Tux?" George, their father, asked.

"For the prom," Kelly said.

"Prom?" George said. "You're going to the prom?"

"Yes," Jimmy said. His father always seemed one step behind when it came to current events in the Hawthorn household, despite always being around when things happened or hearing about them. It was strange and frustrating.

"Why didn't anyone tell me?"

"George, we talked about it last night at dinner," Kelly

said.

"You talked about the prom, but no one ever mentioned anything about going."

Jimmy stood up from the table and grabbed his plate, his mind too high-strung to deal with a conversation like this, and his stomach too tense to handle the heavy spaghetti dinner.

"Honey, you haven't eaten a thing," Kelly said.

"I know, I'm sorry. I'm just not hungry."

"Well, at least sit with us while we finish dinner," George said.

"I can't," Jimmy said.

"Why not?"

"I just need to get out for a while." Jimmy didn't know what else to say. All afternoon he had been thinking about Megan and what he had done after school. It had been way too risky and probably unnecessary, because chances were she wouldn't have found a thing even if she had searched the Hood place. At the time, however, his mind hadn't really thought about the risk and instead just wanted her and her thoughts on the kidnapping out of the way. He also had been excited about the idea of having another girl down there. Two was better than one.

And they are best friends.

It was this final thought, more than any others, that was really tormenting him now because he wondered if he would be able to use that friendship against them. Would he be able to force one to do something under the threat of the other being punished? Even better, would he be able to force the two to compete against each other?

In his mind, he saw both girls on their knees before

him, taking turns giving him a blow job. Whoever made him cum first and swallowed everything would get to spend the night handcuffed to the post while sitting down —no more ropes for a position like that—while the other would be stretched to the very tips of her toes all night long, or maybe even put in a strappado position.

His pants bulged with the thought.

Of course, he didn't even have the handcuffs yet to make such a situation possible, nor did he think he would be able to muster up the courage to stick his penis down their throats, even though it was something he desperately wanted to experience. It was just too risky. In time, maybe this wouldn't be the case and they would be broken enough to do whatever he asked without question, but now that wasn't possible.

I should knock out all their teeth, he thought to himself. *That would solve the problem.*

He wondered if such a thing would be possible. Could he safely remove their teeth without having to worry about infection killing them?

In his mind, he saw the pliers yanking free a tooth. Once they were removed, he would grab a bottle of peroxide and make them swish it around.

This led to another thought. *What if the girls got tooth infections and cavities because they were no longer brushing or flossing?*

God, he hadn't even thought about this. A tooth infection could be fatal if left untreated.

He would have to start having them brush their teeth, or brush them for them if they refused to cooperate.

"Jimmy, why don't you put the plate in the fridge in case you want some later," Kelly suggested.

"Okay," Jimmy said. He had already been planning to

do just that. Moments later the plate was sealed up with Saran wrap and sitting on the bottom shelf.

He headed down to his room, his plan being to head to the fallout shelter once everyone went to bed, the way he used to wait to watch bondage flicks he had ordered in the mail or downloaded, the distance between his room in the basement and their rooms on the second floor making it so he could have the sound on low without worrying about them hearing it. Of course, one hand was always ready to mute things if he heard movement above.

Unfortunately, once he was in his room he couldn't stop thinking about Megan and Samantha, a mix of excitement and terror illuminating the situation.

You shouldn't have grabbed Megan, his mind would say. *Not with her father being the sheriff.*

This was always followed by an image of how hot she looked with her hands stretched over her head, her large breasts thrust forward against her tight shirt, her body waiting for whatever violations he had in mind.

The thoughts led him to look at some bondage sites on the computer, his goal being to find pictures similar to the image of Megan that he carried in his mind. Several of them appeared on screen without much effort, but there wasn't any real thrill or excitement at seeing them. This didn't stop him from saving the pictures to his hard drive, but it did make him realize he wasn't going to wait until his family went to bed to go see Samantha and Megan. Nope. He was going now.

"What are you doing?" Samantha asked.

Megan didn't answer right away and instead focused on turning her purse upside down. It wasn't an easy task, despite how simple it seemed. Every time she hooked her foot through the strap and tried to flip the purse, her foot would slip free, and every time she tried to simply scoot her foot under the purse and flip it over, she would only manage to push the purse farther away. Once that happened she had to hook the strap again and pull the purse back. It was frustrating.

"What are you doing?" Samantha asked again.

"Trying to get my cell phone out," Megan snapped.

Anger at herself for not thinking about the possibility of calling someone this entire time was getting the better of her. The fact that they had gone so long without Jimmy coming back also added to this because it would have given her ample time to get the phone in position, get her shoe off, and dial a number with her toe. Now, however, Jimmy could return any second, and would surely take the phone away, especially if he heard one of the beeps.

She just couldn't believe how stupid she had been.

Five hours.

They could have been rescued by now and Jimmy in custody if she had made the call right away, but instead she had just stood there like a fool, her body getting weaker and weaker, her mind growing more and more terrified.

"Why?" Samantha asked.

"*So I can fucking call someone!*" Megan shouted as her foot once again slipped free. *Goddammit!*

"Don't," Samantha said. "He'll punish us."

"Not if I can get the phone out and call my dad before he gets back." She hooked the purse again, and once again it slipped free.

The phone beeped.

Five hours and twenty minutes.

"*Megan, please!*" Samantha cried. "*He'll hurt us bad!*"

"*Samantha! This is our only chance!*" Megan couldn't believe her friend. "Now help me flip over the purse. You are close enough to tip it with your feet."

Despite her pain, Samantha inched toward the purse, but rather than helping Megan tip it over, she kicked it as hard as she could.

"*What the fuck!*" Megan screamed, her foot stopping the purse at the last second before it slid too far away. "Samantha!"

"He'll hang me again," Samantha cried while trying to kick it again, tears falling from her eyes. "He'll hang me all day!"

Megan tried getting the purse out of Samantha's reach and then kicked at her feet. "Stop it!"

Samantha didn't, and Megan was forced to hit her friend as hard as she could in the shin. The impact hurt her own foot and caused her friend to scream again.

"Samantha, listen to me," Megan said, her voice stern. "We are going to die down here unless someone finds us, and this phone is our best chance at the moment."

Wet sobs were the only reply she got.

Megan couldn't believe her friend yet knew it wasn't fully her fault. Still, one good kick and the purse would have been completely out of reach. One good kick and Samantha could have sentenced them to death.

"Samantha, I'm going to get this phone," Megan said. "Now, if you don't want to be a part of it, just stay right there and don't move, okay?"

Samantha continued to cry.

"If Jimmy finds out, I will tell him you had no part in this."

"It won't matter," Samantha said.

"Are you going to help me?" Megan asked.

Samantha shook her head.

"Fine."

Megan turned back to her purse and quickly tried to think up a way of flipping it over. A moment later an idea struck and she used her left foot to take off her right shoe, something that would have to have been done anyway once the phone was free, and started reaching into the purse with her toes in an attempt to scoop everything out.

It worked and the phone came free, only it landed facedown.

Megan tried to grab it with her toes to flip it, but her socks made it impossible to grab. She needed to remove them.

Beep!

God, he could be here any second!

Needing her other foot free from the shoe, Megan used her right to push against the heel, making it possible to slip free. Once that was done, she attempted to slip the toes of her left foot into the sock of her right and pulled. Once again, the task was harder than it seemed, and she spent several minutes trying and failing, growing more and more desperate, until finally she managed to slip the sock over her ankle and then her heel.

Beep!

The sock was free.

Now she just had to grab the phone with her toes, flip it over, and call her father.

Samantha's foot came out of nowhere and nearly hit the phone, the surprise strike only being deflected at the last second by Megan's ankle, which hurt.

"Goddammit!" Megan screamed at her friend and kicked her as hard as she could, the nail of her big toe cutting into the flesh of Samantha's calf. "STOP IT!"

Samantha didn't, and Megan was forced to deflect several more attacks and then went on the offensive again.

Beep!

Things settled for a moment and Megan went back to trying to grip the phone, her foot hurting from the battle, her eyes going back and forth between the task at hand and watching Samantha, her mind wishing Jimmy had just left her hanging from her wrists so she couldn't reach the phone.

It took three tries before she got the phone flipped over. Once that was done she tried using her toe to start dialing, her mind so focused on her father's phone number that she didn't even realize she could have just done 911, which would have been a whole lot simpler.

Her toe hit the fourth button needed. At the same moment, a sound echoed from the door.

Oh God!

She found the fifth button and then the sixth.

One more to go.

She heard the door start to open.

She got the seventh button. The number was complete. All she needed to do was hit Send.

Jimmy entered the room.

Megan hit Send.

The sound of the phone ringing on the other end filled the room.

Megan looked toward Jimmy and saw his eyes go wide. At the same moment, Samantha managed to kick the phone, which went across the room, and shouted that she had told Megan not to call.

"Megan, is that you?" her father cried into the phone. "Are you all right?"

Jimmy lunged across the room.

"Daddy, help me!" Megan screamed. "Jimmy Hawthorn has got us at the Hood place!"

There was no reply. Jimmy smashed the phone with his foot before she finished screaming. The question was, had her father heard enough to find them?

Jimmy looked back and forth between the smashed phone and Megan, panic building, his mind unable to comprehend anything but the words Megan had screamed into the phone: *Jimmy Hawthorn has got us at the Hood place!*

He didn't know what to do.

"I told her not to call!" Samantha said, her lips repeating the words over and over again. "I tried to stop her!"

"Shut up!" Jimmy snapped.

"I told her not to," Samantha continued.

"SHUT UP!" He grabbed her by the hair while shouting this and yanked her head back so that her throat was completely stretched and vulnerable.

"Let her go, you bastard!"

Jimmy turned and stared at Megan. Beneath his panic was anger, both at himself and at her, all of which would be taken out on her.

Samantha whimpered beneath him.

He let go of her hair and started toward Megan, who took a few steps back, fear momentarily touching her face before being replaced with a look of defiance.

Jimmy grabbed her by her cheeks and said, "I

smashed the phone too soon. He doesn't know you're here."

Megan tried to twist free of his hand but couldn't.

"And now you will pay for trying—"

His voice was cut short as her knee smashed up into his testicles, the sudden sharp pain making his entire body seem too heavy to fight gravity as he tried to back away, his feet managing two small steps before everything simply collapsed.

"Try to get it up now, you fucking pervert!" Megan screamed.

Jimmy heard but didn't really register the words, his mind only able to focus on one thing, that being the strange hollow sensation that encased his groin region.

On the other side, Samantha was sobbing uncontrollably.

Jimmy lay on the ground for a long time.

Slowly the sharp pain fizzled into a dull throb, one that was unpleasant but manageable. The hollow numbness faded as well but didn't go away completely.

He tried to get up, but his legs were barely able to support his weight, and his stomach turned over.

Thankfully, he hadn't really eaten much, so nothing came up.

He stayed on his knees for nearly a minute, his hands palms down on the cold concrete floor, helping to support his weight.

A few feet away, Megan continued to taunt him.

Fear crept into her head as she watched Jimmy struggling on the floor, a feeling that competed with the enormous amount of satisfaction kneeing him in the balls had produced. Fear of both him and the fact that her father might not have heard enough to come rescue her.

Please come, her mind begged. *Please come before he gets up and hurts me.*

Kneeing Jimmy in the groin had been completely involuntary and was something she would have done to any guy who grabbed her like that. Now, however, a part of her wished she hadn't done it simply because she knew it had created a pain debt that Jimmy would make her pay. At the same time, she knew he would do tons of horrible things to her, so hurting him wouldn't really matter much. Fighting back was also better than lying down and letting him do whatever the hell he wanted with her.

Still, she worried what the consequences of the knee strike would be, looking at Samantha while thinking about this.

Her friend whimpered on the floor like a frightened dog, one that feared daily beatings from its owner for stupid infractions.

I will not become like that.
I will not openly show fear.

It took several minutes, but eventually Jimmy managed to stand up and move around, his legs still weak yet finally able to support his weight once again.

Anger filled the void as the pain started to leave, but for the moment, he held it in check because he knew he needed to see if Megan's call had accomplished anything, or if he had broken the connection in time.

What if the police are swarming the Hood place?

Jimmy had no idea what his actions would be, but did know one thing: Megan would not live to see the results of her call. No. If it became apparent that he would not leave the Hood place of his own accord, then the last moments of his freedom would be spent killing Megan, his hands working as slowly as the lawmen up above would allow him to work.

"What's the matter?" Megan taunted. "You gonna go home and cry to mommy?"

Jimmy did not reply, though the words did anger him, and continued toward the door. Once on the stairs of the fallout shelter, he crept up slowly until his body was pressed against the trapdoor, his hand slowly lifting it so that he would not give away his position if anyone were around.

The area above was silent. Nothing seemed to be stirring around the Hood place.

That doesn't mean they aren't on their way.

Jimmy hesitated.

If he went home now, he could get a running start if they discovered he was responsible for the two girls. At the same time, he doubted he would actually be able to get away, and wondered if it would be better to just stay in the shelter and take all the pleasure he could get from the girls before being locked up.

I should have brought the gun.

With the gun, he could hold the police off for a long time, especially if they knew the two girls were down here, his body enjoying them for as long as the food and water supply held out. Things would get pretty nasty after a while, especially without any bathroom facilities, but it would be worth it.

The thought caused the start of an erection, one that hurt like hell yet still felt somewhat pleasurable. It was an odd combination.

Minutes came and went and still nothing stirred, the only sound being a car that drove by on the road, one that seemed to be going the normal speed for cars taking the wooded turn—forty to fifty miles per hour, despite the speed limit sign stating twenty-five.

Jimmy checked his phone a few times, deciding that if no one came around by eight o'clock it probably meant he was in the clear.

Unless they are at your house.

Shit. Megan had shouted his name before the Hood place, which meant they might know it was him but not where he had them.

Do I have anything at home that could point them in this direction?

Jimmy thought back but knew the only thing he had ever brought back from the Hood place was the gun he had found, which had been left inside the fallout shelter, the Hood family having probably forgotten it, given how many guns they possessed and grabbed while fleeing.

The bondage videos.

Nothing he owned was illegal, but if the police found the tapes, they might grow incredibly suspicious of him. Then again, even without the tapes, just the fact that Megan had said his name might make them suspicious as well.

Fuck!

He had no idea what to do. A part of him wanted to ride home and get rid of the tapes, that was, if the sheriff wasn't already there waiting for him. Another part wanted to stay here and take out his anger on Megan.

Don't be stupid. You can take out the anger any time.

This was true.

He looked at his phone again. It wasn't quite eight o'clock yet, but he had a feeling nothing was going to happen here and quickly headed back into the fallout shelter. Five minutes later he was back on the surface of the Hood place, unhooking his bike from the tree he had chained it to, a chain which he had found in the garage at home and used a padlock to secure. Brett and his friends would need bolt cutters to get at his bike, and he doubted they carried them.

Once free, he hopped up onto the bike and then quickly jumped off with a curse, having not given any thought to how painful the seat would be to his swollen testicles.

He tried again a minute later once things cooled off, his movements much slower this time. The pain was still there, but it was manageable.

Megan found herself struggling for breath minutes after Jimmy left, her lungs feeling as if her breasts and rib cage were squeezing them to the point where they couldn't expand. Her wrists also screamed in agony. In fact, they had been screaming since the moment Jimmy had pulled her off her feet, feet that were now desperately trying to find the ground.

Samantha was hanging too, though she didn't struggle, the tears streaming down her face the only sign that she was suffering as well.

Oh God, make it stop!

Megan couldn't take it. Her entire body hurt. Jimmy hadn't even done anything to her after pulling her off the ground, yet it felt like she was experiencing the worst punishment ever.

And his words as he was leaving promised worse to

come when he returned. *What could be worse than this?*

"Ughhhh!" she moaned while trying to touch the ground. Her feet couldn't even get close. It was only about five inches below her, yet it might as well have been a mile.

And her wrists! God they hurt. The ropes felt like they were chewing their way through her flesh, and beyond them her fingers strained to move around, each one trying to find a spot to grab the ropes to ease the pressure but unable to find a hold.

Torture.

This was what torture was. It was something she had never understood before. Now she knew why people confessed. She would do anything to be let down.

Nothing she could do would work, however, and her body would continue to slowly twist in the air, her feet unable to touch the ground until Jimmy returned.

She hoped it was soon, even if worse was to come. She didn't care what it was just as long as he lowered her.

No, don't give in to him!

The part that was in pain ignored the words from the stubborn part of her body, a part that was quickly shrinking.

Her body twisted around and she came face-to-face with Samantha, who stared back at her.

Megan wanted to apologize but couldn't find the words and then twisted away, her body unable to control the sway the rope caused.

She kicked her legs, thinking that if she jerked on the rope hard enough something would snap. Unfortunately, all she managed was to create more pressure on her wrists, which was something she couldn't handle.

Her body twisted back the other way, and once again

she was looking at Samantha. *I'm sorry,* she mouthed, no sound arriving, her lungs still straining to get in normal breaths of air.

Samantha did not acknowledge her. She didn't react in any way at all, her own body slowly twisting away.

The ache in his groin and testicles reached the unbearable mark six minutes into his ride home, and he was forced to jump down from the bike and walk. While doing this he noticed an obvious increase in the amount of sheriff's department vehicles that were patrolling the area, but he was relieved when none of the deputies paid him any attention.

He probably didn't hear my name, just the screams from Megan.

Still, he felt very uncomfortable out in the open like this and wanted to get home. At the same time, he knew that pacing himself would be best because he didn't want anyone to think he was running from something.

No one was waiting for him at home, but just to be sure it wasn't a trap, Jimmy entered through the front door and then hurried out the back door, Alan giving him a puzzled look from the family room couch where he was watching TV.

No one swarmed the house upon his arrival, and eventually Jimmy left the cover of the bushes in back, ones that were completely in shadow now that the sun had nearly set, and went back inside.

"What was that?" Alan asked.

"Oh, nothing, I just wanted to see something," Jimmy lied. "I think Brett was following me."

"Again?"

"Yeah, so I left the bike on the front porch and then ran around to the side of the house and waited. I figured

I could jump him when he tried to take it."

"Did he?"

"No."

"That's good, but you should have had me hide with you. I want a piece of that bastard as well."

"Oh, sorry. Next time."

"Yeah. Battle?"

"Um, okay."

The two battled for nearly an hour, Alan winning every game, even the ones where Jimmy should have dominated given the level they chose. Jimmy wasn't surprised, though. While playing he had only been able to think about two things: one being the fear that the police would find him, two being the image of both Megan and Samantha hanging from their wrists.

Stop! Stop! Stop! Megan had cried while Jimmy lifted her off the ground, her words turning into screams as the rope bit into her flesh, her legs kicking every which way in an attempt to relieve the pressure by finding something to stand on.

Samantha, on the other hand, hadn't protested at all, her body simply sagging against the ropes as he lifted her off the ground, her whimpering the only evidence that she was even aware of the situation.

Watching them both being lifted like that had been incredibly stimulating, and for a moment he had considered sticking around with them just so he could watch as they suffered. But then the fear of the phone call and what Megan's father might have heard once again expressed itself, and he knew he had to head home.

He thought about his bondage tapes, the idea of getting rid of them weighing heavy on his mind. He didn't want to do it. He didn't want to destroy items that he had once waited days to receive, his eyes constantly watching the mailbox, his heart racing every time he saw the mail truck outside, his mind trying to picture what the scenes would be like but unable to even comprehend what it was he had ordered. It had been an amazing moment, though one that he hadn't realized would mark the start of his dissatisfaction with the staged scenes, especially when so few of them had long-term hands-over-the-head displays. He also never again waded through countless hours of piss-poor movies just because there was a chance it would contain a hands-over-the-head scene, something which he had done for years, first with movies and shows on TV, and then, once he had his driver's license, with movies he rented from every video store he could find.

"Another battle?" Alan asked.

"Nah, I have to get some work done."

"Oh, okay."

With that, Jimmy headed into his room and waited, listening for Alan to head back up the stairs. Once that happened, he dug into his closet and pulled out an old box, one that was completely filled with VHS tapes. A series of red numbers marked the front of each. It was his way of coding the tapes so that his parents wouldn't see the titles if they ever stumbled upon them, titles like *Asian Schoolgirl Bondage Vol. 5*, *Pain and Punishment Vol. 2*, and *European Girls Bound and Fucked*.

The first bondage tape he had ever ordered had been *The Witchfinder*. He had thought that with such a title the movie would have countless scenes of medieval dungeons where peasant girls were chained up in shackles and tortured without mercy until they confessed.

Instead, the dungeon location had been nothing more than a painted-on brick wall with modern-day bondage items, the girls wearing costumes that didn't have any historical accuracy to them, their torture more of an erotic torment. Jimmy had still gotten off on it many times, but had also been incredibly disappointed.

Other videos hadn't been so bad, but none of them had ever given him the scenes he really craved. Even the Internet had been a disappointment, though that hadn't stopped him from searching out images and videos daily, his eyes always on the lookout for something good.

The really sad thing was that his favorite bondage scene moments, before grabbing Samantha and Megan, had been ones he had stumbled upon on TV when he was younger. *The People Under the Stairs, The Lair of the White Worm, Slave Girls from Beyond Infinity, Howling II, No Retreat, No Surrender 2, Chained Heat 2, American Ninja 4,* and *Burial of the Rats* had all been movies he saw on TV or rented from the video store without knowing whether or not they would have a scene in them, and he watched with growing anticipation as the story unfolded just to see, his heart always starting to race if a female in the movie was ever taken prisoner. *Howling II* was probably one of his favorite moments. Alan and he had just finished picking out pumpkins to carve for Halloween from a local farm, and he had gone into his room to make sure the VCR was taping the movie, which he had read about in *TV Guide*. The description hadn't said anything about a girl being strung up from her wrists, but it had mentioned they would be in Transylvania and that there would be castles, which meant the possibility of dungeons, which was enough for him to tape it. Sure enough, a scene came on where the main female girl was captured. After that, Jimmy sat down and waited to see where the girl ended up, heart racing, mind unable to focus on anything but the TV screen. And then the scene arrived. It started out with the camera zoomed in on a wall of skulls while a girl moaned in the background. The moan was what really got him excited. After that, the camera started to shift to the left. Jimmy's heart raced even faster, his groin tingling, his mind begging for a hanging-from-the-wrists scene, and then there she was, hanging from her wrists. It was an amazing moment, one that other guys might compare with an early discovery of *Playboy* or *Penthouse*. Afterward Jimmy had watched the scene over and over again, his hand constantly bringing him to orgasm until finally he grew tired of it and went in search of other scenes.

What happens when you get tired of Samantha and Megan? Jimmy asked himself suddenly.

An unpleasant answer followed.

CHAPTER NINE

"Whoa, what is going on?" Tina asked as Alan, Jimmy, and she stepped into the school parking lot that Thursday morning, their tired bodies having barely spoken more than simple greetings as they walked toward the school, a situation that was typical given the early hour. The commotion outside the school, however, was atypical, and for a moment all three of them stopped in their tracks, their eyes needing a moment to take everything in.

"It looks like they have sheriff's deputies at every entrance," Alan said.

"You don't think there was a shooting?" Tina asked.

"No," Alan said. "They wouldn't be letting anyone inside if there had been. It's more like they are directing traffic or something." He turned toward Jimmy. "What do you think?"

"I don't know," Jimmy said with a shrug. It was a lie. He knew exactly what was going on, or at least knew what had prompted whatever was going on, and he now regretted the bag of bondage tapes he had stuck in his backpack, ones that he had planned on throwing away during lunch, because for all he knew they were searching the students.

No, more likely they are asking students questions, he said to himself in an attempt to calm his mind down. *You have nothing to worry about.*

Still, bringing the tapes to school had been a stupid idea. He should have just left them at home and thrown them away that afternoon. Nothing would have happened during the seven hours he was away. No one would have searched his room.

If they do search your room, it's because they know something and the tapes will just be another nail in the coffin.

"Shit!" Jimmy snapped.

"What?" Alan asked.

"I must've dropped my pen back there." He pulled an empty hand out of his pocket while saying this, even though the pen was still inside. "I think I know right where it is."

"I have an extra pen," Tina said. She started to open her purse.

"Nah, that's okay. I really like my pen." With that, he quickly turned and headed back down the sidewalk until he had rounded the corner near the dugout of the baseball field where a beat-up garbage can stood. Nothing but a few pop bottles and an empty pack of cigarettes were inside. A moment later, the plastic bag full of bondage tapes joined them. A sense of loss followed them down. He had spent so many hours acquiring those tapes and watching them at night that he couldn't stand to see them go.

Let them go he did, however, and quickly hurried back to the parking lot where Alan and Tina were waiting, the pen now in his hands, the words "Found it" leaving his lips.

"That was lucky," Alan said.

"I know, but I remembered hearing something drop while I was walking by the dugout, and sure enough, it was right there, so I didn't really have to look much at all." He looked at the school and the mobs of students at every door being filtered inside by the deputies. Getting rid of the tapes was a relief, though it wasn't enough to completely do away with the fear of being caught and arrested for the abductions of Samantha and Megan. Even worse, he doubted anything would ever do away with that fear. Even if he disposed of the bodies really well once he killed them—something that he should probably do sooner rather than later—he knew there was always a chance someone would discover something that pointed in his direction.

Speculation and random bits of chatter met them as they connected with the group of students waiting by Entrance Three—the school had six entrances—most of which was an unintelligible mix of gibberish due to all the different statements colliding and bisecting each other.

"…probably searching for drugs…"

"…they stole a bunch of…"

"…Megan Reed is missing…"

Jimmy twisted around to look toward the girl who had spoken this last bit, but couldn't figure out where the words had come from. He also knew it didn't really matter. Grabbing Megan Reed had been a mistake because of her relation to the sheriff. Any other girl and the sheriff could have still dismissed the idea of a predator stalking the teenage girls of Ashland Creek, though with growing dismay from many in the town, but with Megan he obviously wasn't going to sit back.

You had no choice, a part of his mind said. *She would have found the shelter.*

Or at least she might have caused interest in the Hood place that would eventually lead to the shelter being found.

Or maybe nothing would have come of it.

What is done is done.

Besides, he was enjoying having Megan in the shelter. Seeing her hanging from her wrists was incredible, her body perfect for such a position. In fact, she had looked so good that he hadn't wanted to lower her this morning, but had done so fearing he would accidentally kill her—this based on the gasps her lungs were making when he entered the shelter in the predawn hours. Not that he wasn't planning on killing her eventually—this he had decided last night while lying in bed, his plan being to slowly hang her from the neck—he just wanted to make sure he was able to enjoy it rather than find out it had already happened. Plus, if he enjoyed their deaths, then at least the girls could go into the next life knowing they had meant something, even if they didn't agree with his getting off on it.

The three made it to the door and were ushered in by a deputy who said, "Please head into the gymnasium for an announcement."

"How come?" a student behind them asked.

"Please, just go to the gymnasium," the deputy repeated. "Everything will be explained to you there."

The three did as they were told, all of them deciding to bypass their lockers since they had no coats and would carry their bags with them to class anyway.

* * *

"Fuck this shit," Brett said. "Let's go."

"Go where?" Matt asked.

"To your place, man. I want to see what the fag threw out."

"Who cares?"

"I care," Brett snapped. "And I'll be damned if I'm gonna sit for an hour during some stupid assembly shit while I could be watching whatever is on these tapes."

"Man, they're garbage."

"Yeah, and he just happened to throw them away when he saw the police at the school. What're you, stupid? He was worried the police would see what was on these tapes. Probably thought the cops were searching everyone just like you." Brett shook his head. "And fuck, man, why would you toss out that premium California shit I gave you to hold? Do you know how much that fucking bag cost?"

"What would you do if you saw the police at the school?" Matt snapped. "And fuck, I was gonna grab it on the way back anyway. I just didn't want to be caught with it at school."

Once Matt had seen the police at the school, he had decided to throw out the bag of marijuana that Brett had given him to hold the other day, his reasoning being that his older brother would steal it. Matt didn't like the stuff anyway, and the last thing he wanted was to be caught with the shit right before graduation, especially that much of it. Apparently, he hadn't been the only one tossing stuff out, though he had never in a million years expected to see Jimmy Hawthorn dumping something. The fact that it was a bunch of VHS tapes made it even more unusual, which, of course, caused him to mention it to Brett. Naturally, Brett couldn't let something like that slide—the guy was obsessed—and grabbed the tapes and the discarded bag of marijuana.

"Grab it on the way back from school," Brett said. "Look up, you see that sky? You know what those dark clouds mean? Please tell me you aren't that fucking retarded? God is going to be pissing on us all day from up there, and you think the dope would have stayed good in that garbage can?" Brett shook his head. "The baggers at the grocery store are smarter than you."

Matt didn't reply to this, thinking he only had a few more weeks and then everything was good. He was going away for college, and Brett wouldn't be there with him.

"Come on, let's go to your place. I know no one is home. We'll chill in your basement."

"I can't ditch school," Matt protested.

"Dude, we just tell everyone we thought they wouldn't let anyone in, that there was some sort of emergency like the time that pipe burst in the bathroom and flooded everything."

Matt shook his head again.

"Don't be such a pussy," Brett said while pulling out his car keys. "Come on."

Matt followed him to the car.

"Wow, this is serious," Tina said.

Jimmy nodded.

"Can you imagine being grabbed like that while walking home from school?"

"No," Jimmy said.

"I mean, why would they get close enough to the guy's car?" Tina asked. "Unless maybe they knew him?"

"But that would mean someone in town was behind this," Jimmy said.

"You don't think that's the case?"

"I don't know, but if it was, who would it be?"

Tina shook her head. "You know them better than me. It's scary, though."

Jimmy felt a tap on his shoulder and turned to see a teacher he recognized but had never had class with before standing in the bleacher aisle with her arms crossed. "Pay attention," she said.

"Sorry," Jimmy whispered.

Down below, the sheriff and the school principal continued to talk about staying safe and walking in groups of three and four when coming to or leaving school from now on, how leaving school for lunch was now forbidden, about the phone number that could be called if anyone knew anything, and how a temporary town curfew was being discussed—angry boos followed this last part.

"They better not fuck up prom," a girl below them said, her voice loud enough to turn heads all across this section of the bleachers.

The teacher who had tapped Jimmy on the shoulder headed toward her and quietly demanded to know which one of the girls in the group below had used the dreaded F-word. None of them confessed.

Give them to me, Jimmy thought to himself. *I'll make them confess.* An image of each girl hanging from her wrists appeared in his mind, weights slowly but surely being added to their ankles to loosen their tongues.

Instead, the teacher just told all of them to see her after the assembly, probably because each one of them would have detention unless one of them came forward. Such punishments didn't seem right, kind of like putting a dozen people in prison unless one confessed to the store robbery or something, but no one would cry out against it.

"Man, this is sick," Matt said while watching a tied-up girl in a red leather outfit being forced to suck on a flesh-colored dildo. "Turn it off."

"Wait, this one's probably almost over," Brett said, completely fascinated by the tape they were watching. "The other one didn't last too long."

The two were in Matt's basement, which his parents had allowed him to set up as a hangout for his friends. Most of the time, though, their group would head somewhere else, the basement only used as a place of last resort due to how close the parental units always were. During ditch days, though, the place was great.

Horrible gagging sounds echoed from the TV as the girl's head was pushed farther down the fake penis.

Matt looked away and once again told Brett to turn it off, but his friend wouldn't listen.

"Can you imagine if that was your dick?" Brett asked. "Man, that would feel so good."

"You really want to tie a girl up and make her do that?"

"Fuck no. That's sick. But to have a girl do that just 'cause she wants to. It's like pure heaven."

"Until she loses her lunch all over you." He watched the screen for a few more seconds. The girl was told to stop by a leather-clad woman who got up on top of the fake penis and started fucking it, the tied-up girl using her tongue to pleasure the woman while she did this. "Man, seriously, turn it off. I don't want this shit on in my house."

"What's the matter? Is it turning you on too much?"

"Fuck you," Matt said and went over to the TV to turn it off.

"Fine," Brett said. "Let's see what's on the others." Brett hit the Stop button while saying this and went over to the bag of tapes. "Here, this one says SB nine twenty-seven on it. What do you think that means?"

"I don't know. Man, why would Jimmy watch this shit?"

"Because he's a sick twisted motherfucker."

Brett was right about that.

The next tape started up.

"Great, this one's in another language too," Brett said as something French looking was displayed across the screen.

"I don't think people care what language it's in," Matt said.

"You're the expert."

A shot of two girls appeared, both of them in white blouses and black jumpers. The two looked like schoolgirl students but were probably around nineteen or twenty—Matt hoped—and were both kneeling with their heads bowed in a bright room. The footage was grainy, almost homemade looking, and the sound, despite being in another language, was soft and difficult to hear, the absence of microphones obvious.

"Pretty cute, really," Brett said. "The one with the dangling earrings and the blue eye shadow kind of looks like your sister."

Matt glared at Brett.

"Did your sister ever go overseas?" Brett continued.

"One more word and I'll fucking take that pipe over there and smash your head in," Matt said.

Brett must've heard something in Matt's voice that

startled him, because he didn't say anything else.

On screen, the two girls shifted positions so that they were both kneeling with their butts up in the air. An older woman, once again clad in leather, though less leather than the woman in the other video, lifted both their skirts, exposing their bare butts, and began to spank them with a long thin rod.

The girls' screams sounded real, as did the painful-looking hits.

Two minutes into the spankings, Brett hit the fast-forward button and waited. Eventually the spanking ended and the two girls started playing with each other, and then were ordered to a large black dildo on a small round table. Together the two started sucking on it.

"Same storyline, different girls," Matt said. "That's all this shit ever is."

"Yeah," Brett agreed.

The two continued to watch. The morning hours quickly turned to afternoon hours as they went through most of the tapes, their minds both fascinated and disturbed by what they saw. One video was so intense that Brett was the one to turn it off, the words "I can't watch that shit" leaving his mouth. The fact that the video contained an actual enema scene made his description both literal and figurative.

"What are you gonna do with these?" Matt asked at one point, this after they had watched a man being tied up and fucked in the ass and mouth at the same time by two women with fake penises.

"I don't know, broadcast them on the TVs at school and tell everyone they're Jimmy's," Brett said.

"Yeah, um, I don't think people will believe you. If he were actually in the video that would be one thing, but anyone could have thrown these away. People will think you're just messing with him and then will wonder why you have the tapes."

"Good point."

The two went silent, the only sounds being a woman crying out as she was whipped.

"I wonder if Jimmy's girlfriend knows about these," Brett said after a while.

"What?"

"If she doesn't, maybe we should inform her about them so she knows what a sick perverted bastard he is."

"Again, you have no proof they're his," Matt said.

"Ah, but if she confronts him about it, he may not realize that right away and might accidentally reveal it to be true. Right?"

"Right," Matt said. "You gonna do it today?"

"Nah, I think I have a better idea."

Many years earlier, Megan's father had dragged the family up to Wisconsin to camp out on Redstone Lake, a place he had traveled to a lot with his family while growing up, a place that he claimed was haunted in an attempt to scare them. The family had two small tents for the trip, both of them old Boy Scout tents that their father had used as a kid, ones that had been sitting on a shelf in the garage her entire life, an inch of dust sealing them, hundreds of insects calling the folded-over portions home. At first things had been fun, but then at some point during the night the weather changed and a storm came upon them. Within minutes, the wear and tear the tents had experienced became known as water leaked in from just about every part of the sagging roof. Unfortunately, the floors of the tents weren't as worn out as the tops of the tents, because the water that filtered in through the ceiling and walls pooled easily, soaking everything and making it impossible for them to sleep, even after Megan and her brother had folded themselves into a small, seemingly rainproof corner. Even worse, the storm made it difficult to find the car, which was nearly a mile away, and once there they quickly learned that even though they were no longer being rained on, the mugginess inside the car wouldn't let them dry out or sleep. They also couldn't lie down, thanks to the decision to take the car rather than the van because of gas prices. It had been a horrible night, the worst of Megan's entire life until yesterday, one that she would now give anything to be experiencing over and over again if it just meant she was free from this god-awful place.

At least you're back on your feet.

For a while, Megan didn't even realize she was allowed to stand, nor did she remember Jimmy even coming in this morning—just bits and pieces of him moving about and talking, which all could have easily been memories from the other day. Instead, once she had woken up, she had felt the pain of her body being held up by the ropes, and the shortness of her own breath as she tried to breathe, and assumed she was still hanging. But then her legs realized they were touching the ground, but not standing upon it, and quickly corrected the situation.

Pain followed, and for the first time Megan realized why Samantha had screamed the other day once she had been able to stand up. It was the blood returning to her fingers, only now it wasn't the annoying tingle one got when she slept on a limb all night. This was pure agony, almost as if the blood were shocking the tissue back to life.

Not wanting to scream even though Jimmy wasn't there to hear it, Megan ground her teeth together and waited it out. Eventually it faded, but until it did, Megan wasn't able to think of anything else, her mind completely focused on what felt like millions of tiny razors flowing through her veins.

Time came and went.

Megan had no way of marking its passage. What seemed like minutes may have been hours; what seemed like hours may have only been minutes.

She stared at her friend while thinking this, her body swaying back and forth as it dangled from the ropes, her toes acting like weak anchors on the cold concrete floor.

"Samantha?" Megan said.

Her friend didn't reply.

"Samantha!" Screaming her name sapped all her energy, which was startling. Seeing her friend hanging lifeless was worse, however, so she screamed again, and again, and again, until finally Samantha's eyes fluttered open.

Not dead!

Samantha's eyes moved around a bit and then closed again, her body making no effort to stand, her head not even turning as her eyes took everything in.

"Samantha, wake up!"

Nothing.

"Samantha!"

Anger built.

A part of her wanted to wake Samantha because she felt that while awake it would be harder to slip into death. Another part, the bigger part, wanted her awake because Megan couldn't stand to be alone, and with Samantha unconscious, she might as well have been alone.

Please wake up. Her exhaustion was too much to say it out loud this time. *Please!*

Samantha still didn't stir, and this time when she pissed herself again, no moan of relief followed. This more than anything else frightened Megan. She didn't want her friend to die.

Later she wondered if maybe death would be better. After all, it didn't seem like her father was going to find them.

If only you had tried to call sooner!

With that thought, Megan spent what had to be hours berating herself for being so stupid, the anger she directed at herself unlike any belittlement she had ever experienced. It was awful.

"My mother actually called the school once she heard about Megan Reed," Tina said at lunch. "She wants me staying after and waiting to be picked up."

"What?" Jimmy asked.

The two were eating lunch, only this time they didn't have the second half of the table to themselves because the school had suspended off-campus lunch privileges. There still was a chair space between them and the others who had reluctantly sat down on their side of the table, and no conversation had breeched it, yet Jimmy still felt incredibly closed in by them and guarded his words, not liking the possibility of others listening in, even though what they said wasn't private and those near him wouldn't even care.

"At first I said *no*, but she told the school to put me in detention if I didn't stay on campus and to cancel my prom ticket." Tina shook her head. "I don't think they will really cancel my ticket, but I'm not sure if I should risk it, you know."

Jimmy nodded. "I think staying would be good just to be safe. It would really suck if you couldn't go."

"It would," Tina agreed. "But I bet they would let me in if I came, even if my ticket was canceled. I mean, how would they really know?"

"They might, but still, why risk it? And it's just one afternoon."

"She wants me staying after tomorrow too."

"But seniors get to go home at lunchtime tomorrow."

"She doesn't care. She doesn't want me staying at the house all by myself. I think a part of it is because she knows I went through it and found the prom ticket after she took it from me. It's like a punishment."

"Has she said anything about that?"

"No. It's really weird. The whole thing gives me a bad feeling."

The two went quiet after that, though the lunchroom was anything but. The extra students were making it incredibly loud, so loud that Jimmy and Tina had to shout to each other, though the two didn't even realize it.

"Is the library even open till five thirty?" Jimmy asked after a while.

"I assumed it would be," Tina said. "Why wouldn't it?"

"Budget cuts. The state has missed most of its payments this year, so the school has been cutting several things, the library staff being one of them."

Tina was about to ask where he had learned this, but then remembered that Jimmy had an economy class and figured the teacher had told them all about it.

"I think it now closes at four fifteen or something like

that," Jimmy added.

"Great, what am I gonna do after that?"

"I don't know. Your mother should just let you go home. Nothing's going to happen to you."

"That's what I said. I told her I walked home with you and Alan, but she doesn't care. It's crazy."

"Maybe I should come meet her so she'll be comfortable with me," Jimmy said. "Adults always seem to like me for some reason."

"My mother's different," Tina said. "You could be the greatest guy in the world and I still don't think she would like you."

"Wait, I'm not the greatest guy in the world?"

Tina laughed.

Brett couldn't help but think about the videos he had found while sitting in the waiting area of the dean's office, and the fact that Jimmy got off on them. He had always known Jimmy was fucked up, but never knew exactly what it was that was wrong with him. Now he did. Even better, the school would know soon as well because during the school prom he was going to show everyone what a pervert Jimmy was. It was going to be great.

The inner door to the dean's office opened, and Mr. Williamson stepped out for a moment, looked around, saw Brett, and said, "Mr. Murphy, if you would be so kind as to step inside."

Thoughts of Jimmy disappeared as Brett left his seat and followed Mr. Williamson into his office, the words *They won't do anything to us* echoing through his head. He had spoken them while sitting in Matt's basement after the school had called Matt's house, the caller ID alerting them to the source of the call. Matt, of course, had freaked out and wanted to go right back to school, but Brett told him to quit being such a chickenshit and stay. In the end, they had gone back, mostly because Matt decided to go, with or without him, and Brett couldn't stay there by himself. He also didn't want to go home because his brother would give him shit, so he headed back, the four hours of class time that remained looming before him like a mountain he didn't even want to start climbing. Thankfully, the dean had decided to see him, which cut out a huge chunk of his science class—during a lab, no less, which was even better. The detention afterward wouldn't be that bad either. He had nothing else to really do.

"Not today," Jimmy said. "Her mother is making her stay after because she's scared she'll be kidnapped like Samantha King and Megan Reed."

"While walking with us?" Alan asked. "What, does she think we're the kidnappers or something?"

Jimmy let out a weak laugh at that. "Maybe, who knows? I guess I can understand her concern. The thing is, Tina doesn't think her mother is really concerned for her safety and is just using this as a way of imposing her will on her, you know, because she doesn't really like Tina or how defiant Tina is to her."

"God, it makes you realize how lucky we are that Mom and Dad get along and never got a divorce," Alan said.

"Yeah."

"I mean, look how screwed up that situation is."

"I think it's not just her parents having been divorced, though," Jimmy said. "There's more to it. She hasn't really told me much, but I get the feeling her mother isn't really all that stable. I guess she just left the family right after Tina was born to live with her own mother, which is just weird."

"Still, we're pretty lucky."

"Yeah." He paused. "Hey! Where's my Coke?"

"What?"

"You said you'd buy me a Coke today since you drank most of mine yesterday. Where is it?"

"Sorry, I forgot," Alan said. "You want to go back?"

"No," Jimmy said. They were already halfway across the parking lot, which looked as if it had been rained on at some point during the day, not that it had cleared out the horrible humidity that had descended upon the town. "That's okay."

"I'll grab you one tomorrow, I promise."

"Ha, I get to go home early tomorrow because I'm a senior."

"Shit. Monday then."

"Deal." A second later Jimmy added, "But if you forget, Samantha and Megan won't be the only teens disappearing from around here."

"Oooooh, look how scared I am," Alan taunted. "I'm shaking."

The two stepped from the parking lot onto the sidewalk. Up ahead was the garbage can Jimmy had dumped the tapes into this morning. Given the rain, they were probably ruined, not that he would have grabbed them anyway, especially while walking with Alan.

A sense of loss and disappointment still filtered through him while nearing the can, one that forced him to glance inside while walking by.

He stopped.

The tapes are gone!

Other stuff was still in the can, however, which meant it hadn't been dumped.

Who would have taken them?

What if it was the police? What if they can track who the tapes belong to?

Jimmy had no idea if something like that was possible, but didn't doubt it in this day and age.

"Jimmy, what's wrong?" Alan asked.

Jimmy looked away from the can. His brother was several steps ahead of him.

"You look like you're about to throw up."

"No," Jimmy said. "I think. No." He waved a hand. "I thought I forgot my history book, but it's already at home." Once the lie started, he went with it. "Yeah, it is certainly at home because I was working on note cards yesterday for my presentation next week."

"Okay," Alan said. Something about his tone told Jimmy that his brother wasn't convinced.

The two started walking again.

"I'm sorry, but the library is going to be closing in a moment," a middle-aged woman who looked every bit the part of a high school librarian said. Most students disliked the lady and thought she was a bitch, but Tina had never had any problems with her and always tried to be nice.

"Oh, okay. Um, do you know where I could wait until five thirty?" Tina asked while sticking a bookmark in the novel she had brought with her. "My mother doesn't want me walking home because of the missing girls, so I'm waiting for her to pick me up."

"Oh dear," the librarian said, hands folded against her

chest. "Such a tragedy. Those poor girls." She paused a moment. "It is good your mother is concerned. Most don't seem to care what their children do these days. So many young girls just tossed into the world without care or concern."

Tina waited, but then, when the woman didn't continue, she asked again about a place where she could wait.

"I suggest you go ask in the office because I really don't know where you could go. All the after-school activities are finished for the year."

"That's what I was afraid of," Tina said while grabbing her things. "I'll just head down to the office."

"Oh my, what is that you are reading, my dear?"

Tina looked down at her book. It was *Necroscope* by Brian Lumley, and it sported a wicked-looking skull on the cover, one that often startled people who weren't ready for it. "It's a novel about a young man who can communicate with the dead, who also fights vampires during the Cold War."

"How dreadful."

"It's pretty good. Way better than the romantic vampire garbage that most people read today."

The librarian smiled. "Not a *Twilight* fan?"

"God no!" Tina wanted to add a vomit sound to this but held back.

"Thank goodness. There is at least one sane girl in this school."

Tina smiled. She had heard stories of some of the fights that had broken out when the school got the *Twilight_*books, fights that had gotten pretty vicious, especially when someone shouted that Jacob was a loser. Jimmy had told her all about it, said some crazy mothers had even called the school because they were angry that their sons and daughters—daughters mostly—had not been allowed to use the book for English reports. The teacher hadn't banned the book from being used as a report topic, but instead had only allowed one or two students to do a report on it, and parents had gotten upset because they felt only their son or daughter would be able to do the story justice in front of the classroom.

"I'm an Anne Rice fan myself, though I do enjoy a really good horrific vampire story as well," the librarian added.

"Well, you might want to check out these," Tina said while lifting the book. "My boyfriend loaned me this copy and said that there are a dozen more."

"I will do that. And now I better close this place down. Good luck finding a spot to wait."

"Thanks," Tina said and headed for the doors. Ten minutes later she was sitting outside of the girls' locker room on the far left of the school, her body lounging across a old wooden bench, her book open, her eyes going from line to line waiting to see if Harry Keogh managed to outsmart the Soviet-supported East German police as he searched for the grave of a man he needed to talk with.

It was an exciting scene.

A breeze came out of nowhere and turned several pages forward in the book. Tina swore and flipped the pages back until she found where she had been.

Her eyes did not return to the page, however, but looked over at the deserted field. With school over in two weeks (three for anyone who had to take finals), the practice fields were empty, the sports programs over for the year. An eerie thought settled in as she realized how alone she was. Sure, there were janitors, teachers, and office officials still in the school, but out here, there was no one. Isolating her even more was the area where she had chosen to wait. During the outdoor sports seasons, the area would have been packed with girls coming and going from the locker room, but now there was no one. She was completely alone.

What if the kidnapper is watching me now?

Beyond the sports fields was the sidewalk she always walked home on, one that everyone said Samantha King and Megan Reed had been on when they both disappeared—though no one could understand why Megan Reed had gone that way when her house was on the other side of town.

Tina shivered at the thought of someone coming at her while she was walking home. Thankfully, she always had Jimmy with her.

Were the two even kidnapped? What if this is just some hoax they're playing?

This was a thought some people had voiced today after the assembly, though most thought it unlikely. One girl disappearing right before prom and graduation could be explained with the runaway theory, but two girls, both back-to-back like this, was a stretch.

Then again, they were good friends, so it wasn't completely improbable. Still, Tina now fell into the majority that thought something bad had happened. The question was, *what and why?*

Tina shook her head and went back to reading her book, but unfortunately, her eyes could no longer focus on the story because they kept looking up and scanning the horizon, which was growing darker and darker as thick clouds once again moved in.

Behind her the door to the locker room was thrown open with a bang, causing her to jump up from the bench and twist around, book clutched against her chest. A second later a janitor pushing a huge cleaning contraption that held a garbage can, broom, mop, bucket, and other sanitation tools wedged everything through the door.

Tina eyed the tools on the cart and hoped that one day she would not be skilled enough in their uses to be considered a professional.

The guy stared at her for several seconds and then said, "What're you still doing here?" It was a voice that was trying to hold authority, yet fell short, a voice that would still cower to teachers in the hallway despite being of the same generation as them. Teachers, in turn, would talk down when replying to that voice and treat its owner as if he were a student himself.

"Um, waiting for my mom to pick me up," Tina said. She was still standing, her book clutched against her breasts, which were heaving in and out with each breath.

"School's closed. No students allowed on the grounds." A second later he added, "No loitering. It's against the law." He seemed proud of himself after that statement.

"But I'm waiting to be picked up." A part of her had known someone would probably say something to her while she waited outside between four thirty and five thirty, which is why she had chosen such an isolated spot. Her mind had never pictured a janitor saying something, though, and now she thought about Samantha and Megan, and how often serial killers and perverts took jobs as janitors at schools so they could be around young girls without looking suspicious. "My mom should be here any second."

"Go wait somewhere else."

"I can't," she said, and then once again, just in case he had any ideas, added, "She'll be here soon!"

The janitor continued to stare at her, and for a moment Tina wondered if he was considering how easy it would be to grab her and take her to his car, an act that would probably go unseen and unheard on this side of the school.

"I'm reporting you," the janitor said and turned to head back inside.

Tina sighed and took a much-needed breath, her lungs having halted their production line for a moment. A second later she started to wonder if she would be in trouble for waiting out here like this, and for not doing as the janitor said, but then she let the thought fade because her mother had insisted she wait and the library was closed. Besides, chances were the janitor wouldn't even report her, given the odd social position he carried in the school, one that had him hovering above the students but below the teaching staff. Most likely, the man would feel just as uncomfortable walking into the dean's office as a student would, and even if he did get up the courage to do so and report her, the dean probably wouldn't care. In fact, if she remembered correctly, she once heard secondhand from someone about a janitor who reported overhearing students talking about doing a "bigger than Columbine" school shooting and reported it. Nothing was done until a few weeks later when a teacher reported hearing the same students making similar comments. An investigation uncovered evidence that what the students had been saying was true.

Tina sat back down on the bench and tried to get back

into her book, but once again had a hard time focusing.

A horn honked.

Tina looked up and saw a car pulled alongside the walkway that encircled the school, the driver looking at her through the windshield, face and body blanketed by shadow.

For a moment, she had no idea if the driver was trying to get her attention or that of someone else, and she looked around to see if someone else had been waiting without her knowing.

No one else was present.

"Tina," a familiar yet unrecognizable voice called from the car. "Your mother asked me to pick you up so you didn't have to wait too long."

"Who—" Tina started to ask but then realized it was Scott Goldman, the young man who was part of the same knitting club as her mother, one who she knew her mother was screwing during her nights away because she had pretended to be her mother once when Scott called looking for her.

"Come on, let's go," Scott said.

"She told me she would pick me up at five thirty," Tina called back, an image of the two missing girls floating in her mind.

"Yeah, but she said she knows the library closed and thought you wouldn't have a place to wait and told me to take you home and stay with you until she came home."

Tina shook her head. "Thanks, but I think I'll wait here anyway." Even without two girls missing, Tina would never have considered getting in the car with him, not when his favorite pastime seemed to be knitting with a bunch of women and fucking the ones twice his age. No thank you.

"Tina, your mother wants me to take you home." His voice was growing harsh yet couldn't mask the juvenileness that it still carried. "Now get in this car."

"No." Tina turned and looked back and wished the janitor really had gotten the principal or dean or some school official.

"Tina, I'm not going to ask you again." Scott got out of the car and stood with his arms crossed.

"Fuck you!" Tina shouted and started back toward the girls' locker room.

Scott followed.

Panic developed as she neared the door, but it wasn't overwhelming because she knew he wouldn't follow her inside the girls' locker room.

"Tina!"

Tina grabbed the door handle and pulled, but nothing happened. The door was locked.

Shit!

The panic increased.

"Tina, get in that car right now!" Scott said. His voice was too close.

Tina turned. Scott was standing ten feet away from her, anger covering his face.

"I'm serious!"

Tina ran.

Scott followed.

The main entrance to the school wasn't far, just up and around the corner from the locker room doors. The only problem was she had to scale a large hill that went up the side of the school, one that equaled two flights' worth of stairs inside the building, thereby making the locker rooms a part of the subbasement, even though they had their own outside doors.

Making matters worse, the grass was wet from the rain earlier, and about halfway up Tina slipped, her right leg just seeming to disappear the moment she put pressure on it, the ankle crunching as she landed. A horrible numbness vibrated through the leg, one that made standing impossible.

Thankfully, Scott was having trouble with the hill as well and couldn't reach her level, and by the time he started to get the hang of it, the numbness had cleared and she managed to stand back up.

The rest of the climb was no easier, but she made it without slipping and then around the building to the main entrance, which she charged into, much to the dismay of the hall monitor at the front hallway desk.

"Whoa, slow down," the monitor said. She was the same young lady who often walked around the lunchroom, the school officials thinking the presence of hall monitors would discourage any rowdiness.

"There's a man chasing me," Tina said.

"What?"

"A man is chasing me."

The woman glanced at the entrance, which was still empty, and said, "Are you sure?"

"YES!"

Just then, Scott came in.

"That's him!" Tina shouted.

Another hall monitor had come on the scene now.

"What's going on?" he asked.

"Her mother sent me to pick her up," Scott said. "But she ran away from me."

"My mother told me she would pick me up herself," Tina said. "And he tried forcing me into his car."

Scott put his hands up. "I did not try to force her into

the car. I just told her to stop acting like this and get in the car."

The hall monitors looked back and forth at each other for a moment, and then the young man turned to Tina and said, "Do you know him?"

"Not really. My mother does, but I've never really met him."

The monitor turned to Scott. "Her mother asked you to pick her up, even though you two have never met, knowing two girls have disappeared?"

Scott shrugged. "She just didn't want Tina waiting forever at the school."

"What's going on?" another adult asked, this one having come out of the main office.

The hall monitors explained the situation.

"Okay, into my office, both of you. I want to call her mother and find out what's going on." He then whispered something to the one hall monitor. Tina couldn't hear all of it but was sure one of the words was *sheriff*.

From there the three headed into the office, Tina keeping the school official between herself and Scott.

"Hey, Mom," Alan said. "Have you noticed anything odd about Jimmy lately?"

The two were in the kitchen, Alan helping clear up the dinner mess the family had left. Jimmy himself was down in his room, and their father had flipped on an episode of *The Office*.

"Jimmy? No."

"Really?" Alan asked.

"Have you?" she asked. She seemed to be examining an old sponge while asking this, one that probably added more bacteria than it took away when applied to the dishes.

"Well, I don't know," Alan said, his voice careful because he knew Jimmy had a way of appearing out of nowhere at times, his movements almost naturally stealthy. "He just hasn't seemed himself lately and—"

"I'm going for a bike ride!" Jimmy called, his presence in the entryway having gone unnoticed until he spoke.

"Okay, honey!" his mother called. "Be careful."

Alan waited until his brother left and said, "See, that's what I'm talking about. Why all these sudden bike rides?"

"He just rides at night after dinner," she said while tossing the sponge into the garbage can. "I have friends who go on walks every night or jog in the morning."

"Yeah, but he goes a few times every day. In the morning he wakes up at like five and goes on a ride in the dark, and at night once everyone goes to bed he heads out again sometimes."

Kelly opened a new sponge and wetted it.

"It's…I don't know," Alan added before she could reply.

"He's just restless." She started scrubbing the plates.

"Maybe," Alan said, though he knew it wasn't that. Something wasn't right. It wasn't just the bike rides. Jimmy's entire personality seemed different, almost cautious at times, like he was giving more thought to things. At first, Alan had assumed it was because of Tina and the prom, but now he didn't think that was really it.

CHAPTER TEN

"*Ugh*," Jimmy gasped as he pulled open the heavy door and stepped into the fallout shelter. *It smells like shit.*

Thankfully, it wasn't actually fecal matter that he smelled, just a combination of urine and body odor, but it was still enough to stop him in his tracks and momentarily kill his sex drive. Even worse, he had known something like this would happen, given the small space and lack of circulation, and had even started to notice a growing foulness, but he hadn't done anything about it, his mind able to ignore it at first. Now he couldn't. A smell like this could kill an elephant.

And I can't leave the door open.

No toilets, no shower, and no way to quickly ventilate the space. It obviously wasn't a first-rate fallout shelter the Hood family had created. In fact, Jimmy was pretty sure it had been a last-minute creation, probably one that had originally been a storm shelter that they tried to convert—something they could duck into when the foreign paratroopers dropped in, and wait out their advance until the lines moved beyond the area.

Illinois Insurgency or the II for short.

Jimmy smiled at the thought, but then quickly grimaced at the smell and covered his face with his sleeve, wishing the Hoods had left some gas masks behind for him to use.

And a hose to spray them down with.

Actually, he wondered if he could connect a hose from the house to the sink in the back corner and spray them down. The shelter did have a drain in the center of the floor, so the water wouldn't pool too much. Even better, he then wouldn't have to worry about scrubbing the floor, which was undoubtedly covered in drying urine.

Like the floor of Frodo's cage, he thought to himself. Frodo had been a rabbit Alan owned for many years, one that he had named Frodo due to the *Lord of the Rings* trilogy. Unfortunately, Alan had been pretty young at the time and hadn't been very good at cleaning out the cage, or the giant corner of the basement where the rabbit was free to roam, a three-foot-high foldable fence keeping it penned in. In the end, Jimmy had always been forced to clean the floor, especially when the smell got so great it would waft into his room. Now this reminded him of that, the only difference being the lack of wood-chip litter.

Maybe you should give them each a litter box.

Once again, the smell killed his smile.

He glanced around the room, looking for the bucket. It wasn't far from Samantha's feet, feet that were not holding her up but instead simply glided across the floor.

Shit!

He looked up at her face but couldn't really see much since her head was hanging low, her chin resting on her chest.

Is she breathing?

He stared at her chest for several seconds but couldn't detect any rise or fall.

He twisted around and looked at Megan. She was staring back at him, her eyes looking as if she were trying to burn a hole through him.

"Is she dead?" he asked.

Megan didn't reply.

Jimmy shook his head and then, nose still pressed into his sleeve, walked over to Samantha and put a hand to her chest.

For a moment, all was still, but then he detected a faint beating of her heart and felt her lungs working. Both were weak, however, and he doubted she would be able to keep it up if she continued to hang like this, the weight on her lungs too much, her body needing her feet to support her.

"Let her down," Megan said. "She's had enough."

Jimmy glared at Megan, even though he knew she was right, but then wondered how he would go about securing Samantha if her hands weren't over her head like this. Even if he allowed her to sit rather than keeping her lifted up to where she had to stand, she would be able to work at her bindings once the strength returned and pull herself free.

You need handcuffs or shackles in order to keep them like that.

He didn't have any that would work, however, and had no idea how to get some. Several online sex stores carried them, but ordering them was a problem because he feared it would be traceable. The last thing he needed was for the sheriff's department to know he had ordered a couple sets of handcuffs.

If you drive up into the suburbs, you could buy some from Lover's Lane or even go into Chicago and stop at a sex store.

Lover's Lane was a possibility; driving into Chicago was not. He had only been in the city a few times during his life and knew that he did not possess the skills to drive around such a busy place or navigate the different neighborhoods. Too scary.

"Jimmy, you have to let her down!" Megan said again.

"I will!" Jimmy snapped back. "But only if you behave yourself!"

Megan didn't reply to this.

It's starting.

You care about her.

Jimmy wanted Megan to feel responsible for Samantha and to know that if she misbehaved, Samantha would suffer for it, unless it was something so horrible that Megan herself needed a severe punishment.

"First I need to clean this place out." His words were still muffled by his shirt. "If you don't give me any trouble with that, I will lower her."

Again, Megan didn't respond, even though he knew she had heard him.

Such actions annoyed him, so he quickly said, "Do you understand?"

"Yes," Megan said.

"Good."

He didn't want to say much more after that because each time he opened his mouth to talk the smell seemed to attack his taste buds.

Could this smell kill them?

It was a question he had no answer for, though he did remember a teacher once telling him that people who lived in houses overrun by cats could start to go crazy from the ammonia in the urine. That took a long time, however, and they had only been here a few days. Still, if the oxygen became contaminated enough, it might pose a problem.

Unfortunately, he didn't really have a solution for it, aside from keeping them clean, so it wasn't really something he could worry too much about.

He walked over to the sink in the rear corner while considering this and looked at the nozzle, trying to figure out if a garden hose would be able to attach.

The head didn't have any screw swivels on it, so he figured the answer was no. He would have to fill the bucket with soapy water and scrub them down.

And bring a bottle of Febreze next time.

Jimmy grabbed the bucket from the floor and took it over to the sink to fill. While there, he realized there was no soap, nor any cloth to scrub them with.

He would have to venture into the Hoods' house and see if anything like that had been left behind. Chances were it had been; the question was, had kids destroyed it during their adventures inside?

At the moment, such thoughts didn't really worry him because he was craving the fresh air.

And you've only been in here a few minutes.

He wouldn't let this happen again. From now on, the girls would get a sponge bath every day, right before he fed them.

For a while, Megan hadn't even realized Jimmy was down there with them, her mind having drifted into a wakeful daze that didn't really register anything, almost as if she were having a very plain dream, one that lacked the surrealism most people came to expect and sometimes enjoy during the nighttime hours.

It was his movement that finally alerted her to his presence, movement toward Samantha.

Don't touch her!

The words stayed within her head, her mind and body momentarily fearful of drawing his attention. At the same time, she regretted giving in to this cowardly behavior and tried to break free from it.

The words *let her down you stupid piece of shit* nearly left her lips. In fact, she was moistening her dry lips so that the words would have the needed forcefulness and wouldn't sound weak, when he looked at her, his attention causing the fear to return without any delay.

"Is she dead?" Jimmy asked.

Megan couldn't respond and just stared at him.

Rather than demand an answer from her, Jimmy went and investigated the situation himself.

Megan stewed in her own cowardly guilt for a moment and kept vowing to herself not to give in to the fear. *Make him realize there will be a cost for his actions. Nothing is free.*

Such defiance was easy to imagine, but hard to actually achieve in this situation.

After a few moments, Megan did summon up enough courage to tell Jimmy he needed to lower Samantha. It was only a small victory, though, because she knew Jimmy would realize this himself. She also worried that by suggesting this Jimmy would refuse, not wanting to give in to her.

The worst was when he told her he would let Samantha down, but only if Megan behaved herself. She didn't want to be tied to Samantha like this. She didn't want her defiance of him to harm her.

That is exactly what he wants, though.

Samantha had become her whipping girl.

It wasn't fair.

Thankfully, she didn't have to think about this much because once Jimmy left the shelter her mind went back to the unrelenting pain, which never fully disappeared. She couldn't even put it out of her mind. This led her to think about a statement she had once heard on TV during one of those medical shows. A guy said something about living in chronic pain and how it was horrible because the one who suffered was always aware of it. Making it even more aggravating was the notion other people had about getting used to it. Even Megan had thought this would be the case. Now she knew differently. The ropes were constantly on her mind. At moments, other thoughts seemed more pressing but never fully acquired all of her attention.

Time passed and she suddenly realized Jimmy had not returned, even though he had said something about cleaning them.

What if something happened?

For the first time, Megan realized she couldn't wish for disaster upon Jimmy, not unless he left behind enough clues so people could find the two of them. If not, then they would both die a slow death while hanging like this.

She also realized a part of her was craving his return, even though she knew his actions would be horrible. She wanted him back because the long stretches of isolation were too much, especially with Samantha hanging lifeless.

Don't!

She couldn't help it and quickly grew angry with herself. *You can't let your dependence on him get the better of you!* her mind screamed.

When it came to the population within her mind, this resistance movement was an ever-shrinking figure, despite how much she wished for it to grow.

Don't give in to him, the resistance part said.

Don't give him reason to hurt you, the other part replied.

He doesn't need a reason!

If he didn't have a reason, however, she then wouldn't have to feel guilty about it.

Samantha moaned.

Megan turned her attention toward her friend and realized she also didn't want to feel like she was the cause of her pain.

It's not your fault!

Megan knew this to be true but wondered how long she would be able to accept it.

How long before I turn into a willing prisoner and accept his rule over me?

Megan feared this more than pain.

The fresh air outside the fallout shelter tasted wonderful, and for the first time that day, he didn't care about the muggy wetness that clung to him. Instead, he felt almost as if it was a complimentary cleansing process, one that promised to take the stench of the fallout shelter away from his body.

I could walk away. Just seal it off and walk away.

It was a nice thought but one he knew he couldn't truly achieve because the cravings to see the girls would be too strong. The same thing happened with the porn he bought. After purchasing an online subscription or a video, he always decided that it would be the last time, never again would he waste money on something like that, but then, a few days or weeks later, depending on how strong his willpower was, he would find himself doing it again. He couldn't stop.

Will you stop once the girls are dead?

He feared the answer to this question and quickly pushed the thought from his mind as he approached the back door of the Hoods' house. Many years earlier, the door latch had been broken, and people could come and go at will. Eventually, the sheriff had gotten tired of having to check the place out all the time—mostly because a few kids got hurt while inside, which sparked outrage from the parents—and installed a padlock on the door. Of course, this didn't stop the kids from getting inside, which eventually led to the front door being padlocked as well, something which the sheriff had been hesitant to do because the Hoods still owned the place and could come back anytime and would be furious if they found it locked. What made the situation even more frustrating for the sheriff was that he couldn't have charges filed against anyone who broke inside, because they needed the Hood family to be the one to complain, and no one could reach them. Thankfully for the sheriff, this information wasn't common knowledge. Even Jimmy had been ignorant of this fact until two years earlier when he had inadvertently asked his world history teacher about it. Before becoming a teacher, the man had been a lawyer, and at the time Jimmy was considering using the Hood place as a way of getting bondage videos mailed to him, so he asked him a series of carefully worded questions about the issue, ones that didn't reveal his true plans but got him the answers he was looking for. The plan had never gotten off the ground, though, because when he attempted to mail a letter to himself with the Hoods' address as the delivery location, it never arrived. After this, he decided to wait until he had his own place to buy bondage tapes, but then eventually gave in to the desire, his hope being that his parents would never ask him about the boxes that were arriving, which was the whole reason why he wanted to use the Hood place to begin with. Thankfully, the issue never came up. He lied about his age with a simple "Yes, I'm Over Eighteen" age statement along with a fake birth date, and sent in money orders to get the tapes, which always arrived a few days later in plain boxes before his parents came home from work.

His knowledge about the legality of entering the Hood place never disappeared, and one day he decided to use their basement as a dungeon. His plan had been to grab a girl walking home and tie her up and use her like crazy until he got tired of her, the ski mask he wore making it impossible for her to know who had done this, just in case she was ever discovered. In the end, the plan had been vetoed because he didn't think the basement secure enough, but not before he had broken off the back-door padlock with a pair of bolt cutters and put his own identical one on.

If the sheriff ever did try to get inside, something that wasn't likely to happen because he would need a warrant, he would probably just assume he had misplaced the key and use bolt cutters as well once he failed to get inside. So far, this had never happened, so Jimmy was confident the sheriff didn't really care.

Using his own key, Jimmy opened the lock and went inside to look for a sponge and some soap, the dusty stale air not really bothering him because the stuff in the fallout shelter was still fresh in his mind.

The cobwebs, however, were a different story and

grossed him out, especially when one caught him square in the face.

Waving his arms around to combat the dangling creations and spitting a bit out of his mouth, Jimmy entered the family room.

All the electronics had been picked clean, either by the Hood family as they were leaving or by kids who had broken inside over the years, but the wooden TV canopy was still present, its shelves ready to be filled once again with VHS tapes and DVDs.

I should have left the bondage tapes in here, he said to himself, the thought having never even occurred to him.

Were did the tapes go?

The question went unanswered as he left the family room and headed up the stairs, certain there had to be at least one bathroom up there.

I should just bring the girls over here one at a time to take a shower.

That would be too risky, though. One false move and the girl could get away easily. Again, if he had shackles and connected their feet together, that wouldn't be such a problem, but then with his luck someone would see him leading a girl from the shelter to the house or the house to the shelter. The place was isolated, but not isolated to the point where being seen was unlikely.

The stairs sighed as he stepped into the hallway, his arms once again having to clear away the cobwebs that crisscrossed the open air. While doing this he noticed another horrible smell assaulting his senses, one that almost felt damp when ascending into his nose.

It was coming from the bathroom on his left, specifically the shower.

Jimmy once again covered his nose and mouth with

his shirt and opened the shower curtain.

Mold and mildew colored the once white walls.

He looked around for some soap or body wash, but nothing had been left behind.

The same was true with the top of the sink and the cabinets beneath.

The place had been picked clean.

He left that bathroom and looked to see if there was one in the master bedroom. It too was moldy, though this time the toilet was the really gross part because someone, probably Mr. Hood, had left the seat up before leaving the house. A second less noticeable musty smell was present, one that almost reminded him of the zoo for some reason.

Despite the shirt, he could barely stand the room and for a moment wondered if he should just rinse the girls off tonight and then come back the next day with soap from home.

No, you're here and it will only take a second to check, so just do it.

Jimmy obeyed, walked over to the shower, and threw open the curtain. This time a bar of soap was waiting, but it was one he would never touch, not even with gloves on, because of the mold all around it, and he quickly turned away.

His eyes rested on the cabinet beneath the sink. It was bigger than the one in the other bathroom. Only one of its doors had been broken off, probably by kids, and from where he was standing it looked to be empty.

He couldn't see into the second cabinet, however, and quickly got down on his knees and opened it.

Something growled inside and then lunged at him.

Jimmy screamed while falling backward into the

bedroom as an angry opossum came at him, teeth glinting, and quickly backpedaled himself from the bedroom, his hand slamming the door shut as he entered the hallway.

Panic at what else could be living in the house entered his mind, especially given how dark it was becoming outside.

The opossum continued to scream at him from beyond the door, one that Jimmy knew he would have to open so that the animal didn't get stuck and die in there.

Catch your breath first.

It took a while, but eventually he was able to stand and was ready to leave the hallway and the house, the idea of finding soap far from his mind now. Before leaving, he eased open the bedroom door so that the opossum just had to push it to get out.

Images of other animals entered his mind, ones that could have easily crawled or slithered inside through the broken cellar windows.

Gooseflesh sprang up on his bare arms.

Get out of this house.

Jimmy did just that, his hands scraping free all the cobwebs and grime that had caught hold of him, his body desperately wanting a shower.

Jimmy looked horrible when he came back into the fallout shelter, and for a moment Megan wanted to ask him what had happened, but then bit her tongue as he snatched up the metal bucket from the ground and headed toward the sink.

He was angry, but at what she didn't know. Still, it frightened her a bit.

Bucket filled, Jimmy came back into her line of sight

and looked around for something. Nothing seemed to catch his eye, though.

Frustrated, he headed over to the shelf with the wool blankets and unfolded one. Then, without warning, he pulled out a knife from his pocket, flicked the blade open with his thumb, and started cutting out a large square. Once he was done with that, he took the large square back to the bucket and draped it over the edge.

"Samantha, stand up," he ordered.

Samantha did not reply.

Jimmy grabbed her by the hair and jerked her head back. Samantha moaned. "I said, stand up!"

"Leave her alone!" Megan snapped. She didn't even think about the words; they just erupted.

"I'm not in the mood!" Jimmy shouted at Megan. He then lifted Samantha by the hair until she was on her feet.

Samantha stayed like that for a moment and then collapsed again.

"Fine, be that way," Jimmy said and walked over to where the rope was tied off, undid the knot, and pulled her up until her toes just barely touched the ground.

"You're going to kill her if you keep doing that!" Megan shouted.

"I don't care!" Jimmy shouted.

Samantha started crying.

"Put her back down!"

"Do you want to be lifted up too?" Jimmy asked.

Megan didn't reply.

Jimmy took hold of Samantha's shirt, pulled it up all the way over her head, and wrapped it around the ropes. He then used his knife and cut off her bra, exposing her completely.

"Stop it!" Megan shouted. "Leave her alone!"

Jimmy turned and came at her with the knife, which he pushed up against her right breast, the cloth of her shirt barely masking the feel of the sharp point as it threatened to pierce the flesh just under her nipple. "Don't say another word unless you want to spend another night hanging from your wrists, after I whip the shit out of you."

All Megan could focus on was the knife, her body unable to back up because his other hand was holding her in place.

Please don't cut me!

Her lips stayed sealed.

Jimmy pulled the tip away and went back to Samantha, his hand setting the knife on the floor so he could scrub her clean with the square of cloth he had cut.

Samantha gasped at the water, which was probably really cold, and almost instantly started to shiver, despite how warm it still was within the room.

The smell of wet wool hit the air as Jimmy repeatedly plunged the square into the bucket and then roughly ran it over Samantha's bare skin, his hand pressing so hard that the fabric left red scratches up and down her pale flesh.

Megan got a chill when he scrubbed Samantha's groin, thinking he would probably drop his pants and start fucking her, but that didn't happen. Still, she didn't want him touching her like that—no way—and would do whatever she could to prevent it.

Samantha's cleansing ended eventually, her naked body completely raw looking from the wool as it dangled from the ropes.

Jimmy put the square back in the bucket and came toward Megan.

"Don't you dare touch me," Megan said.

Jimmy stared at her for a second and then said, "You don't want to push me right now. I'm not in the mood."

"And you don't want to touch me right now because I'm not in the mood!"

Jimmy shook his head and grabbed at her pants to undo them, his hand struggling with her jeans as she twisted and turned. The quick movements hurt her wrists, but the pain was worth it, given the satisfaction she gained by making things difficult for him.

Without warning, Jimmy grabbed her throat and squeezed.

Megan tried to breathe, but nothing got through and she gagged.

"Stop fighting me!" Jimmy ordered and then let go.

Megan gasped, but then twisted away again when he tried to undo her pants.

"Goddammit!" Jimmy shouted at her. "Stop!"

"No!" Megan shouted back. She then spit on him with all the force she could muster.

Jimmy's hand came out of nowhere and smashed into the side of her face.

Tears sprang to her eyes, and her busted lip quivered at the blow, but the resistance did not stop.

Jimmy struck her again.

Megan still didn't stop, even though parts of her mind were pleading with her to do so.

"Fine!" Jimmy snapped and grabbed the bucket of water.

Megan saw what was coming and quickly tried to shift herself out of the way, but couldn't and caught the splash full force, her eyes closing at the last second as the water came at her.

"*Ahhhh*," she gasped at the coldness. She then felt her body being lifted into the air just like Samantha's had been, only this time it didn't stop until her feet were once again several inches off the floor.

"I don't know why you fight me like this," Jimmy said. "You always lose in the end."

Megan didn't reply.

Jimmy undid his belt.

Megan had an idea what was coming and braced herself.

"I told you that from now on I will punish Samantha if you act out," Jimmy said. "First I shall show you what it feels like to be whipped."

Jimmy disappeared behind her.

A second later, the belt snapped across her wet back, the thin fabric of her shirt offering no protection whatsoever.

Don't scream!

Megan bit down hard, her teeth trying to lock in place.

Jimmy hit her again.

The only sound that echoed was the leather snapping across her back.

Jimmy hit her again, and again, and again.

Megan just barely managed to stay silent this time.

The next blow was the hardest of all, one that she knew Jimmy used all his strength on. Not screaming once the leather landed was impossible, especially when the tip wrapped around her body and snapped into her breast.

Jimmy hit her five more times after that, his arm

holding nothing back with each blow, the leather cracking as it cut into her, causing her body to sway in the air.

"*Please stop!*" Megan cried, tears running down her checks.

Jimmy paused for a moment, then came around, wrapped the belt around her throat, and pulled.

Megan couldn't breathe at all.

"I could do this all night and would if you two didn't smell so bad. Tomorrow morning I'm going to clean you with soap whether you like it or not, and then I'll whip you again just so you remember how it feels. Samantha too."

He let go and she struggled for air, her violent gasps completely audible.

Jimmy gave Samantha five good strikes after that, each one causing her to scream, and then let her shirt fall back down over her body, which wasn't completely soaked like Megan's clothes were.

He then let her down so that she was on her knees. The position would still be incredibly painful, but nowhere near as bad as hanging from the wrists, or even standing.

Please let me down too, Megan said to herself, her body already starting to shiver from the cold wet clothes. *Please.*

Jimmy did let her down enough so that her toes could support her weight a bit, though she was sure it wasn't a result of her thoughts.

Jimmy looked at the torn fingernail on his left hand in what was left of the sunlight in the Hoods' yard and grimaced. The nail had gotten caught on Megan's pants while she had been twisting away from him, either on the button or the zipper, and before he even realized it the nail had ripped.

At first the rip didn't hurt all that much since the nail itself didn't have any nerves, but then, as the air started touching the sensitive skin beneath, and as the area near the cuticle realized the nail had split down into the root, the pain arrived and it was bad. Anger followed, but it did little to mask the throb pulsating from the middle finger.

Had it been his right hand, he wouldn't have been able to do much more in the fallout shelter, but since it wasn't he still had been able to whip Megan. The actions weren't pleasurable though, which was why he hadn't gone all out. Instead, it had felt like a necessary task, one that he had wanted to finish quickly so he could head home and tend to his finger.

Most of my visits feel like necessary tasks, Jimmy realized. *Almost as if they are pets that I no longer want but need to take care of.*

It was frustrating. His fantasies had never detailed any of this stuff. Instead, he had always seen the girls hanging from their wrists and doing whatever he ordered them to do, their minds too weak and scared to even consider the possibility of disobeying him.

Go back in, cut off her clothes, and leave her hanging naked all night.

Jimmy considered this for a long time but ultimately vetoed the idea, mostly because it seemed like too much of a hassle at the moment. He also had never really cared much for nudity. It seemed boring. He would much rather force her into some humiliating fetish outfit and leave her there. That wasn't a possibility either.

Still, you should have done something more.

Tomorrow morning he would punish her, that was, if he wasn't too tired after cleaning them again.

He took another look at his finger and then headed into the woods to get his bike. Once that was in hand, he started walking toward the street and was just exiting the yard when a sheriff's cruiser drove by.

He froze.

The cruiser continued forward for several feet and then came to a halt.

Run!

The impulse was strong, but he didn't give in to it, having seen enough real-life police shows to know such action would be foolish. Instead, he stood his ground as if he had done nothing wrong and waited for the deputy to back up.

A second later he was face-to-face with Deputy Paul Widgeon, who just happened to be the youngest law enforcement official with the sheriff's department, who had been honorably discharged from the military two years earlier after serving three combat tours. The guy was a town hero, one who everyone had welcomed home after his military discharge with a huge barbecue behind the mayor's office. It had been fun.

"Hey, Jimmy," Paul said. "What are you doing out and about?"

"Just riding my bike," Jimmy said. His heart was racing, even though he knew Paul well. When he and Alan had been younger and Paul in high school, the guy would help them organize games of capture the flag in the woods.

"Looks more like you're walking your bike."

"Yeah, that's because I fell," Jimmy said. He held up

his finger. "Look."

"Ouch," Paul said. "Let me get the first aid kit and fix that up for you."

"Oh, don't worry about it; I know you guys are busy. I'll just clean it at home."

"Nonsense." Paul popped the trunk and got out, the limp he had come home with from the war just barely visible, thanks to all the hours he spent conditioning it. "I'll have it cleaned up in no time."

Jimmy sighed. This was the last thing he wanted or needed, especially this close to the fallout shelter.

"You've been riding your bike quite a bit I hear," Paul said. "Trying to get in shape for something?"

Jimmy shrugged. "More like I'm really restless and am not sure what I want to do now that school is pretty much over. I'll be graduating soon and have no plans really."

"I know what you mean." He took hold of Jimmy's hand and looked at the finger. "Ah, not too bad. Hurts like a son of a bitch though, I bet."

"It does."

Paul gently touched the uplifted part of the fingernail. "I'll have to cut this part off completely," he said. "It'll hurt for a moment but will feel much better once everything is bandaged up, okay?"

"Um…okay," Jimmy said.

He watched while Paul pulled out a small pair of scissors from the first aid kit and got them positioned to cut away the torn part of the nail.

"Hold still," Paul ordered.

Jimmy did.

The first cut wasn't so bad, but then the scissors pressed into the nail bed and everything went white hot, and it was all Jimmy could do not to jerk his hand away. Thankfully, it didn't last long. Two quick snips and the flipped-up part of torn nail that would have snagged on everything was gone.

"That wasn't so bad," Paul said.

Jimmy glared at him.

"Let me just wrap that up and you'll be on your way." Paul started wrapping the finger. "By the way, any idea what could have happened to those two girls?"

"What?"

"You've been riding your bike so much I wondered if maybe you saw something," Paul said. His hands pressed the gauze down hard on Jimmy's finger so that it wouldn't slip free.

"Yeah, but I never saw anything, and I heard they were taken when they were walking home from school, so me and Alan probably weren't even home yet."

"That's the theory at least. The last place anyone ever saw the two was at school, so we assume they were taken while walking home." He paused to tear a strip of white tape. "This is the road they would have been taken on; at least, this is the road Samantha King should have been walking home on. Did you know that?"

Jimmy was going to say no but then realized that couldn't possibly be true, given all the talk at school, and instead said, "Yeah, I'd heard that."

"What I can't figure out is who would do such a thing," Paul said. "If it had just been Samantha King, then I could see someone just coming into town and grabbing the first girl he saw. But you'd think they would leave town right away, not stay around and grab another girl. Too risky, don't you think?"

Jimmy nodded.

"That's why I believe it's someone in town."

"But who?" Jimmy asked.

"That's the question, isn't it? Who could do something like this? Makes you wonder what goes on behind closed doors."

"Yeah, *ahhh!*"

"Sorry, had to press the tape down into it so it sticks."

"Wasn't expecting it," Jimmy said.

"The gauze pad is medicated too, so you don't have to worry about disinfecting it. Just make sure you take everything off in a day or two and put on a fresh bandage."

"Okay."

"And be careful. I know you say you didn't see anything, but you might not realize you did see something, and the person or persons responsible for all this might come after you."

"Okay," Jimmy said again.

"In fact, maybe it would be better if you rode on the other side of town since this area seems to be the focal point of everything."

"I really like this area though."

"Suit yourself. Just be cautious. I don't want anyone else to disappear or get hurt."

"I appreciate that and will be extra careful." *You have no idea just how careful I will be.*

"Great. Can you make it home from here, or do you need a ride back?"

Jimmy didn't want to get into the car. "I'm fine." To prove it, he jumped up onto the bike. "See." He tried not to show how much his finger hurt when gripping the handlebar, but had a feeling he didn't do a very good job because it hurt like hell.

"I see," Paul said. "Be safe."

Jimmy wanted to ask him if they had any suspects but figured that would be too much at the moment and simply started riding home.

Paul followed for a while, but then turned at the next intersection.

Jimmy sighed. He had had enough close calls at the Hood place for a while. Hopefully his trips there would be uneventful from this point on.

Deputy Paul Widgeon followed Jimmy Hawthorn on his bike until the first intersection and then made a right turn at Elm as if he were planning on patrolling another area, but really he was just using the road to wrap around to the left, the three-way intersection half a mile down the road making this possible, which eventually connected back to the road the Hood place was on.

Paul slowed the vehicle as it came upon a turnoff that dead-ended into a cul-de-sac five houses down, the house to the right of the center being the King household. Like all the houses along the right side of this road, their home backed up against the woods, ones that didn't end until they came upon the farm fields a few miles away. The houses on the left also backed up against the woods, but those stretches eventually opened up into other backyards on the north side of town, properties that gradually got bigger and bigger as they headed south toward the Hood place.

After a moment Paul continued his journey back to the Hood house, his eyes noting the last house before their property began about half a mile from the actual home. The land had been in the Hood family a long time, and a decade earlier it could have made them rich beyond their wildest dreams if they had sold it to developers. Now no one would buy it, the last new house having been built back when Paul was in Iraq, back before Wall Street had gone into its first nosedive.

Jimmy, what were you doing out here? Paul asked himself while pulling up alongside the Hoods' crumbling driveway. *What were you hiding from me?*

Jimmy's story about falling off his bike had been bullshit because fingernails wouldn't tear outward when impacting the ground from a fall. Plus he had no other wounds on his body, not fresh ones anyway, and if he truly had taken all the impact of a fall on his hand like that, the broken fingernail would have been the least of his pains. Nothing had been broken though, a fact made obvious by the way Paul had been able to twist his hand back and forth while bandaging it. It also hadn't been swollen. So now the question was, what had Jimmy been doing that would leave him with a torn finger?

No answer would arrive without a little investigating, so he got out and walked around. He was pretty sure that whatever had happened to Jimmy's finger had happened on this property because why come here after the fact— unless he had been going home from the school and took the old wooded path. Of course such a situation would bring up two more questions—the first being what would he have been doing at the school after hours, the second being why he would head home on this path when taking the sidewalk provided to him would be much faster.

Could he have snagged his finger while riding, which is why there were no other injuries?

Paul asked himself this while in the backyard, his eyes looking at the thick brush everywhere. If one were cutting through that on his bike, it would be possible to get a stick caught up under the fingernail and rip it outward, but then why lie about falling?

And why was he out in the woods to begin with?

He knew Jimmy had been riding his bike a lot. He had witnessed it a few times this past week, and others had as well, most concerned by the very idea Paul had planted in Jimmy's head about him being a target in case he had seen something he didn't realize. Paul, however, also wondered if Jimmy could have had anything to do with the two girls having disappeared. Most in the department didn't think a high school student could be behind something like that, but Paul knew differently. Paul had been overseas and had seen what people his age were capable of. Hell, Jimmy was eighteen, and that had been the age Paul had been the first time he had killed someone, fascinated by the damage the grenade had done in the room where the insurgent had been waiting.

If another girl is reported missing this evening maybe... An image of a fingernail being ripped in a struggle filled his head.

Nothing behind the house pointed toward a struggle, and so far, all the reports of missing children that afternoon had been false alarms—most being the result of a late bus home from school, and one due to a parent who forgot his daughter had work that evening.

Paul's radio came to life while he was walking behind the old shed on the corner of the Hood property and reported a car accident on the other side of town, one that sounded pretty bad.

"I can be there in eight minutes," Paul said into the radio and quickly hurried back to his patrol car, thoughts of Jimmy Hawthorn and the missing girls quickly disappearing from his mind.

Brett sat in his room for a long time that night watching the videos Jimmy had thrown away, his mind playing with ideas on how to use the tapes against him. Earlier he had seen his stupid little girlfriend in the hallway during some odd commotion, one that had involved a deputy being called to the school, and he wondered what would happen if he gave some of the tapes to her.

What if she likes this stuff too and gets all freaky with Jimmy? Hell, the two probably were making their own tapes and posting them on some obscure website.

Still, he wanted Jimmy to know he had these tapes, and the best way to do that was to give one to the girl. And if it turned out she didn't know about the tapes or how sick and twisted Jimmy was, it would be even better because she would probably dump him right before the prom.

Now if only Jimmy were in some of these tapes.

Sadly, he didn't think this would be the case. If it were, he would have made plans to somehow show the tape during the dance, maybe on a projector screen or something so that everyone could see what a freak he was.

On screen, he watched as a girl was lifted off the ground by her wrists and then tormented with a pink vibrator. Kneeling next to her was another girl, this one sucking the man's dick while he used the vibrator on the first girl.

Brett couldn't believe people enjoyed stuff like this, especially people like the girls in the video. It was sick.

At the same time, he wondered what he would do if he were one of those guys and knew he could do whatever he wanted with them. Would he join in? If so, he wouldn't have to live with the disgrace of still being a virgin, something that weighed heavily on his mind day in and day out, especially since he knew Matt was no longer one, the jerk having scored some pussy with his coworker at the video store last year.

It pissed him off.

CHAPTER ELEVEN

Megan peed herself halfway through the night while shivering from the cold, her wet clothes making it impossible for her body to stay warm as all the heat was sucked away from the underground shelter once the sun set. It was a miserable situation, one made even worse due to her position. Had she simply been tied up on the floor, she could have scrunched herself into the fetal position, or into a corner, and maybe with one of those wool blankets. Instead, she was stretched out, her entire body exposed to the air.

"You've been hung up to dry!"

She jerked her head toward the sound, but Samantha was the only other person in the room with her—as far as she could tell—and the voice had most certainly not been hers.

"Not funny," she said.

No one replied.

Megan stretched open her eyes and looked around a second time, her body slowly twisting so that she could see the back of the shelter.

You're imagining things, she said to herself.

It was the lack of sleep and food.

Her eyes relaxed, the heaviness of her lids making it hard to keep them focused. She could not sleep. At points, she managed to doze off, but it was never deep, which was why her mind was now trying to dream while awake. It was trying to force her body into that much-needed rejuvenating state.

Megan tried to fight it, but to no avail. Hanging like this in wet clothes made it impossible. Hell, hanging like this in dry clothes would have made it impossible too.

She twisted toward Samantha, who was asleep, and envied her position again. The girl was lucky. Jimmy had allowed her to stay on the ground.

"The cold concrete ground."

Again, the voice didn't seem to be her own, yet she knew it was.

"The two are working together!"

Megan shook the thought away and once again tried to focus her mind. It didn't work. A permanent haze hung over everything, one that seemed to grow thicker and thicker with each passing moment. It was so bad that Megan didn't even realize she was peeing in her own pants until after the fact. Instead, she felt an annoying ache in her lower regions followed by relief and pleasant warmth, one that sadly faded quickly.

Disgust followed once she recognized the act.

It would have been one thing if she had been holding the need in for hours, the pressure building and building until she couldn't take it anymore and had to open up. It was another for it to just happen.

Memories of Samantha lying on the ground the other day, urine flowing freely down her leg, arrived.

No! No! No!

She didn't want to become like that. Worse, she didn't want to be aware that she was becoming like that.

"*It will happen!*" This time the voice seemed to echo across the shelter.

Please, God, NO!

She struggled against the ropes, tearing free the fresh scabs where the skin had torn the other day and then started to heal during her inactivity.

A little bit of blood dripped down her right arm.

Shivers followed.

And then the haze grew even thicker. Several hours passed without her being aware of it.

Jimmy was now in the room.

Megan said something about him bringing back the warmth.

"What?" Jimmy asked.

Megan didn't reply, though this time it wasn't a result of defiance. Instead, she simply had no idea what she had said, the words a minced-up mess even within her own mind, and couldn't repeat them, the thoughts that had generated them having quietly fled.

Jimmy yawned and then went back to the tin bucket, which he had filled with soapy water. He also had a pink loofah sitting on the floor.

Once finished with that he stood up, walked over toward her, and said, "If you fight me this time, I will really make you suffer."

Megan heard the words but couldn't really understand what he meant by them until he started undoing her pants. Once she realized this, she started to struggle, but then found herself too exhausted and let him do what he needed.

It felt good having the wet clothes removed.

His work with the loofah felt even better, despite how cold the water was.

Afterward she felt as if a pound of grime had come off her body.

Don't let him do this, her mind screamed.

Megan ignored the statement. Later, once she got her strength back, she would resist his advances. Right now, she just didn't have the energy.

"I'm going to lower you a little," Jimmy said.

Her body fell before she even understood what his words meant, and had it not been for the rope and his hands, she would have hit the floor hard. Instead, he eased her down until she was allowed to sit.

The relief was short-lived as the cramps began, her muscles and blood vessels all springing into action as if an alarm had awakened them.

The pain was too much.

She had to scream.

Jimmy waited.

Once again, the haze made it difficult for her to judge how much time had passed. Eventually the pain faded, though it didn't disappear completely. Thankfully, it had retreated enough for her to drink some water and eat.

Jimmy regulated how much she could have.

"I don't want you getting sick," he said while pulling the water bottle away.

She cried as if he were taking it away for good. In reality it was only for a minute, and then he would allow her to drink some more. Drink a little, take it away, drink a little, take it away. Every now and then, he would also give her some pretzels and other dry foods from the shelf, his hands having to hold it while she chewed because her fingers weren't working. Some of it was stale, but Megan didn't care. It was the first thing she had eaten since... her mind couldn't even figure it out and didn't really care.

"She was so pissed off, it was great," Tina said while the three were walking to school. "But she couldn't really say anything because everyone at the school was saying I did the right thing and that it was better to be safe than sorry."

"And the police actually took him away?" Jimmy asked, even though she had already said they did.

"Just for questioning," Tina said. "They didn't arrest him or anything, but they made sure the threat of that possibly happening if he didn't cooperate was there."

"God, I bet the sheriff just wanted to take him into some deep dark basement room and beat the shit out of him," Alan said.

"Do you think he's really responsible for the two girls?" Jimmy asked.

Tina shook her head. "No. The guy is odd, but harmless. I mean, his favorite pastime is knitting with a bunch of middle-aged ladies."

"Still, who knows what goes on inside his head? Maybe he has a thing for high school girls and that's why he is spending so much time with your mother, and other mothers who knit, so he has easy access to you and their daughters."

Tina seemed somewhat spooked by this statement but then brushed it away. "He and my mother have been seeing each other since before I moved here. I don't even think he knew I existed back then."

"Still..." Jimmy started but didn't finish. He didn't want to push it too far.

"Oh, don't worry, the guy is a creep, no question about that, and I won't be caught dead alone with him. And I'm guessing he will think twice before offering to do my mother any favors in the future."

The three went silent for a while, and then Jimmy asked, "Do you have to stay after today?"

"My mother didn't say anything about it. She probably wants me to, but I won't. I mean, we get out at what, like noon today?"

"Yeah." Jimmy turned toward Alan and smiled. "Two of us do."

Alan gave him the finger.

"Then there is no way in hell I'm staying at school," Tina said. "What would I do all day?"

"You know, this isn't fair," Alan snapped. "Instead of letting all the seniors have a half day, they should let anyone with a ticket to the prom have a half day."

"But then lower classmen like yourself would have one less day to prepare for finals, which wouldn't be good." Jimmy never understood why seniors didn't have to take finals during the second semester, but he didn't mind. He had a feeling it had something to do with tallying up who would graduate and who would not, especially since the graduation ceremony was the weekend after finals. Still, it seemed odd.

"It's still stupid, and why does everyone need a half day to prepare for a dance that isn't until Saturday night?" He turned toward Tina and asked, "Do you need all day to do your hair?"

"Um, no," Tina said. "I really have no idea what I'm going to do all afternoon in that empty house all by myself."

Jimmy heard the words and then saw the look Alan

gave him, but he wasn't sure what to say.

"It's going to be lonely," Tina added.

Jimmy stayed silent and calm, despite the questions jumping around in his mind. A fantasy also began, one that he couldn't shake.

Brett watched and waited for the two to split up before classes, eager to give the girl the video he had picked out for her, barely able to hold back the desire to run up and down the hallway shouting that Jimmy liked watching bondage sex movies.

The two stood by her locker for a long time, both having gone right to it, since Jimmy didn't seem fond of using his own all that much and instead just carried all his books from class to class.

Dork!

Anger at the guy oozed through his veins. He so desperately wanted to walk over there and punch him right in the face, consequences be damned.

Somehow, he held back and waited for the two to part ways, Jimmy heading toward the science hallway, Tina toward math.

Halfway toward the math class Brett intercepted her, the words, "Hey, cutie, how's it hanging?" leaving his lips.

"What do you want?" she asked while trying to slip between him and the wall of lockers.

Brett put his hand up against the locker to stop her.

"Tina, isn't it?" Brett asked.

"Yeah," Tina said. She started to walk around him the other way, but he reached out and grabbed her by the arm. "Hey, let go of me." She tried to twist away, but his grip was too firm.

"Not so fast. I just have a question for you. Do you know if I can borrow Jimmy's handcuffs one day?"

"What?"

"You mean you don't know?" Brett asked.

"Know what?" She tried twisting away again to no avail.

"That Jimmy is a huge bondage freak and loves to see girls and boys all tied up."

"You're sick," Tina said.

"Hey, you don't have to believe me. Just watch this tape." He reached into his bag and pulled out the VHS tape, only she wouldn't take it. "There are a whole bunch more where this one came from too, and I'm sure Jimmy will show you his others if you want."

"Why don't you get a life?" Tina snapped and tried to pull free again.

In the hallway, other students were rushing by them as they tried to get to class. No one paid much attention to them, and those who did made no move to intervene.

"It's your little friend who needs to get a life," Brett said. "Take the tape."

"Let me go!"

"Take the tape and I will."

Tina grabbed his arm and dug her nails into it.

Brett winced and grabbed hold of her backpack, his fingers easily opening the flap and dropping the tape inside.

Above them, the bell rang.

"Enjoy," he said and hurried away. In his mind, he saw crowds cheering his brilliant move. Others came forward to shake his hand.

The excitement wore off quickly though as he headed into his English class. He hated the class and the teacher and would have gladly skipped the class if it wasn't something he needed in order to graduate. Most had completed the English course the year before. He had failed it, and now had to sit in the class with a bunch of juniors while listening to the stupid fag tell them all about all these great authors. It was such a waste of his time. If they were so great, why hadn't he ever heard of them before?

"Samantha," Megan said again. "Just try."

Once again, her friend ignored her, only now Megan wasn't going to back down.

"Samantha, get off your lazy ass and start undoing those ropes!" Megan screamed.

Several hours earlier screaming like this would not have been possible, but the food and water Jimmy had given her during his morning visit had helped clear her mind a bit. She was still sluggish, and her exhaustion still felt like a boulder strapped onto her head, but her thought process was once again able to focus on things, which was good. Even better, the hallucinations had disappeared for the time being, though she was sure they would return sooner than later, especially if she continued another day without sleep.

"Do it!"

"No," Samantha moaned.

Megan couldn't stand her friend anymore. *Why wouldn't she at least make an effort? Why not do everything in her power to get free?*

You didn't make an effort this morning either, her mind countered. Thankfully, her inner voice no longer sounded like it was coming from someone else.

Frustration followed.

She had made no move against Jimmy while he was cleaning her, even though he had been pretty vulnerable, especially when bending over to clean her feet.

Don't let a moment like that slip by again!

She pictured an image of her getting the better of Jimmy and killing him. It was a pleasant fantasy, one that had permanently replaced the visions of her father coming to the rescue because that wasn't going to happen—*which is all your fault!* If she had thought about calling him earlier while the phone was beeping, Samantha and she would be free and Jimmy locked away. If she had called earlier, she could have told her father exactly where the fallout shelter was and he would have come down, broken the door from its hinges, and cut them free. After that, he would have gone after Jimmy and made the bastard pay.

Now that wasn't a viable possibility, and if the two of them ever wanted to be free, they would have to do it themselves. More importantly, Samantha would have to undo her own ropes, and she would have to do it while in her current position, one that would allow her to stand up and put the knots to her mouth, knots that she could untie if her determination to be free inspired the strenuous activity.

Once you're free, you can untie me, and we will both get Jimmy when he comes in. Megan had said this out loud several times since Jimmy had left for school that morning, but her friend didn't seem to be able or willing to take part in the escape attempt.

"Samantha! Please!"

Her friend didn't respond.

"All you have to do is stand up and untie the ropes with your mouth."

Nothing.

"Do it!" Megan screamed and moved forward a bit so she could kick her friend.

The distance between them was just enough to make it impossible for Megan's foot to cause damage, but only because of the rope holding her hands. If she had been low like Samantha, she could have easily reached her and hit her hard, but then, if she was low like that, she wouldn't have to rely on her friend at all. Now Samantha was her only hope, and it, like the hope of her father coming to the rescue, was fading fast.

"If you don't untie yourself, we will die down here," Megan said.

Again, her friend did not reply.

Megan screamed.

Her voice bounced off the concrete walls several times and then faded.

Megan tried kicking her friend again with her naked leg, but once again couldn't reach.

Tears threatened to fall after that, but she held them back, thoughts of killing Jimmy herself helping to distract her mind.

If you kill him, you will die.

But at least it would be more satisfying than waiting for him to kill her and then get away with it.

And once he was dead and Samantha saw it, maybe she would snap out of her fear-induced submission.

The school day passed quickly for Jimmy and Tina, both of them having only had to go to their morning classes. Normally a half day would have seen them going to all their classes, each one shortened considerably so they could all fit, but this half day wasn't like that since the other grade levels still had a full day.

"I feel bad for your brother," Tina said as they left the school. "It really is silly that we get to leave so much earlier than him."

"Yeah, but he only has three hours to go," Jimmy said. "He will survive."

"Yeah, three hours isn't really that long."

"No, and there are worse things than having to sit in class during them."

An uneasy silence followed.

The two stepped out of the parking lot and onto the sidewalk that would take them around the small lake and into the neighborhood, Jimmy's eyes once again glancing at the garbage bin he had so foolishly thrown the videos into.

"What is it?" Tina asked.

"Oh nothing," Jimmy said. "Do you think your mother will be upset that you didn't stay?"

"She'll be upset, but I don't really care."

"How come?"

"Because she doesn't deserve any of the credit. When she left, she made the decision she didn't want to be my mother, but now she is trying really hard because the court says she gets a second chance. It's stupid. This country is so focused on blood relations as if there really is a connection there, but there isn't. They could have put me in a house with a lady that had no idea who I was, who'd never even set foot in Illinois, and she would be just as connected to me as Rebecca is."

"Huh," Jimmy said. He really didn't know how to add anything to that.

"What's worse is how often people in this country will side with a mother because of the fact that she carried the baby for nine months, even if the father would be the better parent. If Rebecca had wanted to, she could have probably gotten custody of me without much trouble when she left. It's stupid."

Jimmy thought about a girl in one of his classes who had once said she would rather have an abortion than sign her child up for adoption because she couldn't stand the thought of *giving up* her child. The statement had confused him at the time, but now that he was a few years older and had gotten a better idea of the world, he had come to realize she wasn't alone in her thoughts. It was weird.

"But what can you do about it?" Jimmy said. He had planned on sharing the story of the girl, but then decided against it.

"Nothing, I guess," Tina said.

"Exactly."

No matter how loud she shouted, no one was going to be convinced, so why even bother?

Tina's house appeared on the left.

The two stopped.

Jimmy's mind replayed the statement she had made earlier about being all alone and wondered if she wanted him to come in. How did one go about asking that? How

—

"Do you want to come inside for a while?" Tina asked.

"Um, if you think it's okay," Jimmy said. "I don't want you to get in trouble."

"Come on, it'll be fine," Tina said and took hold of his hand.

Jimmy felt a pleasant tingle run up his arm as she pulled him toward the door, and when she let go to open the door, an impression of her hand stayed against his skin.

The house was quiet.

"You're sure she's not home?" Jimmy whispered.

"Rebecca!" Tina shouted.

Jimmy jumped.

No answer followed.

"See," Tina said with a smile.

Jimmy returned the smile.

"Come on." She took hold of his hand again and led him up the stairs.

Jimmy's heart was racing. Were they going to have sex? Did she want to have sex?

She wouldn't have taken you up here if she didn't, his mind said.

But maybe she would? Maybe she just wants me to see her room.

If he made a move and it turned out she didn't want to have sex with him, it could ruin everything. But if he didn't make a move and she did want sex, that might ruin things too.

"My room in Glen Ellyn was better," Tina said as the two entered.

Jimmy looked around and said, "Looks cool to me."

"Believe me, it isn't." She tossed her backpack into the corner while saying this and took a seat on the bed.

Jimmy stayed where he was, unsure what to do.

"Come sit by me," Tina said.

Jimmy did, placing himself a few inches away.

Tina quickly closed the gap, and without warning, her leg was touching his through his jeans. The tingle that developed from this was considerably greater and more pleasurable than the one that had entered through his hand moments earlier.

Jimmy didn't know what to do. In his mind he saw himself reaching around and kissing her, his body eventually pushing her down onto the bed, her own hands touching him while also undoing all the obstacles between them.

The action stayed within his mind, however, and rather than making the move, he just sat there.

Do something! he shouted at himself.

Nothing happened.

Silence settled.

Just kiss her, or touch her leg, or touch her breast.

Jimmy raised a hand to do the latter but then quickly pulled it back, the fear of upsetting her getting the better of him.

Tina watched the hand come up and thought to herself, *Here we go, he's going to do it,* but then saw the hand fall back and felt her heart sink. He wasn't going to make a move.

You do it!

All she had to do was reach over and start touching him, maybe press her hand against his groin, which had an obvious bulge in it, and start rubbing. Once she did that, he would finally realize what it was she wanted and would take over, his body pressing into hers as the two indulged in the lovemaking process.

Just touch him!

Her hand didn't move at first, but then she gently placed it on his thigh and said, "I really like you, Jimmy."

He didn't respond right away and when he did, his voice was caught up in his throat, the words "I like you too" badly mangled.

Her hand rubbed a bit against his leg, yet still he

didn't make a move.

Move it closer!

She ignored this cry, her mind wanting him to take charge—*needing him to take charge.*

Kiss him.

This she could do and quickly leaned in and touched her lips to his.

Jimmy seemed surprised by this and pulled back as their lips touched, but then moved in and kissed her back. His hand then came up, took hold of her head, and held it in place so he could kiss her harder, his lips pressing into hers with quite a bit of force.

After a few seconds, Tina had to pull back.

Jimmy looked surprised and said, "I'm sorry."

"No, it's okay."

Jimmy stood up from the bed. "I should…I—"

Tina reached out a hand, took his, and pulled him back toward her. "I liked that, Jimmy," she said.

"You did?"

"Yeah." She grabbed him by the front of his jeans. "I liked that a lot."

She stood up after that, her body pressed up into his because of the bed, and kissed him. Down below she could feel his erection pressing into her and quietly slipped her hand down into his jeans to touch it.

Jimmy quivered as she did this and then, without warning, took charge and pressed her back down onto the bed, his hands first holding her head as he kissed her again and then moving down to explore the other parts of her body, his fingertips teasing her as they gently crisscrossed her most sensitive areas.

What followed was amazing and completely unexpected, and by the time it was over she felt thoroughly used up, her body barely able to move.

Jimmy lay next to Tina for a long time afterward, pleased yet angry, though not with Tina but himself, because of how much he had enjoyed what had just happened. It wasn't just that, though. It was the enjoyment he had felt with her compared to the lack of enjoyment he been feeling with Samantha and Megan, something which he should have been enjoying more than what he had just done, because it was what he had been dreaming about for years.

It didn't make sense.

There had been absolutely no bondage involved in what Tina and he had done, yet the moment she had slipped her fingers around his penis and slowly started to stroke it while kissing him, he had known this was going to be the greatest moment of his life, and that his orgasm would be intense.

And then when she had licked him and swirled her tongue around him, one hand holding his penis while the other tickled his balls, all before slipping a condom onto him and then getting on top of him and easing his penis into her pussy and riding him until he came—God, he could have died a happy man after that. It had been incredible.

*And if she was tied up while doing it, her only goal to please me while also taking pleasure in what I did to her…*that is what heaven would be like in his eyes.

But how would I go about getting her to do this?

Worse, what if I drove her away by asking this and she never again did what she just did to me?

What if she really enjoyed it and was completely submissive like those girls in the videos I watched?

The questions tugged at his mind as he lay there with Tina, his body feeling completely satisfied yet strangely craving more. He didn't want another round right this minute, but he knew he would want to do this again, and again, and again.

With a pair of handcuffs.

God, how could he even ask her something like that?

She would think he was crazy.

Tina too lay there amazed at what had just happened, though she had no thoughts of bondage or the possibility of bondage—that would come later. Instead, she had been overwhelmed by what Jimmy had been able to do with his fingers and how easily they had brought her to one orgasm after another. Eventually she couldn't take it anymore and grabbed his hand while his thumb was playing with her clit, his index and middle finger inside of her, and pulled him out.

For a moment, he had looked confused, but then she had flipped him over onto his back and slid down between his knees, her hope being to give him as much pleasure as he had just given her. To do this, she undid his pants and pulled them, along with his underwear, down his legs, surprised but also impressed by his shaven penis, something she hadn't even noticed while reaching down inside. The lack of hair changed her mind about what she was going to do to him. At first, she had been planning to use her hand, her palm rubbing the head the way she had read in *Cosmo*, but then decided to see what it felt like to put her mouth around him, the disgust at such an activity completely disappearing due to how clean he was.

Of course, her hands still played with him as well, his

impressive size making it so there was enough to go around, and she worked on him for a good fifteen minutes, his knees often bucking from the intensity.

Once she finished that, her lips and hands having brought him close to orgasm several times but never actually to the point of no return, she pulled a condom from her purse, tore the package, and gently slipped it onto his erection, her mind thinking, *Here we go, this is it.*

A quick sharp pain hit as she eased herself onto him, his large penis slowly but surely tearing away her virginity. Once that happened, however, the pleasure masked the pain and she moved up and down, her athletic legs able to maneuver her hips so that he never slipped free. At first she stayed straddled on top of him, but then after several minutes she laid on top of him, his penis still inside, so that her breasts were pressed into his chest, her lips in line with his. They kissed and kissed and kissed while she worked back and forth with her hips, the position causing his penis to push up against different areas within, ones that were incredibly sensitive.

"*Oh God!*" Jimmy cried at one point, his knees again bucking up against her. "I'm going to cum!"

"Give it to me!" she cried back. "Give it—" She felt warmth through the condom and for a moment worried that the condom had actually broken, but then, when she slipped herself free, the thing was still covering his penis, though he had cum so much some had actually slipped down the shaft beyond the edge of the protection.

She had pulled the condom free after that and tossed it toward the waste bucket—it fell short—and then pulled the bedsheet out from under them and eased both their bodies beneath it, her arms around Jimmy.

"That was amazing," she said while pressed up against

him.

"Yeah," Jimmy said.

Nothing else was said for a long time because words were not needed.

Alan glanced at Tina's house while walking home that day and wondered if Jimmy and Tina were inside, and if so, were they having fun? A smile crossed his face while thinking this, one that then faded as he pictured Jimmy and Tina together in bed. Ugh. It wasn't something he wanted to think about—at least not when Jimmy was involved. Tina he could think about all he wanted and, in fact, he had even imagined himself with her from time to time, especially when sitting on the shower floor. She was a beautiful girl, one who was nicely built but not stuck up, one he knew would be fun in bed because she wouldn't be shy or embarrassed to try things. That was the trouble with girls in high school—at least that was the trouble with the ones he had had sex with. They were all so unimaginative and thought sex was just about having a guy stick himself into them and pound away. Alan knew differently. He also knew that there were things high school couples could do that were incredibly pleasurable but didn't have the risk of getting pregnant attached, things that health classes should talk about rather than the stupid "abstinence" theory. Abstinence was the equivalent of telling a person with diarrhea to just hold it. It was ridiculous.

A deputy cruiser drove by him while he was walking, the deputy inside—he couldn't make out who it was—not hiding the fact that he was staring at Alan.

Alan waved.

Ever since the sheriff's daughter had disappeared the

police presence had been pretty heavy, yet there still hadn't been any significant developments. Rumor had it that search parties would be started soon, ones that would comb the woods and fields looking for bodies. Why they hadn't started those parties yet was something Alan didn't understand. He hoped there was a good reason for it, but doubted it. He also had a feeling that these two disappearances would ruin Sheriff Reed's career. People were already voicing complaints about the way he had handled things, and they would remember their dissatisfaction come the next vote.

Another deputy cruised by as he neared the house and caused him to wonder if there would be a heavy presence tomorrow night at the dance. He hoped not because he wanted to try to get Rachel alone somewhere to fool around. He had even hinted at this while in art class with her today, and she had teased him with a dozen *maybes* and *we'll sees.*

Maybe we will see if you are able to resist my charm, Alan said to himself with a smile.

An image of her pulling her dress down to reveal what had to be beautiful breasts stayed with him all the way into the house.

"Jimmy, you here?" he called out.

No answer.

His smile grew. What if Jimmy was really getting it on! If so, he was happy for his brother, though again he really didn't want to think about it too much.

The vision of Rachel with her dress pulled down returned. It was a better thought, one that followed him around the house as he got a snack and then went to watch TV.

Nothing good was on, so he headed to a news station

to see if there was any mention of the missing girls. Nothing was said. Had there not been so much focus on the oil spill and who was to blame for it, then maybe some of the affiliates in Chicago would have been interested and driven the three and a half hours south to get here, but kidnappings and suspicious disappearances weren't the fad right now.

Megan's wrists screamed as she purposely lifted her legs into the air so that they would become covered in urine when she peed. Unfortunately, she was unable to go when in this position and eventually put her legs back down, much to the relief of her arms, and simply leaned to the side so that it all wouldn't just splash all over the floor. The position wasn't perfect and a lot of the urine was wasted, but a good amount still went down her bare leg, the dark yellow liquid almost sluggish as it found the path of least resistance.

Finished, all Megan could do was wait and hope that Jimmy would respond the same way he had this morning when he had cleaned her legs. Worry was present too, along with a small bit of disgust at what she had done, despite its potential for saving her life.

Only if your timing is perfect, her mind said. *You will get one shot at this, and if you fail…*

She looked at Samantha and knew that what the girl had gone through as punishment for her escape attempt would probably be nothing compared to what Jimmy would do to her.

Jimmy and Tina grew hungry after a while and left the comfort of the bed to head into town. They ate at a local sandwich place, one which was often frequented by kids during the lunch hour at school, but now was pretty quiet thanks to the midafternoon time and provided them with a nice cozy atmosphere to talk about what they had just done, a topic which they danced around at first but then jumped into once the subject was fully broached. It was great.

Afterward, the two walked home holding hands.

"You don't have to walk all the way back to my house," Tina said once they came close to his house, which was closer to the downtown area than her house. "I'm sure I'll be fine, and I know you are tired."

"I am tired. You wore me out"—he smiled—"but I also like spending time with you and want to see you all the way to the door."

Tina returned the smile and allowed him to walk her back to the house. Once there, he kissed her goodbye, a long passionate kiss that left her warm and tingly, and watched her go inside.

Once inside, Tina went to the window and watched him walk away, curious why he took a right from her house as opposed to a left, but then she decided maybe he wanted to enjoy some time to himself with more walking—though if he was like her, he was really sore from the afternoon activities—and went into her room.

Her eyes stumbled upon the condom, which hadn't made it into the waste bucket, and she picked it up, once again thinking about what they had done and how wonderful it had been.

He is a great guy.

She wrapped herself in thoughts about him and climbed back into bed.

Jimmy didn't head home right away, because he knew

Alan would be there by now and he didn't want to walk in just to leave a second later. Originally, he had planned on heading to the fallout shelter that night, but now he wanted to get it over with, especially given how suspicious his activity around the Hood place would be if he were caught near dark again.

They probably will be suspicious of me now as well if I'm caught over there again.

This was why he had decided to head back toward the school rather than straight to the Hood place. That way he could cut through the woods all the way there. It was an easy and well-known path, but one that would be completely hidden by the road, and therefore it was doubtful any law enforcement types would see him. He also doubted there would be any people on the trail, the idea that they could disappear next keeping them from going into places like the forest, which was perfect for him.

What am I going to do with them?

The question had been bouncing around ever since he and Tina had walked back from the sandwich shop. A part of him just wanted to kill the girls and get rid of them like he had the bondage videos. Another part knew this wasn't a good idea because he would grow desperate again—unless Tina was into the bondage stuff as well.

But would that be enough to stifle the cravings?

The idea of her willingly allowing him to tie her up was very appealing, but at the same time, he liked the idea of a girl being helpless. Still, there was something to be said about the enthusiasm Tina had shown today, and how powerful his pleasure had been because of it. Samantha and Megan did not show enthusiasm like that. They didn't care about making him enjoy himself and probably never would.

Unless I train them to only think about my pleasure.

Was that even possible?

Could he turn them into sex slaves whose only goal in life was to make him happy?

Could he get them to the point where he could leave the door open and they would not flee—only in theory, because he would never be stupid enough to risk it?

Or should I just kill them and end it?

In his mind, he saw them both hanging from their necks, their faces turning red while their legs kicked, painful choked gasps escaping their lips. From reading stories online (the Internet was full of breath play sites), he also knew that their pussies would get really tight when doing this, so if he was inside them at the time, it would feel great.

The idea turned him on, even though he had already ejaculated that day, and if the walk through the woods had been a closely contested race, his erection would be what people looked at during a photo finish.

If I hang Samantha from her neck, would Megan give me a blow job to save her life?

Having felt how wonderful it was for a girl to suck on his dick, something that he had been fantasizing about for years, he now craved it again and wanted to see what it was like to cum in their mouths. He wanted to watch them taste his cum and swish it between their lips before finally swallowing it.

In his mind he watched as Tina rolled the condom onto him and slipped him inside her, her fingers at first having trouble getting him positioned properly but then finally finding the tiny opening, which swallowed him up. It had felt wonderful, but not as pleasurable as her lips and hands, yet for some reason he had cum quickly while inside her. He didn't know why this was.

Up ahead the trees started to clear as the Hood house drew near. Jimmy slowed down and approached the place cautiously, wanting to make sure no one was present before he made himself visible.

All seemed quiet.

Still, being as cautious as possible, he stepped off the path and crept through the woods until he was right in line with the shed and then emerged from the trees, thereby cutting down the risk that someone would just happen to walk by and see him.

Megan had been in a sort of daze when the door finally opened later that afternoon—what had seemed like an eternity after peeing on herself—her mind and body unable to stay focused for long periods of time due to her unbearable and drawn-out situation. She had also wasted quite a bit of energy being angry at Samantha shortly after peeing on herself, the disgust at her actions having gotten the better of her and forming the spearhead of her anger, her feelings being that had Samantha untied the ropes with her mouth like Megan had suggested, then she wouldn't have had to pee on herself again. Samantha hadn't fought back, but that wasn't needed, because Megan's mind had played both sides and berated herself for falling into Jimmy's trap to begin with and for not making the call to her father when she had the chance.

It was the latter mistake, her failure to call, that shamed her the most, not just because it would have ended their ordeal, but because it could, in reality, have been one of those rare life-and-death moments, one which she had fucked up. It wasn't even her life that she thought about, but Samantha's. If her friend died, and by the looks of it that moment wasn't very far away, she would be responsible. Not "trigger-pulling" responsible, but responsible nonetheless.

Pissing all over herself would be her redemption, but only if it spurred Samantha into action. If not…

Megan didn't want to think about what would happen if that became the reality. If she killed Jimmy, and Samantha still stayed in her coma-like condition, then they would both die.

These thoughts weren't present when Jimmy finally did enter, but they hadn't disappeared either. Instead, they had simply embedded themselves in her.

Jimmy grimaced at the smell of the room.

Megan didn't know if it was because of the freshly dried pee on her leg and the floor, or just the standard "two people living down here" smell that he had attempted to clean away this morning.

The question was answered quickly.

"Did she piss herself again?" Jimmy asked and nodded toward Samantha.

"No," Megan said, her eyes looking toward the floor as if in shame. "I did."

Jimmy looked at her leg. "Why didn't you use the bucket?" There was anger in his voice, though something else seemed to soften it. She didn't know what, though.

"I—" she started.

"Goddamn, I left it there so you two wouldn't make me clean you like this every fucking day!"

"I'm sorry," Megan shouted, tears somehow falling from her eyes. "I forgot about the bucket. I'm so tired from standing here like this. I'm"—she briefly wondered if whining this much would get her punished—"can you please clean it off? I won't do it again. I promise."

Jimmy stared at her for several seconds.

"I'm going to make sure you keep that promise, because I think you peed on yourself just to keep me from fucking you, but it isn't going to work. From now on I'm going to fuck you every time I come down here, no matter how disgusting you make yourself." With that, he went into the back to grab the washcloth he had set on the sink to dry this morning, wetted it, and returned.

Heart racing, Megan waited for him to get down and start cleaning her leg.

One chance at this!

Jimmy took the cold washcloth and started rubbing her leg, his hand purposely pressing hard while the other held her leg in place.

For a moment, Megan feared he would keep hold of her leg the entire time, but then he started to kneel to get at her ankle and let go.

Now!

Her limp body sprang into action, her legs quickly hooking Jimmy by his throat and pulling him directly into her groin.

One moment Jimmy was leaning forward to clean off Megan's foot, the next she had her legs wrapped around his throat, choking him, his mouth pressed right into her exposed pussy, his lips gasping for air.

It happened really fast, so fast that Jimmy couldn't even really evaluate the situation. Instead, he just reacted, his hands trying desperately to pull her legs free. Unfortunately, despite his strength, his arms were no match for her thighs, even in her weakened state, and the more he pulled the tighter they seemed to become, almost as if she were fighting his attempt by squeezing harder.

Without thought, his fingernails plunged into the flesh of her legs and sliced toward the ground, his nails like a farm tractor tearing up packed-in dirt.

Megan screamed but didn't let go.

Jimmy felt her flesh curled beneath his nails as it ripped free, but still her legs would not loosen.

A fuzzy darkness began to appear around the edges of his vision. At the same time, he heard his own lips trying to suck in air but getting nothing but pussy hair and sweaty fluids.

"Die, you bastard!" Megan cried.

Her legs got even tighter.

He tried punching her in the kidneys but couldn't muster enough force. From there he tried reaching up toward her eyes but couldn't make it.

Her legs continued to squeeze, and suddenly the darkness began to cloud his entire vision span.

His arms flailed around, looking for something, for anything, but finding nothing.

The darkness got thicker.

His lungs screamed for air.

He continued to flail his arms.

Up above he heard laughter.

A horrible dry gasp echoed from his lips.

Urine flooded his pants.

This was it. He was about to go—

His knuckles crashed into something hard, something that *PINGED!* when he hit it. Without any thought, he grabbed the object by the thin handle and swung it upward.

* * *

"Die, you bastard!" Megan cried, her lips working without her mind processing anything, her only real focus being her legs and keeping them tight despite the pain in her wrists—pain that was intensified because Jimmy was adding weight to her body.

An eerie laughter followed, one that she never realized was her own.

Jimmy's struggles started to cease.

She had no idea how long she had been holding him like this, but knew she had to hold on for a long time, even after he blacked out, because he could be faking.

To emphasize this, she squeezed her legs harder and harder, thinking this would be much easier if his neck would just break. The added force within her muscles inflamed the cuts his nails had made and caused more blood to well up, but she didn't care. Later, once she was free, those scratches would be minor annoyances, ones that would fail to cloud her happiness.

Something came toward her, something big.

She tried twisting out of the way at the last second but couldn't and felt everything flee her mind as the object crashed into her face, her nose audibly crunching beneath it as the object pulped the cartilage, a heavy *THUNK!* bouncing back and forth within her skull, scrambling her brain.

She felt her legs loosen even as her mind tried to hold them in place.

A second blow landed.

Blackness followed.

Jimmy fell to the floor after the second blow, his left knee and right ankle tangling together and absorbing most of the landing. The metal bucket followed him down, its impact echoing through the small room as it was ripped from his fingers and sent bouncing across the cement.

For a moment he knelt where he had landed, his mind and body trying to focus, but then a foot came into view and crashed into his face—not hard, but enough to knock him off-balance—and sent him scurrying away, his left knee screaming each time it pushed off from the floor.

The heavy metal door stopped his retreat, and rather than standing up and fleeing the room, Jimmy flopped over onto his side, closed his eyes, and gulped in one giant lungful of air after another.

He lay there for a long time, barely able to comprehend what had just happened, his only focus being the ability to breathe again, the sting of the air on his raw throat a welcome pain because it meant he was still alive.

You have survived every escape attempt.

Jimmy thought about this for a few seconds but then let it fade from his mind. Later the observation would return, and when it did he would really wonder about it, but now all he cared about was lying back and taking the deep breaths. Nothing else mattered.

Oh God! Tina thought to herself while watching the video Brett had given her, having not expected to see what she saw, her fingers frantically trying to find the Mute button so her mother would not hear the screams that echoed from the screen.

Disgust quickly followed and drove her fingers toward the Stop button.

Wait.

She continued to watch, a strange fascination coming over her as the scene unfolded.

A moment later, she turned it off, the disgust having returned. Anger followed, and for a few minutes she actually considered heading over to Brett's place and demanding to know why he had given her the tape.

The darkening skies outside stopped her in her tracks. Why risk ending up like the other two missing girls because of a stupid tape?

Why does Brett have tapes like this?

The pig had said they belonged to Jimmy, but that probably was a lie, one designed to hurt Jimmy because that seemed to be Brett's main goal in life.

Besides, if they belonged to Jimmy, how would Brett have known about them? It didn't make sense. Instead, Brett was probably the one who owned the tape and realized he could use it against Jimmy. However, if he owned tapes like this, that probably meant he was interested in this—or someone he knew was—and if he was interested in seeing it on screen, it only made sense he would be interested in seeing it in real life too.

The first scene from the video appeared in her mind, one that showed two girls in a dark dungeon, one in a cage, the other standing with her wrists chained to the wall. After a few seconds a leather-clad man in a black mask walked in and started ripping the clothes off the girl chained to the wall, the girl in the cage forced to watch as he then sexually molested her. Finished with her, the man left her dangling in her chains and went over to the one in the cage, who fought like a cat at the vet to stay inside, but was eventually ripped free and dragged kicking and screaming to a table where she was locked down, stretched, and raped. The faces of the girls in her mind were different from the ones who had been on screen. The faces in her mind belonged to Samantha King and Megan Reed. And the man in the mask, well, that was obviously Brett Murphy.

You should give this tape to the sheriff and tell him Brett gave it to you.

She remembered the look the sheriff had when taking in Scott after he had followed her into the school yesterday and knew he would probably be even more aggressive with Brett once he saw the video. At the same time, she wondered if the video really was connected to the two girls disappearing, and if it really was Brett's.

What if it does belong to Jimmy?

But how would Brett have gotten his hands on it?

Unfortunately, this didn't push the idea away completely, and even worse, it kept interfering with her thoughts on what the two had done this afternoon. Rather than relishing the recent memory, some of which she could still almost feel on her skin, she kept seeing Jimmy yank her from the bed and pull her into the dungeon from the video, where he ravaged her like the man in the video had done to the girl in chains.

Tina shivered.

The horrible vision would not leave. In fact, the more she tried to push it away, the more determined it seemed to become, and not only did it recreate what the two had done in a dungeon-like setting, it added several more scenes as well, scenes that she would never in a million years want to take part in and felt herself growing sick just thinking about.

Jimmy didn't remember falling asleep, nor did he know what time it was when he woke later. He also didn't care, his only real thought being the pain as he tried to move, his neck and back feeling as if he had spent days on the concrete floor rather than whatever short amount of time he had actually been asleep.

What if it was days! his mind cried. *What if you missed the dance and everyone is looking for you?*

Jimmy shook the thought away while standing up and looked over at Samantha and Megan. The last image he had of them had been the lifeless poses each had succumbed to, Samantha on her knees with her head hanging down against her chest, the ropes seeming to barely hold her up, and Megan dangling from the ropes, the blow with the bucket having knocked her into unconsciousness so that her feet no longer supported her body and instead just acted like two flesh rudders as she slowly swayed back and forth, her weight never seeming to be able to settle in one spot.

Is she still unconscious? Jimmy wondered and realized he should check.

His neck protested the upward movement as Jimmy forced his body to his feet, his hands having to guide himself up the door due to the dizzy spells that swirled the room.

Once up, he stood with his eyes closed for several seconds, fighting everything that threatened to knock him back down, and then, once recovered, carefully walked across the room to check on Megan.

Her back was to him.

Jimmy took hold of her right arm, his hand slowly but forcefully twisting her around to face him.

A gasp erupted, followed by the sound of the bucket once again bouncing across the floor as Jimmy backed away from the grisly image and tripped over it.

The metal door stopped his fall, his poor elbow taking all his weight as he crashed into it, pain messages reaching his brain quickly along with the order to cry out.

The sound faded.

Samantha and Megan did not react.

The urge to vomit followed, but nothing was in his stomach, the lunch Tina and he had eaten earlier long since digested.

God, what did I do to her? he demanded while leaning against the wall, the image of Megan's busted face refusing to leave.

You did what you had to do to survive!

The sensation of the bucket connecting with her face returned to his arms, as did the sense of satisfaction that had momentarily followed—until he found himself falling. At the time, however, he'd had no idea just how hard he had smashed the object into her face, his only thought being to free himself.

Is she even alive?

The question did not sit well, and despite not wanting to look at that face again, he knew he had to check and forced himself to cross the room again.

Her face wasn't as shocking the second time around, but was still repulsive, the metal side of the bucket having completely flattened her nose. Her mouth had suffered as well, the upper lip having busted like a fat blood-filled leech and her teeth having been knocked loose into her mouth.

The snot-filled blood was the worst part, though, and it pretty much covered her entire lower face and breasts, which were large enough and thrust out far enough to catch most of the drippings.

In the midst of all this destruction a slight wheeze could be heard, one that signaled the work of her lungs as her body struggled to breathe.

She's alive.

But would she stay that way?

Only time would tell.

CHAPTER TWELVE

Alan was in the middle of making a pot of coffee, his body still fighting the urge to go back to bed, his eyes barely able to stay open, when Jimmy walked into the kitchen and said, "Remember, only five scoops."

Alan turned to reply but stopped and instead said, "Whoa, what happened to your neck?"

"What?" Jimmy asked, his voice panicked, a hand rising to touch his throat.

"It's all bruised up," Alan said.

Jimmy hurried from the kitchen and went to the mirror in the front hall.

Alan followed.

"Holy shit," Jimmy said.

"What happened?" Alan asked.

"I don't know."

"Bullshit," Alan snapped. "You didn't come home until really late last night and now say you don't know what happened?"

"I was with Tina," Jimmy said.

"Not all evening you weren't. I called to find out because we were supposed to go pick up our tuxes when

Mom came home, remember?" Alan had been pretty angry about this and had even driven around the neighborhood looking for his brother, thinking maybe he had gone on a bike ride after seeing Tina, but then upon coming home realized the bike was still in the garage.

"Sorry, I forgot." He continued touching his throat. "We can go today, though."

"Yeah, and it will be packed, and we will have to try them on to make sure they fit, which means we will have to wait in line for the dressing rooms."

"So what?" Jimmy snapped. "It was probably packed last night too, and the day before. We're not the only ones going."

"Still, where were you? Mom and Dad were worried and thought maybe you were the next to disappear." This was a lie. His parents had been a bit concerned, but that was all, and they hadn't really thought anything bad had happened. Alan, however, had thought differently.

"Gee thanks, two girls and me," Jimmy said. "Nice."

"Hey, you never know with people like this. Maybe they would want a teenage guy to go with the two girls. Maybe they are like crazy scientists from U of I that want to breed humans for some sort of illegal testing."

Jimmy shook his head. "What time does the tux place open?"

"I don't know, nine, ten." Alan shrugged. "Maybe earlier than usual because of prom?"

"Okay, then let's go around eight thirty, and if they aren't open we can get some breakfast at the bagel place, my treat."

Alan nodded. "Fine, and we need to go to the flower place and pick up some corsages while we're out."

"Pick up what?" Jimmy asked.

"Corsages."

"What the hell are those?"

Alan shook his head. "Flower things, you idiot, for the girls to wear. Every guy gets them for their date. It's tradition."

"It sounds stupid."

"Most traditions usually are."

Jimmy sighed. "How much do they cost?"

"I don't know." The fact was Alan hadn't thought about the corsages either, not until Rachel had called to remind him to pick one up for her. "I just hope the place actually has some, because I think you're supposed to order them in advance."

"Great. Anything else I should know about so I don't make a fool out of myself?"

"Yeah, but you'll want to grab a pad of paper and a pen before I tell you." He started to fill the coffee pot with water and went to pour it into the machine.

"What?"

"I'm just fucking with you."

"Alan!" Kelly Hawthorn snapped while walking into the kitchen.

Jimmy smiled.

"Um," Alan started, nearly dropping the coffee pot. "What?"

"Just want to make sure you used five scoops and only five scoops before you hit Brew."

Jimmy cracked up laughing. His parents knew swears were just stupid words that got people needlessly worked up and didn't care if they used them sparingly.

"Jimmy, what happened to your neck?" Kelly asked.

"I don't know. I must've slept on it weird." He touched it. "It doesn't hurt."

His mother eyed him suspiciously for a few seconds and then turned toward the coffee pot, which had started to brew.

Coffee in hand, Jimmy returned to his room where he browsed the Internet for a while, but then grew bored of that—even the bondage sites he visited (it was all the same stuff repeated over and over again)—and headed into the bathroom to look at his throat.

The bruises weren't too bad but were obviously noticeable enough to draw unwanted attention, especially the really purple one under his right ear, which was where Megan's ankle had smashed into when she first grabbed him. Thankfully, he had a feeling his tuxedo shirt would cover the bruise, so not too many people would ask him about it. Then again, he doubted many people would talk to him anyway, so it didn't really matter all that much.

Actually, if they were worse they could be a good conversation starter, he said to himself.

Had the bruises arrived from another more honorable situation, Jimmy wouldn't have minded talking about it, but given the source he would prefer it if people didn't notice.

An idea occurred.

He flipped off the set of lights closest to the mirror and looked at himself again. The bruises were pretty hard to see when the light wasn't focusing on them directly, and since the lights at the dance would most likely be set on low to produce a more formal atmosphere, he probably had nothing to worry about.

She planned this, he said to himself. It was something he had been thinking about ever since coming home, showering, and lying in bed, where he had not slept but merely rested because sleep had never arrived.

Megan had purposely peed on herself so he would clean her legs and the floor and make himself vulnerable for attack, all without any possible way of escaping afterward, which was startling.

Megan didn't care if she died, as long as she took him with her.

The thought chilled him to the core.

At the same time he knew he didn't really have to worry about this kamikaze attitude from her any longer because the chances that she would even be able to attempt anything like this again were pretty slim. Future girls might try, though, which was why he would have to be more careful once he felt he was ready to start grabbing them again—his mind still unsure if he should wait until he had his own place or continue to use the fallout shelter.

If you had simply tied her legs together, this wouldn't have happened.

Binding a girl's legs together had never really been part of his fantasy, but it didn't really detract from it either, so he figured he would experiment with it. The only downside was that he enjoyed seeing them kicking their legs when lifted off the ground, their feet trying to find something solid to balance on and relieve the pressure on their wrists.

Make a spreader bar.

Though he had never before considered it, he knew he could make the item fairly easily and that once it was in place a girl would not be able to bring her legs together unless she broke the bar, which would require a considerable amount of strength. He also was pretty sure he had everything he needed in the house, but then, such a bondage item wasn't necessary now because Samantha and Megan were not in any condition to fight with him.

An image of Megan's face arrived, causing him to shudder.

Busting up a girl's face had never been a part of his fantasy and was something he never wanted to do again. Hell, just slapping Samantha across the face the other day had soured his stomach.

Actually, the more he thought about it, whipping the girls with his belt like he had done wasn't all that appealing either. In the videos he watched it turned him on and got him off, but in real life, well, he liked watching things like that and seeing the reaction of the girls rather than being the one to administer it.

You liked taking part in the sex with Tina.

But your favorite part was watching her go down on you and watching your cock being swallowed up by her mouth and pussy.

He had also enjoyed seeing the look on her face when he had used his fingers on her, something he had never before done to a girl but seemed to be good at, probably thanks to all the videos from Kink.com where forcing girls to have orgasms over and over again seemed to be the main goal.

Torture her with pleasure!

That was exactly what he had done to Tina. He had made her orgasm so many times with his fingers that she had forced his hand from within her and rolled him over onto his back, her screams of pleasure and cries for him to stop having been replaced by his own moans.

If I had known Tina and I would do that, I would never have grabbed Samantha.

His mind didn't have a response to this statement,

though not because it was true, but because he actually feared it was false.

The thought that followed was even more disturbing: *If given the choice between the two last week, which would you have chosen?*

Jimmy knew the answer but didn't want to admit it to himself, even though it was impossible to hide from his own thoughts. Instead, he tried distracting himself by heading back into his room and watching TV while he drank his coffee, and then, not long after that, going into town with Alan to pick up the tuxedos.

"What?" Tina demanded as her mother knocked on the closed bedroom door.

"Can I come in?" Rebecca asked.

"Why?"

"Because I want to talk," she said.

"Call one of your knitting friends."

"I want to talk to you!"

"Fine." Tina had been looking at her blue homecoming dress, somewhat depressed because she hadn't been able to buy something new for prom, and now got up to unlock her door.

Rebecca stepped inside and said, "Do you know how many mothers would smack their daughters silly for speaking to them the way you speak to me?"

"Do you know how many mothers wouldn't have left their daughters, even if their marriage was a little difficult?" Tina asked back.

"Do you know why I left?" Rebecca asked. "Did your father ever tell you?"

Her father had given her many theories on why her mother had left, each one of them seeming to make sense even though they both didn't have a clue as to which one, if any, was right. Rather than say this, Tina kept her mouth shut.

"No?" Rebecca asked with a laugh. "I bet he told you lots of different reasons, but never the real one because in his mind it wouldn't have been a reason at all."

Tina had a feeling she wasn't going to like what she was about to hear.

"He never saw what he did to me that night as wrong, even though I protested against it and screamed at him to stop." She clasped her hands together and looked up as if getting ready to pray but instead laughed. "He thought he had earned it after spending so much time and money on me, and the more I fought with him the more aggressive he became."

Tears started to gleam in her eyes but did not fall, her face still more hysterical than sad.

"I knew what he wanted when he suggested we get some fresh air, but I was so overwhelmed with the entire situation that I didn't even protest that, and then, when he started kissing me out on the football field behind the bleachers, I kind of liked it, and would have cherished the memories if it hadn't gone any further."

Tina didn't want to hear any more and stood up, but to her surprise Rebecca grabbed her by the shoulders and threw her back down on the bed, her body using strength that Tina would never have expected.

"*Don't you dare leave!*" Rebecca snapped. "For nearly eighteen years your father filled your head with lies, and now it is my turn to tell you the truth. You father raped me that night behind the bleachers, and when I screamed for him to stop he put a hand over my mouth." She shuddered. "I still remember the sweaty taste of his palm and then the blood as I bit his thumb. I can still hear the sound of his shouting with pain even as he exploded inside of me, and to this day I truly believe that if he hadn't ejaculated so quickly, I would have cut through the bone and severed the thumb."

Tina was going to say something but then suddenly remembered asking her father about the scar on his thumb when she was younger.

My friend accidentally closed a car door on it, he had said with a smile. *That's why I'm always so careful to make sure you're clear of the car when I close the door.*

"I still have the dress if you'd like to see it," Rebecca said. "If you don't believe me, you can see the tears and the rips and the mud."

"Why didn't you tell the police?" Tina asked.

"Because I didn't think they would care and I was ashamed of what had happened, and then when I realized I was pregnant—"

"NO!" Tina screamed, finally realizing where this was going.

"I knew I had to take care of you, but I couldn't without your father's help, especially since my mother wouldn't speak to me and kept calling me a whore."

Tina tried to block out the words but couldn't.

"I tried to love you after you were born, but I could never look at you without thinking about that night. Even now, seeing you sitting there makes me remember what he did to me."

"Shut up!" Tina snapped.

Surprisingly, Rebecca did.

Silence settled, though Tina couldn't appreciate it because the words didn't fade.

After a few moments Rebecca said, "I've said what

you needed to hear," and left the room.

Tina burst into tears after that.

Anger followed.

"I look ridiculous," Jimmy said while waiting for his BLT bagel to cool down. "My body is not designed for formal wear."

"But Tina will love it, and that's all that matters, right?" Alan had ordered a bacon, egg, and cheese bagel all on a toasted egg bagel.

"I don't know. Tina isn't like other girls and will probably think I look ridiculous too."

"She'll love it," Alan said. "You just worry too much."

"Maybe." He took a bite. The sandwich tasted wonderful.

Alan followed suit but then grimaced and said, "Ugh, they put American cheese on it. Don't I always order cheddar cheese?"

"You forgot this time," Jimmy said with a smile.

"And you noticed? Why didn't you say something?"

"Because it's funnier this way." He took another bite. "Umm, this is really, really good."

"Bastard," Alan muttered and then, "You know, you paid for it and now I'm not going to enjoy it, so you aren't getting your money's worth."

Jimmy hadn't thought about this.

Alan took another bite, grimaced, and said, "I'm going to see if they'll just give me a piece of cheddar cheese for this and scrape off this crap." His phone rang as he was standing up, stopping him in his tracks. "Oh, it's Rachel."

Jimmy thought about saying something funny that would get Alan in trouble, but then held back.

"What?" Alan said and then listened for a second. "No, I figured we would just take my mother's car."

Jimmy took a bite.

"Are you kidding me? I don't think I can get one. It's too last minute."

Now Jimmy was curious and mouthed the words: *Get what?*

Alan shook his head and said, "I'm sorry, you should have said something the other day. It's too late now." He listened. "No, it's not going to ruin the entire night."

Jimmy actually could hear the angry reply that followed.

"Fine, I'll see what I can do, but believe me, the dance will still be fun even if we don't have a limo." He rolled his eyes. "Yes, it will be. I promise."

Alan pulled the phone away from his ear because the shouts were really loud this time. Once they were finished, he put the phone back and said, "Okay, see you tonight."

He closed the phone.

"What was that all about?" Jimmy asked.

"Apparently I have already ruined Rachel's prom night experience because I failed to get a limo to take us there."

"A limo!"

"Yeah. The school is less than a mile away from her house, and she wants a limo to take us." He picked up his bagel sandwich to take a bite, looked at it for a second, and put it back down. "You know, if these dances get any more serious, they are going to have to start handing out marriage licenses at them."

Jimmy nodded. "I hope Tina isn't upset that I didn't get a limo."

Alan didn't reply.

Jimmy thought about calling her and finding out but then decided it would probably be better not to say anything so that the idea wasn't planted. At the same time, he was pretty sure she would be happy without one.

Alan sighed. "You know, I don't care. If she wants to make a big deal out of this, that is fine. I'm not going to let it ruin my night."

"But then Rachel won't 'love it,' and isn't that all that matters?" Jimmy asked.

Alan glared at him.

Jimmy put up his hands. "Hey, I'm not the one who said it."

"No, but it doesn't really apply to me because I'm not dating her, so if I fuck things up and just walk away it's fine. You, on the other hand, are in a relationship, which changes things."

"How?"

"You still want to be dating tomorrow or the next day or next week?"

"Um, yeah."

"Then she better enjoy herself tonight. With me, I don't plan on ever really talking to her again after tonight, so it doesn't really matter. I'm just going to have fun."

His phone rang again.

He picked it up, saw that it was Rachel again, and didn't answer it.

"Having fun?" Jimmy asked.

Alan gave him the finger.

Rebecca was sitting in the family room reading a romance novel when Tina came downstairs, the statements about her father still the main focus of her mind, but now for a different reason.

She stepped into the family room.

Rebecca looked up.

"Can I ask you something?" Tina said.

"Go ahead," Rebecca said.

"Why did you wait until now to tell me all this stuff about my father?"

Rebecca closed her book around her finger and sighed. "Because it was important for you to understand what he did and why I had to leave the marriage."

"Bullshit!" Tina snapped. "If all of that was important and something you were concerned about, you would have told me all of it months ago. Instead you waited until today, all so you could try and ruin my night."

"No, I—"

"You are a bitch!" Tina snapped. "A no-good, spoiled, stuck-up bitch, one who probably begged to be fucked that night but then convinced herself she had been raped because she couldn't live with the fact that she was a whore."

The book came at her quickly, but Tina managed to move out of the way before it hit her square in the face.

"Get out," Rebecca said.

"Oh, does the truth hurt?" Tina asked.

"Get out!"

"Don't worry. As soon as the courts let me, I will be on my own and you will never have to see me again. Until then, well, you're stuck with me, and trust me, if you ever try to convince me that my father was anything but a good man, I will hit you so hard you'll wish you died in childbirth."

Rebecca didn't reply.

Tina picked up the book that had been thrown at her, looked at the cover, which had a really strong shirtless man on it, and said, "Wow, Scott has a lot to live up to if this is what you want in your men," and threw the book back. "But then again, he's probably cheaper than buying a vibrator, so I understand why you put up with him."

The anger that appeared in Rebecca's eyes was unlike anything Tina had ever seen before, and for a second she wondered if she had pushed the woman too far, but then she dismissed the thought. Any pain she caused her was deserved.

"Just one more, this time out by the flower garden you and Jimmy planted," Kelly Hawthorn said, her camera once again ready.

"Mom, no," Alan said, an apologetic look toward his date. "Please, we really have to go."

"And they will take professional pictures of us at the dance," Rachel Hayes said. It was one of just a handful of statements that had left her lips since her arrival ten minutes earlier. "You'll be able to buy as many as you want."

"But they won't have the flower garden in them, now will they?" Kelly said and quickly ushered the couple out the front door toward the flower garden that Jimmy and Alan had slaved over in the predawn hours of Mother's Day as a surprise.

Jimmy watched from the doorway as his mother took several more pictures of Alan and Rachel, her statements that attempted to encourage smiles making the two even more glum. Eventually she stopped and told the two to have a good time.

Though he couldn't tell for sure, Jimmy thought he saw a look of relief spread across Alan's face as the two headed toward Rachel's car, one which she had insisted Alan drive since it was a Lincoln and much nicer than the car he and Jimmy had planned on driving.

Kelly Hawthorn came back into the entryway, watched for a moment as Alan opened the passenger door for Rachel, and said, "I don't like her."

"How come?" Jimmy asked. He noticed his tie was crooked and started to fix it in the mirror, but only managed to make it worse.

"She's a stuck-up little brat. *'They will have professional pictures at the prom that you can buy.'* No shit, Sherlock."

Jimmy laughed.

"And she acted all superior to us, especially with all that 'let's take my daddy's car because it's nicer and more formal' crap," Kelly added.

"I think you just don't like it that Alan is going to the prom with a senior, even though they are only two years apart."

Kelly didn't reply to that and instead asked, "When are you picking up Tina?"

Jimmy looked at the clock on the wall and said, "In a few minutes." He looked at the camera. "And no, I won't be bringing her by for pictures."

"Oh, come on, I promise I won't go crazy." She looked at the back of the camera. "Besides, I don't even have much film left anyway, so you have nothing to worry about."

"You know Alan and I bought you that camera for Christmas," Jimmy said. "So I know it doesn't take film."

"Well, the card is almost full."

"Nice try." He looked at the clock again. "I better

head out."

"Okay, fine. But I want to meet her one of these days. You promise?"

"I promise."

Jimmy gave his mother a hug.

"Have fun, but be careful."

"I will. Love you."

"Love you too."

Jimmy headed out to the car.

Less than five minutes later he was pulling into Tina's driveway, his eyes surprised to see Tina waiting for him by the front door rather than inside out of the heat.

She started toward the car.

He quickly stepped out so he could be a gentleman and open the passenger door for her.

"Jimmy, the brake!" Tina cried.

At the same time, his foot was knocked out from under him as he tried to step onto the shifting pavement, and without much thought, he jerked his hand toward the gearshift and threw the car into park.

Protests rang out from the engine as the car bounced to a halt.

"Whoa," he said while standing up, his hand touching his head.

"Are you okay?" Tina asked.

"Um, yeah." He shook his head and then rubbed his leg, which had been twisted pretty badly but wasn't hurt. "I've never done that before." He slowly started around the car. "Here, let me get the door for you."

Tina cautiously sat herself into the car.

Jimmy closed the door and started back around, the words *you stupid idiot* echoing inside his head.

Neither spoke for a moment.

"You okay?" Tina asked again.

"Yeah," Jimmy said, though his heart was racing. "I still can't believe I did that."

"I've done it before too," she confessed. "It's like your brain just skips a step for no reason."

Jimmy nodded.

"Of course, I didn't get back in and stop the car."

"Really? What'd you do?"

"Watched in horror as my dad's car smashed two bikes and then hit the tool bench in the back of the garage."

"Oh no."

"It was really bad, and then when my dad came outside I burst into tears."

"Did you get in trouble?"

"No, he was just glad I didn't get hurt and said the shock of what happened was probably enough to make it so I never made the mistake again."

"I wonder if your mother would have been as forgiving as him had I smashed into the garage."

"Ha, she'd try to have you thrown in jail for reckless endangerment and destruction of property."

"And they would probably convict you of being an accessory since it was mostly your fault."

"*My fault!*" Tina cried. "What?"

"Well, if you weren't so breathtakingly beautiful, I wouldn't have been distracted, and would have remembered how to drive."

"Wow, that is…so unbelievably lame."

"Yeah, well, I see you smiling over there. And believe me, it's true. The moment I saw you standing there and saw how beautiful you were, my mind went blank."

Tina blushed. "You're sweet."

"I really am," Jimmy said and then leaned over and

kissed her.

"Modest too," Tina said once the kiss was finished.

The two laughed.

"Okay, let's hope I didn't kill the engine by shifting it to park so quickly," Jimmy said while shifting the car into reverse.

"Fingers crossed," Tina said.

The car backed out of the driveway without any trouble, and soon the two were heading toward the school.

"Aren't we going by your house first?" Tina asked.

"What?"

"Alan texted me just before you got here and said your mother wanted to take pictures of us."

Deputy Paul Widgeon had been placed on the far corner of the parking lot, his vehicle backed in at an angle so he could see everything that happened from his corner to the rear of the gymnasium where the dance was taking place. His presence there was to be a deterrent against someone grabbing a girl, but in all actuality he had a feeling he would be a bigger deterrent against teens who wanted some private "feel each other up and maybe start the process of bringing a new life into this world" time. The fact that he had lost his virginity during his prom about twenty yards from where he was now sitting wasn't lost on him and actually brought a smile to his face. Her name had been Ellie. He wondered what had happened to her. The two had broken up when he informed her he was joining the military. Apparently, she had been of the opinion that turning the other cheek after September 11, 2001, was more appropriate than attacking the terrorist camps.

Was it worth it? he asked himself.

No answer arrived.

He pushed the thoughts away and once again focused on the parking lot, wondering what the sheriff was doing right now.

Across the parking lot, a group of young men awkwardly escorted their dates into the school, their tuxes too formal for their age and giving the impression that they were trying to pull a fast one.

The pictures didn't really take all that long, yet were still annoying because his mother just kept insisting on different shots while also bringing up tons of different subjects in an attempt to get to know Tina, whom she had never met before. After that, they then had to go inside and talk to his father because he too wanted to meet Tina. By the time it was finally over, Jimmy felt like going to bed and hadn't even arrived at the dance yet. Thankfully, the idea of being there with Tina kept him from allowing the exhaustion to overwhelm him, and soon the two were standing in line at the school, waiting for their tickets to be verified.

"Hey, do you remember when he rented that video a few years ago? What was that shit called?" Brett asked while sitting on the Hoods' back porch.

"I don't remember, man," Matt said. "Something kinky though. You know, I should never have told you guys about that because the fucker almost beat the shit out of me after you guys told everyone."

"Man, he couldn't do shit to you," Brett said. "The guy's a pussy."

"Didn't he knock you on your ass the other day?" Ron

asked while sipping a beer.

"Yeah," Matt said.

"The fucker elbowed me in the gut right when a hall monitor was making me let him go. What was I supposed to do? If it wasn't for her, I would have had him shitting his pants in front of everyone."

"Yeah, whatever," Matt said. He took a sip from the bottle Brett had brought and winced as it scorched his throat. "Shit, Brett, what is this?"

"I don't know, something my brother had in his room. Good stuff, right?"

"No," Matt said while reaching over for a beer from Ron, who had somehow managed to get them two cases. "It's awful."

"You fuckers don't know what's good," Brett said and took a huge swig from the bottle. A moment later tears appeared in his eyes and he gagged.

Matt and Ron laughed.

"Man, that is awful," Brett said. "God, give me a beer."

"See, should've tasted it before bringing it over," Matt said. His throat still burned.

"Yeah, your brother probably knew you'd take it and mixed everything strong he could find together."

"You know, you're probably right because he did that once to a guy on his construction crew who was stealing his Gatorade. Filled the bottle with salt water and dyed it blue and then just set it by his stuff so the guy would swipe it and chug it." He popped the top on the beer, took a huge swig, and sighed. "That's better."

"So, what're you gonna do with the tapes?" Ron asked.

"I thought about playing them at the dance, but those

damn police wannabes won't let anyone in without a ticket."

"You gotta do something," Ron said. "I mean, what's the point of having them if they're just gonna sit in your room?"

"Honestly, I really just want to beat the shit out of the motherfucker once and for all, especially now that school's almost out."

"So then let's beat the shit out of him," Ron said.

"But he's at the prom," Brett whined.

"So?"

"So, that means I can't just go there and beat the shit out of him because there are deputies everywhere who will like club me before I even lay a hand on him, and then he'll say he beat the shit out of me. Plus I don't have a ticket, so I can't even get in."

"Matt, don't you have a ticket?" Ron asked.

"No," Matt said.

"Yes you do. You bought one because you thought that chick Caroline was going to go with you, but then she totally shot you down when you asked her." Ron mimicked a plane crashing to the earth. "Ka-boom!"

"So what?" Matt said. "I don't see you at the dance."

"Because prom is for pansies," Ron said. "And I'm not gonna spend hundreds of dollars on a girl without even the promise of getting laid. No way. I'd rather drive three hours to Chicago and pay twenty bucks on a street corner."

"Better start getting used to that trip then, because that's the only pussy you're ever gonna see," Brett said.

"Fuck you."

Matt finished his beer, crushed the can, and threw it into the woods, wondering what the hell he was doing here with these two idiots.

"Anyway," Ron said, "Matt can go tell Jimmy you've got his tapes and are waiting for him to come get them, and then we beat the shit out of him."

"No, *I beat the shit out of him*," Brett said while grabbing another beer. "I don't want you two stealing my glory."

"Fine, you beat the shit out of him while I film it on my phone and post it on Facebook."

"Great idea," Matt said. "You'll get us all in trouble because the police will watch the video." He then turned to Brett. "If you want to beat him up so bad, you go get him."

"Dude, didn't you hear what I said? If I go, we'll get in a fight right then and there and the wannabe police officers will break it up before I can really give it to him."

"Yeah, don't be such a freaking pussy and just go get him," Ron said, even though he really didn't care what happened.

"Man, you guys suck," Matt said while standing up. He started walking toward the trees.

"Where you going?" Brett asked with a laugh.

"To go get Jimmy so you can beat him up!" Matt shouted back. *More like I'm getting him so he can beat you up, you stupid piece of shit. Post that on Facebook.*

"Don't walk, take the car." Brett held up the keys.

Matt gave him the finger and stepped onto the path that would take him by the school. Going to the prom to get Jimmy was stupid, but it would be even stupider if he did it in a car after drinking—especially with all the deputies keeping an eye on things.

Tina was stunned by how beautiful the gym was but then grew worried because that had been exactly what her mother said she had felt. *Stop it. Don't let her ruin it.* How could she not, though? It wasn't every day a girl found out she might have been the result of a rape.

"It's nice, isn't it?" Jimmy said. His words pulled her from her thoughts.

"Yes, yes it is," Tina said.

The place had been decorated with streamers and tissue paper. A stage had been set up and a band was playing on it. One part of the gym floor was open for dancing, the other part filled with round tables and chairs. At the far end was a long table with drinks and simple snacks. She wondered how long it had taken to set everything up. Turning the gym into a nice romantic atmosphere couldn't have been easy.

"Where do we sit?"

Jimmy looked around and finally found Alan and Rachel sitting at a table. Earlier at the house, Rachel had worn a shawl that covered her shoulders and cleavage; now she didn't, the dress hardly holding her in. The two weren't talking, just sitting, each one staring at something else. "Over there," Jimmy said while pointing.

"Okay," Tina agreed.

They walked over hand in hand.

Alan saw the two and stood up. He introduced Tina to Rachel. Rachel gave a high-pitched, ditsy hello and then turned back to face the dance, each movement of her body exaggerated.

The four sat down.

Tina looked around at the gym again. People were dancing to the music. She wanted to join them.

Jimmy was just looking off into space. She nudged him and asked, "Could we dance?"

"Oh, okay." He stood up, led her to the dance floor,

and then confessed, "I've never danced before."

"Me either," she said and laughed. "Just act like everyone else." She pulled him close, her breasts pressing up against his chest.

Jimmy tried to hide his erection but couldn't, and she felt it poking her as they swayed to the music. She liked it.

For the next five minutes, the two clumsily danced along the floor, both stepping on each other's feet from time to time and bumping into other couples, who gave them frustrated looks. It was a sight worth watching, which was what Alan did while sitting next to Rachel.

After the dance ended, the two walked off the dance floor and sat down, each with a large grin.

"That was something," Alan said. "You call it pinball dancing?"

Tina laughed.

Jimmy gave him a look. He then turned to Tina and said, "There just wasn't enough room out there for us, right?"

"Not enough room," Tina agreed.

Jimmy looked down at her right foot. "Your toes okay?"

Tina laughed again. "Yeah, I think so. It's a good thing they aren't open-shoed, or whatever the hell you call them."

"Open-toed," Rachel said. She sounded annoyed, her words almost asking *how could someone not know that?*

Tina looked at Jimmy, who just shrugged back.

Rachel looked at Alan and said, "Why don't you get me something to drink." It wasn't a question.

"Sure." Alan started to stand.

"Hold up a sec," Jimmy said. He turned to Tina. "You

want anything?"

"Yeah, anything's fine."

"Okay." Jimmy got up and walked with Alan to the buffet setup. There weren't many people there at the moment, and the sound of the gym seemed to fade as they got closer. The two were actually able to hear each other without shouting.

"Having fun?" Alan asked.

"I really am," Jimmy said. He took two cups and dipped them into the punch. Without realizing it, he also dipped the bottom of his left cuff.

Alan did the same, only without staining his sleeve. He then looked around at the crackers and cookies, but decided against trying to balance two cups and a plate. "Tina seems to be enjoying herself."

Jimmy glanced back toward their table. "You think so?" he asked hopefully. "I really made a mess out of that dance."

"Don't worry, she's having fun. I can tell."

Tina didn't see him looking at her. Instead, her gaze was on the dance floor, waiting.

"What about you?" Jimmy asked.

The two started walking back.

"Rachel isn't talking much. I'm not sure she really likes me the way she let on and only wanted me to take her so she could be here." He shrugged. "You know, so she didn't miss her senior prom."

A second later, the two returned to the table.

"Thank you," Tina said as Jimmy handed her the drink. Then, "Oh no, what did you do?"

"What?" Jimmy asked.

"Your sleeve." She took hold of his wrist and turned it over for him to see. Her face betrayed her determination not to laugh.

"Damn," Jimmy said loudly, though no one could hear it because of the music. "That's gonna cost me big time." The tuxedo had come with a list of offenses that would result in more charges. Stains were one of them.

"Well, go to the bathroom and try washing it out," Tina said, her voice taking on the tone of a concerned mother.

Jimmy eased his wrist away and sat down. "I'd rather stay here with you." His voice had cooled. "Besides, it won't come out."

The song ended, along with the current dance. Tina looked at the floor and then at Jimmy. "Want to get in on the next one?" she asked.

"Sure," Jimmy said.

Halfway to the school Matt stopped and realized that even with a ticket they probably would not let him into the dance due to his casual attire, and he wondered if he should go home and change into something formal.

Thoughts of Caroline and how she had said no to him a few weeks earlier followed. A mixture of resentment and embarrassment came next, especially since he had been unable to keep himself from tearing up as she let out a laugh, his emotions so high-strung from working up the courage to ask her that they broke easily after she turned him down.

It had been one of the worst moments of his life, and afterward he had been too scared to try to ask anyone else, fearful that he would be rejected a second time.

God, what if I see her there?

What if I beat the shit out of whomever she is with?

The thought would never become a reality.

The same was probably true with the idea of Brett and Jimmy going at it tonight, because even if he got inside he doubted Jimmy would take the bait.

Just go home.

As appealing as the idea was, he continued toward the school so he could at least say he had tried. If they turned him away, which he was almost certain would be the case, he could tell Brett to go there himself and wait for him. If not and somehow Jimmy did take the bait, he would get to see Brett get his ass kicked—he was pretty certain of this as well—which would make it all worthwhile.

He continued toward the school, his hand ready to pull the ticket from his wallet where it had been stored next to his one and only condom, both of which he held on to just in case something unforeseen happened. Unforeseen but dreamt about often.

In the end he didn't need the ticket, but only because Jimmy was already outside.

"You know what this reminds me of?" Tina said as the two headed down the hallway toward the door so they could get some fresh air.

"What?" Jimmy asked.

"You promise not to laugh?"

"Maybe," he said with a smile.

She playfully punched him in the arm. "Promise."

"Okay, I promise I won't laugh."

"It kind of reminds me of the Harry Potter books."

"Um, how come?" Jimmy asked.

"Because, we are in a decorated school at night having fun, yet we have to be guarded by the authorities because something bad could be lurking outside."

"Oh."

"Okay, it's stupid, but I can't help it."

"No, I know what you mean. I read the books when I was younger, and I can see why it feels that way." In his mind, he wondered if that made him Lord Voldemort. "Of course, in the books the Dark Lord and whatever horrible thing that threatened the students of Hogwarts were usually already inside or found their way inside, which makes you wonder if the same is true here."

Tina's grip around his arm tightened. "Okay, you just caused a chill to run down my spine."

Jimmy smiled.

At the door, the school official who had checked their tickets asked them where they were going. Like before, a deputy stood next to him. Unlike before, they both had cups of punch, and the deputy also had a cookie.

"Just going outside to cool off," Jimmy said. "It's really warm in there."

"Okay, but just be aware that there are dozens of deputies out there, and they will be keeping an eye on you."

"We really are just going out to get some air," Jimmy said.

The man nodded.

The two stepped outside. "I hate it when adults do that," Jimmy said.

"Do what?" Tina asked.

"Assume we are up to no good because we are teenagers."

"I guess that means I'm not going to get lucky while out here, am I? And to think I made that whole story up about being hot and wanting some fresh air, all for nothing."

"Hey, I didn't say he was wrong," Jimmy said quickly. "I just said I don't like it when adults automatically assume we are up to no good."

"Really?" Tina said. "Well then maybe we should walk a little farther from the school."

"Maybe," he said back and kissed her.

She returned the kiss, a small laugh escaping, and then pushed him away while saying, "I really think we should walk a little farther from the school."

"Okay," Jimmy said and took her hand.

A few other couples who were standing outside watched them start to walk away, knowing smiles on their faces, some of the guys thinking, *Lucky bastard.*

Together they headed down the side of the hill toward the school plaque, their direction taking them toward an unofficial walkway that went between the football field and parking lot.

"Um, Jimmy," Tina said as they headed toward the bleachers. "Not over there."

"How come? I don't see any deputies over there, and it's nice and dark."

Tina stopped walking, her hand tugging at his. "Please, not over there." The look on her face told Jimmy this was not something he wanted to argue with, though now he was curious as to what the problem was.

Don't ask now, it might ruin the moment.

Strangely, it wasn't the hint at having a sexual moment that his mind was thinking about, but the entire prom experience.

"It's okay, we don't have to go over there if you don't want to," Jimmy said.

"Thank you," Tina said while embracing him, her head against his chest. "Thank you so much."

For a moment, Jimmy didn't know what to do but then simply placed his palms on her back. He could feel her heartbeat through the thin fabric of her gown. It felt wonderful.

He tightened his hold.

It was a perfect moment in time.

And then…

"Well, well, what do we have here?"

Jimmy lifted his head and looked at Matt. "Leave us alone."

Matt held up his palms. "I just wanted to let you know that Brett has your bondage videos and is waiting for you at the Hood place."

Deputy Paul Widgeon was watching a good-looking girl in red lead a not-so-good-looking young man in a black tuxedo across the soccer field, getting ready to follow them so he could let them know they were being watched and should stay within the school bounds—and not have sex out on the field—when he caught sight of a small guy in a leather jacket appearing from between two houses on the sidewalk and stepping into the parking lot. Normally such a situation wouldn't be all that unusual, but given his clothes, which weren't adequate for the event, and his hurried pace, Paul had a feeling he was up to no good and decided to keep an eye on him. While doing this he also radioed a deputy named Carl.

"What's up, Paul?" Carl asked.

"I got a girl in a red dress leading a guy out onto the soccer field on my left and a guy who looks like he is up to no good walking toward the school on my right. Can you take the couple on the left and make sure they find their way back to the school?"

"Where are they exactly?" Carl asked.

Paul looked out to the field and to his dismay saw that they had now disappeared. "They were about twenty feet into the field five seconds ago, so there is no way they could have cut across it already. I'm guessing they are lying down about thirty yards to the right of the far goal."

"Got it," Carl said. "I'll be over there in a jiffy."

"Thanks." He turned back toward the guy in the leather jacket and suddenly said, "Oh shit, I got two guys fighting near the football field. Guy in a tux just laid out a guy in a leather jacket and is beating him senseless."

"Jimmy, stop!"

Jimmy heard the words but didn't really let them register, his mind only focused on the words "bondage videos" and "Hood place" while he smashed Matt's head into the blacktop parking lot, his lips demanding to know what Brett knew and what he had told people.

"Jimmy!"

A hand touched his shoulder, but he shrugged it away. At the same time, he realized he wasn't going to learn anything else from Matt, not after smashing his head so many times into the ground, and quickly headed toward his car.

Tina didn't know what to do and just stood there in the dissipating exhaust smoke for several seconds, tears falling from her eyes. She had chased Jimmy all the way to the car after he had stopped beating the guy on the ground, pleading with him to stop, but to no avail, and now he had driven away.

"Hey, you!" someone shouted in her direction.

Tina looked toward the voice and saw a town deputy standing over the guy.

"Me?" Tina asked.

Her voice barely registered, yet the deputy seemed to understand what she was asking and nodded while saying, "Yes, you, come here."

Tina obeyed.

Others came as well, most curious onlookers who had witnessed the brief fight from a distance and now wanted to see what was going on.

Several of them gasped when they arrived, the blood leaking from the guy's ears startling them.

"This is Deputy Widgeon over at the Ashland Creek High School prom. I need a paramedic here for a head trauma ASAP!" Deputy Widgeon turned toward Tina and said, "Who was the guy you were with, and where did he go?"

Tina just shook her head.

Another deputy arrived on the scene and said, "Good God, what happened?"

"I don't know," Deputy Widgeon said. "One moment this guy was walking toward the school, the next he was being knocked senseless by the guy that was with her."

The second deputy turned to Tina. "What happened?"

"I-I-I don't know," Tina said. She wrapped herself with her arms.

"Yes you do!"

"They just started fighting."

Voices started to mix and mingle behind her.

"*Hey, what's going on?*"

"*Someone beat the shit out of someone!*"

"*Huge fight!*"

Tina looked around but didn't see a single familiar face in the growing crowd. Up near the doors of the school, students were flooding out of the building as if a gunman had opened fire within, news of the fight having reached them.

"Stay with me, young man," Deputy Widgeon said. "Help is on the way. Do you know what your name is?"

Tina was close enough to hear him say "Matt," but anyone beyond her would have thought he was nonresponsive.

"Okay, Matt, can you tell me what happened?"

Nothing.

"He's in and out," the other deputy said. He turned toward Tina. "The guy you were with, the one who did this, what was his name?"

"Um, Jimmy."

"Jimmy what?"

"Hawthorn. Jimmy Hawthorn."

Her voice was loud enough for a few people in the crowd behind her to hear, and the next thing she knew Jimmy's name was being said back and forth, the words "*Jimmy Hawthorn beat the shit out of someone*" bouncing from person to person until everyone had an idea that Jimmy Hawthorn was involved in something.

"And where did he go?" the deputy asked.

"I don't know." Tina really didn't.

Her emotions suddenly got the better of her. First, the thoughts about her father and mother under the bleachers, and then Jimmy's comfort as he hugged her and said it was okay, and then the fight, and now him driving away from her. It was too much. She couldn't take it and sat against the car next to her, crying.

* * *

Alan noticed several people racing from the gymnasium as he and Rachel walked onto the dance floor and wondered what was going on.

"...Jimmy Hawthorn..."

His head jerked toward the voice, his brother's name being the only part of the sentence he heard, and said, "What about Jimmy Hawthorn?"

The guy, who had been talking to a girl who was wearing a really risqué cocktail dress, looked at Alan and said, "Was I talking to you?"

Alan let go of Rachel's hand, grabbed the guy by the collar, and thrust him backward into a table.

The girl next to him let out a brief, "Oh my," and stepped aside.

"If it involves my brother, you better tell me what you said!"

"Hey, man, sorry, chill. I was just saying Jimmy Hawthorn beat the crap out of some guy outside and then took off in his car."

Startled, Alan asked, "Took off where?"

"How should I know? The police are everywhere though, and when I was coming in I heard an ambulance."

Alan let the guy go, who gasped while pushing himself away from the table edge, and headed toward the door.

Rachel stood and watched him go, confusion distorting her face.

Alan didn't say a word to her as he headed outside, having to push himself through the crowd that had gathered at the door, several cries of "Excuse me" and "Get out of my way" leaving his lips.

Once outside he found himself looking down toward the parking lot. Flashing lights danced across everything as an ambulance pulled in, its siren blaring.

To the left the crowd was being pushed aside to make room for the emergency vehicle, while another couple of deputies knelt by a young man lying on the ground. Next to them, Alan saw Tina sitting on a car, but no Jimmy.

He hurried down toward her, his legs taking him to the right so he could detour in between the parked cars, thereby making his journey much easier than if he had tried pushing through the crowd.

"Tina!" he called as he neared her. "Tina!"

Tina looked up the second time he shouted her name, saw him coming toward her, and quickly stepped between the cars to meet up with him.

"Are you okay? What happened?" Alan asked.

"Jimmy got in a fight," Tina said. The makeup she was wearing had been streaked by tears and now was smeared as she wiped at the wetness with her arm.

"Do you know where he went?" Alan asked. He noticed she was shivering and quickly took his coat off and draped it over her shoulders.

"I don't know," she said, her hands hugging the warm jacket to her body.

"Tell me what happened, okay?" Alan said. "Take a deep breath first."

Tina did what he said and told him about the guy shouting something to them while Jimmy was holding her and how Jimmy had snapped. "He just went up to the guy and punched him right in the face," she said. "I heard the sound of Jimmy hitting him, and then the guy fell to the ground and Jimmy started smashing his head into the ground."

Good God, Alan thought. Jimmy was going to get in so much trouble, even if the other guy started it, especially with this happening on school grounds.

"What exactly did the other guy say?" Alan asked. "You said he mentioned Brett?"

"Yeah." Tina looked up for a moment and then, "He said Brett had his bondage tapes at the Hood place. I think Brett is waiting for him."

Jimmy stopped at home before heading to the Hood place and hurried down into his room, his mother calling to him from the family room, asking what was wrong.

"Nothing," Jimmy called back while heading out again. "I just forgot something."

With that, he got back in the car and hurried toward the Hood place, his mind focused on one thing: Brett.

"The fucker must've gotten lost," Brett said while opening another can of beer. It was his eighth or ninth of the evening and he was feeling great. Ron hadn't had as many but was probably feeling the same. The guy was a lightweight. One beer for him was like three for Brett.

"Probably passed out or something," Ron said. "You know Matt doesn't drink that often."

"He just better do his job and get Jimmy over here," Brett said. "After that he can go piss all over himself for all I care."

Ron nodded.

Tires screeched to a halt.

"Shit, what was that?" Brett asked while struggling to stand, his hand guiding him up along the porch wall.

"No fucking clue," Ron said. He had an easier time standing up.

The two stepped out into the yard just as Jimmy came around the corner of the Hood place. The dork was still wearing his tux.

"I see you got my message, shithead," Brett said with a smile while raising his fists. He was going to beat the fucking shit out of him now.

Jimmy raised his right hand. "Yeah, I got the message, you motherfucker. Where are my tapes?"

"Like I'm gonna—" Brett stopped

"Fuck, man, that's a gun," Ron said. He started to turn toward the trees.

"Don't you fucking move," Jimmy warned while pointing the gun at Ron. He looked back at Brett. "Where are my tapes?"

"I, they, I—"

Jimmy fired.

Brett felt the impact before he even heard the gunshot and fell to the ground without a sound, his legs simply seeming to vanish beneath him. A scream followed.

"You shot him," Ron said, eyes wide, mind suddenly sober.

"Yeah, and I'll shoot you too if you don't tell me where the tapes are." He started to turn the gun toward Ron while saying this.

Ron bolted.

Jimmy aimed at the running figure and fired, but Ron kept running. He fired two more times as Ron disappeared into the woods, missing both times.

"Fuck," he said as Ron disappeared into the trees. Word about this would spread quickly. He needed to hide Brett. If his luck held, people would just assume Ron had had too much beer and hallucinated the entire thing.

Brett was writhing on the ground when Jimmy approached. The pain and sudden loss of bodily control was terrible. Nothing mattered. He just wanted it all to end.

Jimmy grabbed his leg and began dragging him. Brett screamed as his insides shifted. Piss ran down the other leg.

Alan heard the gunshot and nearly collided with Ron as he came running out of the woods to the sidewalk. Even though he didn't know the guy personally, he recognized him as one of Brett's buddies.

The guy did not stop to chat, and after avoiding the collision, he kept running. What did that mean? Had Brett gone crazy with a gun?

Alan quickened his pace. Behind him, Tina still struggled to keep up in clothes that weren't meant for running, the two having easily walked away from the school during all the commotion.

If you shot him, motherfucker, I'm going to rip your heart out, Alan shouted to himself. Exactly how he would disarm Brett was a mystery, but he would find a way. He never even considered being shot himself.

Alan pushed himself through the woods. In the darkness, it was difficult to find his way. For a moment, he worried that he had made a wrong turn, but then everything opened up.

He stepped into the yard of the Hood place. Overgrown bushes and long grass made it almost impossible to see what was going on.

He looked to the left toward the street but couldn't see anything. Once he neared the driveway of the house, however, he could make out the back of their mother's car on the street, half of it sticking into the road where another car could easily plow into it if the driver wasn't paying attention.

Tina came up behind him. She was out of breath and could hardly stand on her sore feet. Between sucking in deep mouthfuls of air she asked, "Was that a gunshot?"

Alan nodded.

"Does Jimmy"—deep breath—"own a gun?"

"No."

There had been several shots and then nothing but silence. What did that mean? Was that all it took, or had they been fired to get Jimmy's attention? Perhaps Jimmy had been beating the crap out of Brett, so he pulled a gun to stop him but didn't actually shoot him. Was Brett capable of killing someone?

"I want you to wait here," Alan said to Tina. "Go by the car or something, but stay out of sight until I yell that it's okay. Got it?"

"Okay."

"Good." Alan turned and looked at the bushes. *God, what am I doing?* he asked himself and then pushed through them rather than just walking around them, a stick instantly swiping his cheek. The cut stung like hell, yet would be nothing compared to a bullet cutting through his insides.

His hope was that he could sneak up on Brett and Jimmy and that the two wouldn't even know he was there. That way he could tackle Brett if he had a gun.

Alan emerged into the far side-yard of the Hood place slowly and looked around.

All was quiet. There were no shouts, no cries, nothing. Only Alan knew something was going on. Jimmy and Brett had to be around somewhere.

The silence chilled him.

What was Ron running from?

Was it so bad that he didn't want to be a part of it, or did he flee in fear of his life?

Heart thumping, Alan rounded the corner of the house. The first thing he saw was the case of beer on the steps of the porch and cans scattered across the lawn. He then looked at the shed and saw something that didn't make any sense—light was coming up from the ground.

Alan walked closer and realized that there was a trapdoor leading down into some sort of cellar beneath the shed. When it was closed, one would only see the dirt floor of the shed.

A small but steep stairway led down to another open door. Light came from within. Blood marked a path on the steps. More was pooled in a puddle on the ground, some of it smeared through the doorway as if something had been left there for a second and then dragged in.

Not something, someone.

A figure passed by the doorway, causing the light to flicker.

What is Brett doing to Jimmy inside?

Alan started down the steps, wishing he had his own gun.

He was halfway down when there was a sudden movement in front of him and a cry of, "Oh shit." The bullet punched through Alan's shin before the sound of the shot even reached his ears.

"Ahhhh!" Alan cried while falling down the remaining steps, both hands going to his right leg. It felt like someone had taken a red-hot sledgehammer to it.

He hit the concrete with his shoulder and rolled over onto his back. Screams shattered the night, and for a moment, nothing but the agony mattered.

Then a dark figure was looming over him, gun in

hand. He braced himself for a bullet to the head.

"*Alan?*" the figure asked.

The figure twisted, which allowed the light to illuminate him. It was Jimmy. His older brother had shot him in the leg.

"Oh God!" Jimmy shouted. *What have I done!* "Alan, what are you doing here?"

He had been so focused on getting Brett into the fallout shelter and trying to set it up to look as if he had been the one who kidnapped the girls—all the details weren't in place, but he knew he could make it look good if given time—that he had forgotten to close the trapdoor.

"Jimmy," Alan said. The word was swimming in pain. "You shot me!"

"I didn't mean to," Jimmy said.

Alan looked down at his leg.

Jimmy followed his gaze and could see bone within the hole.

Alan's face went white.

"Here," Jimmy said and quickly went to the shelf and got a blanket, his eyes glancing at the two girls and then at Brett, who was silently convulsing on the floor, bright red blood bubbling up from his mouth and nose, all within Alan's line of sight, but so far seeming to go unnoticed. He returned to Alan and handed him the blanket. "Press this against your leg."

Alan did.

"Let me help you sit against the wall," Jimmy said. He took his little brother by the shoulders and shifted him around so that he didn't have to balance himself while holding his leg. "How's that?"

"Better," Alan said through clenched teeth.

"Alan!" a voice screamed.

Jimmy pointed the gun toward the door, but this time managed to hold his fire as Tina came down the steps, her tight floor-length skirt making it difficult to maneuver down them, her blue heels held in her hand.

Jimmy lowered the gun before she could see it and said, "Tina, go back up."

At the same moment, her bare foot came down in the pool of blood.

"Jimmy?" she questioned while looking down at the ground, a gasp starting to build. "Oh Jesus Christ!" Her eyes saw Alan and then shifted toward Jimmy.

"Tina, it's okay," Jimmy said. He then watched as her eyes focused on something beyond his shoulders.

Outside, police sirens began to echo.

"Jimmy?" Tina said quietly, fear running through her veins. "Is that Samantha King and Megan Reed?"

Jimmy followed her gaze and said, "Yeah."

The two girls looked dead, their bodies just hanging there, toes able to touch the ground yet not even making an effort to support their weight.

Not far from their feet was Brett, head cocked toward them, mouth slightly open, eyes wide. He wasn't moving. Blood stained his lower face and the floor beneath his mouth.

"Shit," Alan said and then winced.

"Tina, can you help him hold his leg?" Jimmy asked.

Tina saw the blood soaking through the blanket that Alan was pressing against himself and said, "Did you shoot him?"

"It was an accident," Jimmy said. He then looked at

the gun. "It's okay. I won't hurt you."

"Jimmy, why don't you put down the gun," Alan said.

Jimmy looked back at the girls again, and then down at Brett and then at the gun. Tina had no idea what was going through his head, or what was going on period, yet in that brief moment he seemed to decide something.

"I can't," Jimmy said to Alan, and then to Tina, "Please help him hold his leg."

Tina did as she was asked, her shoes dropping to the floor as she quickly bent down to press her palms against the bloody blanket.

Alan groaned.

"He needs a hospital," Tina said.

"I know," Jimmy said. He looked toward the doorway. The police sirens were louder. "They will be here soon."

"Jimmy, what's going on?" Tina asked.

Jimmy didn't answer. Instead, he looked at the gun, and for a moment Tina thought he was going to shoot himself, but then someone appeared up by the door and shouted down, "This is Deputy Paul Widgeon with the sheriff's department. Is everything okay down there?"

A dark look came over Jimmy.

Alan must have seen it too and recognized what it meant because he suddenly shouted, "Jimmy, no!"

Tina followed his cry with, "Jimmy!"

Rather than listen to the two, Jimmy pushed by them into the doorway, waited a second, and fired.

Tina screamed.

More shots erupted.

Jimmy dropped the gun and turned toward them. He took two steps into the shelter, a stunned pale look on his face.

A hand went to his chest, where blood was starting to

darken his exposed shirt. He then looked at Tina and Alan and said, "Sorry."

Blood spurted from his lips with the word.

Silence somehow settled upon them, despite the sirens above.

Jimmy took another step, but this time his foot didn't hold his weight when it came down, and he fell to his knees, eyes rolling back as his body settled into the corner between the doorway and the stairs.

"Shots fired, officer down," Deputy Lawrence Milberg said into the radio while kneeling next to Deputy Widgeon.

"I'm okay," Deputy Widgeon said. His voice was incredibly weak, but that was to be expected given the impact he had sustained. "Just help me up."

"No, stay down for a moment," Lawrence said. Then, "Who's down there?"

"I don't know. They shot at me and I shot back. I don't know if I hit them."

Another deputy arrived on the scene and peeked down the trapdoor. "I got a body on the stairs!" he shouted.

"Help us!" a girl cried from within.

"Come out with your hands in the air," the deputy replied, gun pointed down the stairs.

"Don't shoot," the girl said as she appeared in the doorway. Her eyes looked down at the body on the stairs "Please, we need help."

"Is anyone else down there armed?"

"No!"

"Come on up."

She looked down at the body again and then back at

the deputy. "I-I...please, I can't."

"Larry, can you cover me?" the deputy asked. His name was Blake. Deputy Blake Bradley, or BB as they sometimes called him.

Deputy Milberg nodded and came over, gun drawn. "Go ahead."

"I'm coming down," Blake said. "Just stay right where you are."

Paul watched as Blake disappeared down the stairs, the words "Sweet Jesus" suddenly rising from within, followed by, "We need several paramedics here now!"

CHAPTER THIRTEEN

The following newspaper clippings can be found in a scrapbook kept by Tina Thompson, most of which were cut from the *Ashland Creek Weekly Chronicle*:

Underground Torture Chamber

Last night, what started out as a simple but vicious fight in the parking lot outside of the Ashland Creek High School prom quickly escalated into a police shootout at the abandoned Hood residence, one that left two local high school students, Jimmy Hawthorn and Brett Murphy, dead, and another high school student, Alan Hawthorn, wounded in the leg. Deputy Paul Widgeon, veteran of the Iraq and Afghanistan wars, was shot as well but sustained only minor injuries due to his police-issue body armor that the town purchased two years earlier for all its deputies. Following the shootout, which took place around the shed on the Hood property, deputies discovered a secret underground chamber, which held captive the two high school senior girls, Samantha King and Megan Reed, who had gone missing earlier in the week. One of the girls, Megan

Reed, was pronounced dead at the scene, the cause of which has not yet been disclosed. Samantha King was taken to the local hospital and is listed in critical condition. Witnesses to the events report hearing Sheriff Reed screaming for them to "cut my daughter down!" while being forcefully kept away from the scene, all while the near-dead body of Samantha King was being loaded into the waiting ambulance. When asked about this, an unnamed deputy said, "We left her body hanging there because we didn't want to disturb the crime scene." The investigation into who was responsible for the abduction and torture of the two girls is ongoing...

Jimmy Hawthorn Kidnapped Me!

Early this morning, police reported that Samantha King identified the late Jimmy Hawthorn, shot and killed by Deputy Paul Widgeon, as being the one responsible for her kidnapping. Unspecified evidence found within the shelter is reported to support this claim, though no official charges have been brought. The sheriff's department also will not comment on whether Jimmy Hawthorn may have acted alone or had an accomplice, or what his motive may have been...

Jimmy Acted Alone

The investigation by the local sheriff's department, state police, and FBI has concluded that Jimmy Hawthorn acted alone in the kidnapping, rape, torture, and murder (Megan Reed) of the two girls who were discovered in a secret underground room on the abandoned property of the Hood family. Earlier claims that the late Brett Murphy was involved due to the tapes found in his bedroom, tapes his friends said were taken from Jimmy Hawthorn, have been dismissed...

Hawthorn Family Asked Not to Attend Funeral

The funeral of Megan Reed, which is expected to draw many mourners tomorrow afternoon, will not be attended by the Hawthorn family due to a request by the Reed family. It is also unclear at this time if Samantha King, recently released from the hospital, will be in attendance. When asked how their daughter was doing, the King family said she was "recovering slowly." The events of Samantha King's captivity have not yet been made public, and investigators refused to comment...

Alan had just given himself a pump from his pain medication device when there was a knock on the door, followed by Tina stepping into the hospital room.

"Hi, Alan," she said.

"Hi," Alan replied.

Tina took a seat next to his bed, her face and body looking completely worn-out, which, of course, was to be expected after everything she had been through.

"How's your leg?" she asked.

Alan glanced down at the leg, which had been encased in a futuristic-looking device, and said, "I would be lying if I told you it was fine." He sighed. "Thankfully, I got this nifty little thing." He pushed the button on the pain pump to signify what it was, his mind knowing this time around the press would be useless because he had already used up his ration of afternoon painkillers.

"Does it really work?"

"It takes the edge off and makes you loopy to the point where you don't care, but it doesn't really kill it completely." He yawned, a nice swirl of nothingness filling his head. "They should really call it a Pain Duller or Memory Masher or…I don't know."

Tina smiled.

"It really helps when you want to try and sleep at night." He yawned again.

"I didn't wake you, did I?" Tina asked. "If you need some rest, I could go."

"No." Alan shook his head. "Please stay."

"You sure?"

"Yeah. Aside from the police and that really grumpy detective, you're the only one who has visited me."

"What about your parents?"

Alan shook his head. "I think…I don't know what's going on with them." He knew they were having a difficult time in town with locals and reporters.

A quiet rumble came from the foot of the bed.

Tina twisted toward it.

"It's just my blood-clot thing," Alan said. "It tightens every now and then. The nurses keep getting mad at me because I take it off, and because I'm not blowing in this thing every couple of hours." His hand motioned toward an odd-looking clear device with a blue mouthpiece and measuring scale. "They—" He stopped when he saw the look on her face and softly asked, "How are you doing, Tina?"

"I'm tired," she said. "The police keep asking me questions and today I actually had to talk to the FBI, and these stupid reporters keep hounding me wherever I go." She hesitated. "You know, they are pretty sure Jimmy was the one who kidnapped those girls."

Alan didn't reply.

"Do you think they're right?" she asked.

Alan nodded.

Tears welled in the corners of her eyes. "But he was so good to me. How could he do that to them and then be so good to me?"

Alan didn't have an answer for this. Instead, he kept playing over the events in his mind, angry with himself for not putting all the pieces together.

"I knew about it," Alan said without much thought.

"What?" she snapped.

"Deep down inside I knew, and I should have realized it because I had seen his video."

"One of the bondage videos Brett had?" Apparently, the tape Tina had watched had been just one of many.

"No. The tape he made when he was younger. I found it when looking for a tape to record…" He thought for a second, but the title didn't come to mind. "I don't remember what, but I couldn't find a blank tape by the TV in the basement and went into his room to see if he had one because he was always taping stuff, and I found one that looked good because it didn't have a title on it and put it into his VCR to see if it really was blank."

Tina nodded.

"It wasn't. Instead, it was full of scenes of girls hanging from their wrists, one right after another, that he must have taped from TV. I was so young I didn't really understand it, but now that I look back, it makes so much sense. And I should have put it together with how strange he was acting and the girls disappearing and all his bike rides.

"And you know what's worse?" Alan said before Tina could reply. "I don't even care and get mad when I see the people on TV saying all these bad things about him and the nurses talking in the hallways. I just want to scream at them that he was a good person, and whatever it was that made him do those things, it wasn't who he really was."

Tina stared at him for several seconds and then said, "I feel the same way, but then when I hear what he did I get angry at myself and at him because I feel like I was tricked and lied to." She also felt cheated, but didn't want that to slip out.

"I'm really sorry," Alan said.

"Why are you sorry?" Tina asked. "You had nothing to do with it."

Alan looked away for a while and then started to say, "I know. I just…" But he stopped because the words weren't there. He couldn't express what he felt.

"But really, why make a big deal out of it, right? I mean, I finally find a guy I really like who seems to like and respect me, but just happens to be a blossoming serial killer who has two girls locked up in a secret underground chamber. No big deal." She put a hand to her face and started crying. "Why did he do this to us?"

Alan didn't have an answer for that.

"And why did he force the police to shoot him right in front of us? I can't get it out of my head."

This was another reason why Alan liked the pain pump. It helped push aside memories like that when they became too much to bear. Watching Jimmy's body vibrate with bullet impacts and then turn and look at them before collapsing had been a chilling sight, one that would stick with him for the rest of his life.

Tina wiped at the tears in her eyes. "I'm sorry, I know you're supposed to be resting, and now I'm stressing you out with all this."

"No, it's okay," Alan said. Like him, she had no one to really talk to. "You can talk to me whenever you need."

"Thank you," Tina said. "It goes both ways, okay?"

"Okay."

The next morning the FBI came to talk to Alan again, but once again he couldn't really tell them much, which seemed to frustrate them and made them accuse him of hiding something.

Eventually they left.

Alan watched the door after that, wishing Tina would come back, but she never did. A few hours later, however, a nurse came in and started disconnecting all his IVs and his pain pump.

"What are you doing?" Alan asked. His voice was panicked. He didn't want to lose the painkillers.

"You get to go home today."

"No one told me that," Alan said.

The nurse shrugged. It was the same one who had let him sit in bed with a full bedpan for over two hours the other day, one who seemed to think he was responsible for the things his brother had done.

Will that always be the case? he wondered. *Will I eventually have to change my last name so no one knows who I am?*

It was a troubling thought, mostly because he didn't like the idea of being forced to sever himself from his older brother, despite the awful things he had done, things he still couldn't see his brother doing.

"Ahhh," Alan cried as the nurse yanked the IV from his arm.

"Sorry," the nurse said with a smile.

Alan watched her like a hawk after that, wanting to be prepared for any pain she attempted to cause.

Eight hours later, Alan wished he were back in the

hospital because the painkillers they had prescribed him were nowhere near as effective as the ones that had gone right into his bloodstream. He also didn't like getting in and out of his bed without being able to raise it up and down. Worse, his parents weren't easy to get ahold of when he needed something, though they were still better than some of the nurses had been. Bottom line, he wished his leg were all better and pain free.

I wish Jimmy hadn't shot me.

This led to a long line of things he wished Jimmy hadn't done, though none of them concerned his suicidal attack against the police because, having thought about it, he was glad his brother was in the grave rather than a prison cell, one which he would have rotted in for the rest of his life.

At nine o'clock, he popped an extra pill to try to help him sleep. Within minutes, the extra dose kicked in and he felt himself drifting.

Glass shattered.

Screams followed from his parents downstairs.

Alan opened his eyes and saw light dancing on the dark bedroom wall, light that was coming from down the hallway.

"Mom!" he cried.

There was no answer.

"MOM!" he screamed again.

"Alan!" Kelly Hawthorn cried. Her voice sounded very far away.

He could smell something burning, and a second later the first tendrils of smoke drifted into his room.

Oh God!

Alan reached around in the dark for his crutches, ones that barely helped him walk, thanks to the pain in his leg and the heaviness of the device holding everything in place, and forced himself to his feet.

The room swirled when he did this, the painkillers having really started to kick in.

"MOM!" he cried again.

This time no one answered.

Thick dark smoke started to follow the path left by the thinner smoke.

Alan tried to duck beneath it as he made his way to the bedroom door but couldn't due to the crutches.

His taste buds suddenly examined the flavor, while his nose desperately tried to suck in fresh air.

Smoke filled his lungs and he fell to the floor, his leg screaming despite the painkiller, the sounds of something cracking, maybe one of the support pins on the device, reaching his ears.

"MOM! DAD!" he screamed around his choking sobs. "HELP ME!"

No one came.

Knowing he couldn't use the crutches, not with the heavy smoke at head level, he started to crawl into the hallway.

Smoke was billowing up the stairway and into the hallway without any resistance, and he realized it wouldn't be long until the entire second floor was toxic.

GO! his mind ordered.

He crawled as fast as he could toward the stairs, the smoke getting lower and lower.

His parents' bedroom was to the left of the hallway.

Alan looked in and saw that it was empty, the bed still not slept in since that morning given the decorative pillows, which meant his parents had probably been downstairs when the fire started.

But why didn't they come for me?

The answer to that didn't matter at the moment, and he twisted himself away from their doorway and continued toward the stairs, the sounds of stuff burning now reaching his ears.

A part of him could also feel the heat of the flames, even though he couldn't yet see them, almost as if his skin were simply anticipating the burn that would arrive.

Alan made it to the top of the stairs.

Flames had reached the bottom steps.

His heart sank.

The front door was only four feet away from those flames, but the chances of him making it there and getting out without the flames scorching him weren't good.

Two tall windows bordered the doorway. Through one, he thought he saw movement.

If you just get to the door, they can pull you out.
You will be burned.

The smoke continued to get lower and was now only two feet above his head.

If you stay here, you'll be dead.

Alan closed his eyes and took a deep breath, not relishing the thought of the pain that was about to come.

He pushed himself forward, his shattered leg screaming as the metal contraptions bounced on each step edge.

A thick cloud of smoke hit.

Alan tried to get out of its line but couldn't and started gagging as it filled his lungs.

Next, his hand slipped as he tried forcing himself out of the smoke, and his body went sliding down the second half of the stairs, the metal device clanking away, excruciating pain speeding back and forth along his nerves.

When Alan hit the bottom of the stairs, he felt himself go into a daze, one that he couldn't force himself out of right away.

And then the flames touched his left arm.

He felt the skin start to cook and managed to pull away, but the flames followed, hungry now that they had tasted flesh, and came at him.

Alan tried twisting himself back around so he could climb up the steps, but he couldn't maneuver himself like that.

Screams touched his eardrums.

He didn't even realize they were his own.

At the same time, he heard someone say the door was locked. It was his father. Beyond that, he could hear his mother screaming for him to open the door and get Alan.

One of the windows next to the door shattered.

An explosion followed, and the last thing Alan saw was a burst of flames coming toward him, the fire racing down his throat and scorching his lungs as he tried to scream. A blissful blackness followed.

News clipping from the *Ashland Creek Weekly Chronicle* collected by Tina Thompson:

Deadly Fire at Hawthorn House

Arson is suspected in a fire that destroyed the family home of the late Jimmy Hawthorn last night, the young man responsible for the kidnapping and torture of two high school girls, one of whom died before being rescued by sheriff's deputies. Jimmy Hawthorn was also responsible for the shooting death of high school senior Brett Murphy. Alan Hawthorn, little brother of Jimmy, who was recovering from wounds sustained in the shootout with police during what is now known as the Prom Night Shootout, died in the fire, his charred remains discovered just steps away from the front door. Jimmy Hawthorn's parents could not be reached for comment, though witnesses say the two were seen fleeing the back door of the house shortly before the fire was called in by them, and that they raced around to the front of the house to try to rescue their youngest son. A false alarm 911 call made from a pay phone at a gas station on the outskirts of town shortly before the fire started is being investigated, and is being blamed for the delay in firefighter response to the blaze. No suspects in the arson have been named yet.

Two months later, sitting in the locked bathroom of her parents' house, Samantha King stared at the pregnancy test she had secretly bought earlier that day, after it became clear that her missed periods could be more than just a result of great emotional stress and pain.

A moment later, she screamed while throwing the item against the wall, the broken pieces falling to the floor. Tears followed.

"Samantha, are you okay?" her mother asked while rattling the knob.

"Yes," Samantha said around her tears, staring at the newly opened bottle of sleeping pills she had set on the counter before peeing on the stick. "I'm fine."

CPSIA information can be obtained
at www.ICGtesting.com
Printed in the USA
FSHW01095129072I
8366IFS